D0790318

MEET ME IN MADRID

VERITY LOWELL

carina
press

If you purchased this book without a cover you should be aware
that this book is stolen property. It was reported as "unsold and
destroyed" to the publisher, and neither the author nor the
publisher has received any payment for this "stripped book."

**carina
press®**

PLEASE RECYCLE · THIS PRODUCT IS RECYCLABLE

Recycling programs
for this product may
not exist in your area.

ISBN-13: 978-1-335-63100-8

Meet Me in Madrid

Copyright © 2021 by Verity Lowell

All rights reserved. No part of this book may be used or reproduced in any manner whatsoever
without written permission except in the case of brief quotations embodied in critical articles and
reviews.

This is a work of fiction. Names, characters, places and incidents are either the product of the
author's imagination or are used fictitiously. Any resemblance to actual persons, living or dead,
businesses, companies, events or locales is entirely coincidental.

This edition published by arrangement with Harlequin Books S.A.

For questions and comments about the quality of this book, please contact us at
CustomerService@Harlequin.com.

Carina Press
22 Adelaide St. West, 40th Floor
Toronto, Ontario M5H 4E3, Canada
www.CarinaPress.com

Printed in U.S.A.

Orange gleams athwart a crimson soul
Lambent flames; purple passion lurks
In your dusk eyes.
Red mouth; flower soft,
Your soul leaps up—and flashes
Star-like, white, flame-hot.
Curving arms, encircling a world of love,
You! Stirring the depths of passionate desire!

—"You! Inez!" by Alice Dunbar-Nelson, 1921

MEET ME IN MADRID

Part One

Chapter One

Madrid, Charlotte pondered. There had to be someone she could call on short notice in Madrid.

She was sitting alone waiting on the bill in the rather stuffy restaurant belonging to her rather stuffy hotel near the Academia de Bellas Artes. Again, the middle-aged man at the bar turned around to look at her with an alarming lack of subtlety. And again she busied herself with her phone, hoping to give the impression she was waiting for someone.

It was just after 10:30, a perfectly typical time to finish dinner in a city that sleeps even less than New York. She'd had an excellent three-course meal including a lobster bisque, cardoons with salt cod, and four kinds of mushrooms a la plancha, plus a generously poured glass—make that two—of tasty Rioja. She was well-fed and tired, but given the time change, a little restless, too.

The best thing about Charlotte's job at the museum was the travel. The worst thing about Charlotte's job at the museum was the travel. It was as if someone gave you a Porsche 911 Turbo with all the bells and whistles (and horses) and said it was yours as long as you never did more than drive it under the speed limit to the local grocery store and back—without stopping anywhere along the way. And as long as you left *right now* and came back ASAP.

That's what a courier trip feels like.

Most people don't think about how priceless works of art get from one museum to another for a blockbuster show. Which was why her job chaperoning American paintings and sculptures to the Prado or the Louvre or the National Gallery in London sounded so glamourous when she explained it: she was the one personally responsible for making sure the Mary Cassatt or John Singleton Copley loaned by her institution arrived at its destination without a scratch.

So, yes, her job description required travel, usually business class, to great museum cities around the world. And yes, "all" she had to do was ride along, drop it off, and show up for work the next day. And yes, she liked to think of her role as a cross between Secret Service agent and sexy librarian. But in reality the trips abroad were usually just plain head-buzzing, eyes feel like they're bleeding, weak-kneed, exhausting.

Across the Atlantic and back in three days, door-to-door, and she would be once again drinking coffee in her cubicle in New Haven.

The upside? Once in a while, maybe every third trip or so, something went delightfully sideways. Mishaps usually boiled down to logistics. Bad weather, schedule mix-up, house registrar out sick, striking preparators. These were the flies in the ointment she pinned her hopes on. Unexpected delays translated into extended stays, and that, in a city as vibrant and sophisticated as the Spanish capital, was just what she wanted.

Thank God for saints.

James, Charlotte's museum colleague in operations, was a dapper, some would say needlessly fussy, fellow who had handled travel at the museum for two decades. It wasn't at all like him to miss an official foreign holiday. But somehow in the process of carefully piecing together Charlotte's hour-by-hour itinerary, even perspicacious James hadn't factored in the Immaculate Conception.

Nor could he have planned on the arctic squall that unexpectedly descended on the city the very day of the Marian festival in the first week of December.

Someone or something had conspired to keep her in Madrid just a little longer.

But what to do with the unforeseen gift of free time?

She'd go out, obviously. But that was easier said than done well in a city she'd only visited once. The most annoying thing about these junkets was that she actually knew (or knew of) some attractive and intelligent people in many of the places she was sent to. If only she'd been given the time to see them.

In anticipation of her first-ever courier trip last year, Charlotte had written well in advance to one of her dissertation advisors at Yale, who was visiting at Oxford. Sadly, their planned pub crawl in King's Cross never happened. As she'd sat backstage at the V&A counting the elapsing minutes, a forklift's transmission gave out and the crate containing the rare, full-length Eakins portrait in her care couldn't be opened and inspected until several hours after her predicted quitting time.

This had been Charlotte's initial schooling in the futility of trying to add pleasure to a business trip.

But now that the wine had started to ease away the day's stresses, a local contact hovered just beyond the tip of her mind. Madrid or the Prado or the Thyssen or the city's other important museum, the Reina Sofía, had come up in a quasi-recent post in one of her personal feeds. Or was it someone she followed? Or had it been a tweet?

Charlotte oscillated between platforms, scrolling and searching until she found what she was looking for. Adrianna Coates. The name alone filled her with a delightful little charge in what James would jokingly call her "nether regions." And it had been a minute.

The last time she'd seen her, Adrianna was wearing her

newly issued robin's-egg blue academic regalia, rising in turn with the other would-be professors to receive her doctoral degree under a crowded tent in one of the grassy quads. Though somewhat older than Charlotte, Adrianna was only four years ahead of her in the doctoral program in art history. They'd actually met when Charlotte was still an undergrad at Yale. Adrianna had been a graduate TA in one of Charlotte's last big lecture classes. Adrianna had been new to teaching but she was every bit as intimidating as the full professor she was there to assist.

As PhD students, they'd only had one seminar together—in Adrianna's final year. Charlotte had put herself *together* for those beyond-daunting weekly class meetings, dressing as she might for a job interview, if not a first date. With Adrianna to impress up close, she'd read more thoroughly and carefully than for any other class. The paper she wrote that term was the reason she'd received honors. It was published the year she graduated, helped get her a museum job—and was the last original scholarship she really felt good about.

She still remembered the first time they'd run into each other socially. It was Charlotte's third year in the program and she'd gone out to celebrate the end of her first term of teaching—Corot to Manet—with her all-male entourage of grad student queer boys because "real lesbians don't study the Impressionists," as they were fond of telling her.

There were still one or two actual old-school gay bars in New Haven in those days. The most storied, One Fifty-Five Lancaster, a two-roomed garden-level cave with a great patio, was practically across the street from the art history department. Although it had to have been close to eight years ago now—she must have been about twenty-five—Charlotte could summon that night to mind as if it was last week.

She and the boys were sitting around a big table near the bar when Adrianna came in trailing some extremely hot and considerably younger student type. The two of them, arranged precisely in Charlotte's sight line, had hardly ordered their dry martinis before they started making out at the bar like prom-goers in the back of a limo. It was dark to begin with, and they were in the back corner. But there was something about the way Adrianna, always so formal and frighteningly whip-smart in the classroom, had allowed the woman's hands to slip inside her blazer. Something about the way her kiss seemed to deferentially answer to the younger woman's aggressive advances had stayed with Charlotte; all these years later, she vividly recalled what it felt like to watch them. It was funny and a bit sobering to realize she was now probably about the same age Adrianna had been at the time; she'd have to be in her early forties by now.

But here were the Instagram photographs Charlotte had been thinking of. Carefully composed, really quite sensual imagery of lipstick-stained espresso cups on marble café tables; of the hems of women's skirts, their legs tucked underneath; of stray cats regarding each other across the pebbled paths of the public gardens. If Adrianna's moody snapshots were taken in Madrid, it was not the city Charlotte had yet discovered.

Cross-referencing them with Adrianna's FB page, Charlotte determined (she preferred to think of it as good spycraft rather than stalkery behavior) that Adrianna was currently residing in Madrid on a prestigious sabbatical fellowship. According to her latest posts, she was there to document a group of objects housed at a convent near the palace. Made up of paintings, elaborate jewels, and tapestries, the collection had originally belonged to a seventeenth-century nun who spent her life assembling art in a cloister of royal women.

All very interesting. But did she dare send *La Reine des glaces*—the ice queen—as they used to call her, an after-dinner message on a snowy night?

Adrianna Coates had had a long day. She'd spent the morning at the National Library ordering up baroque manuscripts and poring over them in a very cold and crowded reading room. She'd then gone to the dismal basement cafeteria for her usual late lunch: a crust of hard, saltless bread, a few pieces of chorizo, and a *pincho* de tortilla—as Spaniards referred to a narrow slice of cold potato, onion, and egg pie. A demi glass of cheap white wine was her reward.

After the sun went down, she'd Metro'd to the city center in anticipation of a tiresome but mandatory dinner meeting of her fellow fellows in the loud, smoky bar next door to one of the city's oldest restaurants.

She had quickly come to hate these monthly gatherings. Of a group of fifteen, she was, and would continue to be, the only woman of color and, as far as she could tell, the only queer person. It was a true boys' club. The two other women were a pompous sexagenarian emerita from Columbia who continually asked her where she was "really" from and a mousy blonde from Dartmouth in a constant state of anxiety (understandable, Adrianna granted) over the well-being of her three-year-old twin sons still residing with their overwhelmed father back in New Hampshire.

It was always a two-stage affair. The Ivy that funded their fellowships was fond of following the fellows' interminable happy hour "reports" with the same kind of vaguely narcotic, drawn-out, fish and cream-sauced dinner the restaurant had been serving since—and maybe during—the Spanish Civil War. She never got through all the courses but she always left feeling like a snake who had swallowed an ostrich egg.

The thing dragged on forever and as it did, hands and conversation began to wander from the scholarly to the salacious, none of it tasteful or even funny, with alarming speed.

Adrianna waited until the discussion took an especially off-color turn, which it inevitably did, to excuse herself for an unnecessary trip to the powder room. En route, walking the long wood-paneled hall to the back of the building, she felt her phone's vibration through the sides of the Goyard bag that accompanied her everywhere.

She didn't receive many communiqués at this time of the night. Most people stateside would assume she'd be either out for a late dinner or asleep. Adrianna was curious enough about the sender to plop down on a bank of tufted leather benches outside the W/C and have a look. In any case, it wasn't like she actually had to go.

Charlotte Hilaire.

Now that was a blast from the past. What in the world might cute little Charlotte want—contact info for a colleague, perhaps, or a good word for a job?

How striking she must be as a grown woman, Adrianna mused. With an ease that surprised her, she could conjure up Charlotte as she was when they'd first met, a formidably intelligent, tennis-playing type who'd gone straight through to grad school and couldn't have been more than twenty-two. A wearer of sundresses. Small-boned and curvy with olive skin grown deeply tan from days at the beach or on the courts. Freckled. A shy but devastating smile.

Supremely shy. In fact, if memory served, outside of the seminar, they'd barely spoken to each other. The one exception might have been a few ridiculously chaste coffee dates provisionally arranged to discuss "professional development" or suggested revisions for Charlotte's brilliant, as Adrianna recalled, thesis on the color line and Impressionism in New Orleans.

Wasn't she *from* New Orleans? Some old-guard Creole family?

Adrianna realized all this reminiscing had played out even before she clicked into her direct messages to see what, if anything, Charlotte Hilaire wanted from her.

She'd forgotten they were Facebook friends. But there it was.

Hers was the kind of stilted, charmingly awkward correspondence Adrianna sometimes received from younger, though usually queer, female scholars who hoped she would read their incipient articles or participate in a panel at a conference.

Dear Dr. Coates, it began. The remainder of the paragraph said in four or five multi-claused sentences what she might have led with: *I'm in Madrid on a courier trip with a couple of extra days on my hands due to the storm. Might you have time for a drink?*

Chapter Two

Adrianna checked the time. It was just past eleven. For Madrid, especially during a holiday week, this was truthfully a little early for a nightcap. But it might be perfect timing for a quiet get-together at her favorite unofficial women's bar, a little spot near the Plaza de Chueca.

But what was she thinking? This wasn't a date. The girl was emphatically straight. In her mind, Charlotte had always been at the center of a gaggle of preening, tight polo-wearing, meticulously shaven gay boys when Adrianna saw her around Yale. She was just the kind of pretty girl their kind loved to gossip and drink with; a fashionable enhancement of their brand.

Dealer's choice, though. If Charlotte Hilaire wanted to kill time with a local in Madrid, she'd be wise to do it at a place of Adrianna Coates's choosing. For her part, she had little interest in traipsing across the city on a stormy night to meet the girl at her uptight hotel near the museum.

Adrianna paused a moment, then wrote: Dr. Hilaire! Call me Adrianna, please! How nice to hear from you. I'm actually out right now. Can you get a taxi to Chueca in 30 or so?

No reason to be coy, she thought, pleased with the lack of hesitation that characterized her post-"divorce" self. But then it suddenly and unpleasantly dawned on her that Charlotte might be thinking of the old Adrianna. That back in grad school she might even have witnessed Adrianna's undistinguished exploits during the death throes of her last, very long-term, relationship. A time when she was definitely not herself.

Even now she felt ashamed of mid-thirtysomething Adrianna. There was an entire embarrassing year she tried not to remember—when the pain of betrayal filled her with a furious desperation she hoped never to experience again. For the whole of her first two terms of assistant teaching she'd been careless and unfaithful—a vengeful response to the humiliating infidelity of Vera, her eventual ex. Never again.

Single now for the better part of two years, she was neither hungry nor thirsty. Her sex life was like the feeling of fullness that eventually comes with fasting. In the academic realm, near-superhuman productivity had garnered her scholarly acclaim and no small jealousy from her less single-minded peers. And it was all sustained by an occasional one-night stand or porn marathon. She was as untethered as a balloon, free to float through her forties with few responsibilities or attachments besides the life of the mind and the commitment to stay that way.

Her phone pinged. A restrained five-minute delay suggested Charlotte's desire not to seem overly eager while being at the same time unwilling to miss their reunion.

Perfect.

They would meet at the Chueca bar at midnight. Adrianna was surprised Charlotte hadn't balked at the appointed time as too late to leave her hotel, as it might have seemed to other Americans. An image of her former classmate nervously accepting a plastic glass of wine at a long-ago campus reading flashed through Adrianna's mind. Back then those modestly downcast eyes were a source of frustration, coming from an emerging scholar who had every reason to be confident. But perhaps this Charlotte was less restrained and timid. Maybe now she was a woman of the world.

Spanish bars are small and El Jardin, around the corner from the square and tucked between a florist and a hair salon, was smaller than most. Adrianna started there most days. It was a good place to sip a well-priced café con leche and read a few pages of *El País* before she set out on her walk to the National Library.

She'd only realized the place was run by two women when she overheard the older of the couple, gray-haired with a plunging neckline, shouting at the other one, also gray-haired but wearing a man's shirt and boot-cut jeans, about how after twenty-five years you'd think she'd know how she wanted things set up in the kitchen. After that, Adrianna thought of the place, really more of a café with unbelievably long hours, as a lesbian bar.

It was only a few minutes before midnight when she arrived. She was relieved Charlotte hadn't beaten her, which would have made her seem like a bit of an asshole for being late to her own meeting. Adrianna took off her coat. She folded it neatly and sat down beside it on the banquette, facing out so that she'd see, and be seen by, Charlotte when she parted the heavy velvet curtains over the door.

She ordered a cognac and a coffee, taking a moment to look around. Across the room, the server, a girl with an asymmetrical haircut, used a pair of silver tongs to place two butter cookies on a plate. Adrianna's phone pinged. The streets were pretty bad, Charlotte apologized, but the taxi was close. She should be there soon.

Snow was falling thick and fast now. Inside looking out there was nothing but a white screen interrupted by the occasional appearance of a human—or canine—form passing before the glass in silhouette. The girl with the tongs had cued up a Sarah Vaughan album from the sixties. The few other customers, a couple of young women working on their laptops, three probably students, and a pair of close-bearded men who seemed romantically linked, conversed in hushed tones.

Straight or not, Adrianna became aware that she was feeling a feeling about seeing Charlotte again. It was the feeling when you're waiting for someone to arrive and you almost don't want them to because the sensation of expectancy is so sweet. It was that setting on the emotional dial somewhere between *don't let it be over* and *make it stop*; not to be confused with the esteem-challenging fear that you might be about to get stood up.

Charlotte had eliminated that possibility for Adrianna with her thoughtful text.

No, this was more akin to sheer, unabashed anticipation. *Quelle surprise.*

The phone pinged again. Driver having trouble with location.

She began to respond with more detailed directions—Charlotte would probably need to walk a bit anyway, as the one-way street was super narrow and Spanish cabs weren't in the habit of dropping you off at exactly the requested address. She hadn't quite finished typing when she felt a whoosh of icy air as the little bell tinkled over the entrance. She didn't think to look up since Charlotte was clearly still in the taxi.

"That you, Adrianna?" asked a voice with just the slightest Southern lilt.

Something in Adrianna quickened.

She had meant to take off the reading glasses she'd recently begun to need for fine print and her phone. Instead, she quickly looked up and over them.

Damn. The elegant woman before her, and she was definitely that, stood wrapped in a long wool coat with a high collar, looking as much like an actress from the forties as a Titian painting. While stylish, her garment wasn't nearly heavy enough for the city in this season. Charlotte's glossy dark hair was pulled back into a loose chignon sprinkled with beads of melted snow. After removing her leather gloves, she brushed off the water and loosened the belt casually tied around her waist.

"Charlotte," said Adrianna, standing. "I was just texting you. My God. It's been forever. I'm so sorry about this disgusting weather."

"Oh, that's funny. I guess the signal has to bounce back to the States before it can make it across town," she said, bemused. "And this weather is an absolute dream!"

Charlotte dropped her coat in a pile at Adrianna's side. "If it weren't for this, I'd be on the red-eye tomorrow. To Tweed!" She made a sad face.

Tweed was New Haven's tiny regional airport. While it was only minutes from downtown, getting anywhere from there always required a harrowing connector flight to Philly, making it both more convenient and less appealing than flying out of Hartford.

Adrianna took full advantage of the moment, moving in for a friendly hug.

Charlotte was engulfed in an aura of frosty air; Adrianna felt the storm's cold coming off her skin and clothes. Her breasts were soft and full under her navy blue cashmere sweater and as they embraced Adrianna thought she sensed an invitation to press a little closer, so she did. Charlotte was a good three inches shorter. Her slight frame was slightly padded. And it certainly suited her. With tonight's sleepy eyes and easy, radiant smile, she was adorable and sexy and definitely not the shy, boy-crazy girl Adrianna remembered.

★ ★ ★

The server came over and Charlotte ordered a glass of red wine on the grounds that she should stick to what she'd started with at dinner. But really, it was to keep her shit together. Had she just imagined that surely more-than-collegial squeeze from Adrianna, who smelled delectably of what her mother would call "white flowers"—orange blossom, jasmine. Frangipani. However good a Bourbon rocks sounded she had a feeling she'd want to be relatively clearheaded for what was about to transpire.

They fell quickly into conversation, catching up on life since grad school.

To Charlotte's mind there wasn't much to say. She'd finished three years ago, gone immediately into a one-year visiting gig at NYU but failed to get a tenure-track job that season. The next year, she'd taken yet another visiting job, this time at Bard, and had again failed to land the teaching job she'd spent seven years training for. She'd been suggested as a candidate for the curatorial position at the Woodley Center for American Art and, with nothing else on the horizon, had taken it.

She'd always hoped she'd end up teaching at a liberal arts college where she could get to know her students and they could get to know her. She'd definitely imagined teaching smart students who gave a damn somewhere. But publicly, her complaints were few. The museum job was interesting if not especially demanding, and it drew on her expertise in nineteenth-century art.

Privately—and she didn't mention this to Adrianna—she profoundly missed being in a classroom, trying to make things less horrible for POC. And she also missed the more scholarly side of the art world. Given the required schmoozing and fundraising, she feared she wasn't cut out to be an upper-level curator—it was a prejudice that severely limited her career prospects. Then there was the museum's legendarily charismatic, but in reality racist and homophobic, director looming over her like the sword of Damocles. But that was a story for another night.

Charlotte admired Adrianna for doing exactly what Yale expected of them. While still in her final term, she'd landed a coveted job at UCLA. She'd been successfully teaching there since and was now on a cushy sabbatical-year fellowship to finish the research for her first book.

"Do you like LA?" Charlotte asked.

"I actually love LA," Adrianna answered, eyes sparkling. "As a proud Chicagoan, I never thought I would. But it's so fucking sunny, for one. And so diverse. Lots of people like us." She winked at Charlotte.

Charlotte wasn't sure what to do with that. If Adrianna was fishing for something, she figured she'd make her work for it. She certainly wasn't going to put herself out there. Not yet.

"Lots of academics or lots of queer people or lots of brown people or…?" she asked.

Adrianna nodded.

"Sorry," she said. "What I meant was lots of people of color. Of course, there are a shit ton of lesbians there, too. I always assumed you weren't queer. But I guess I don't know how you identify."

Charlotte eyed her carefully, weighing what felt like a whiff of condescension against Adrianna's obvious desire to pin her down.

"Why did you assume I wasn't queer?" she asked.

Adrianna took a strategically timed sip of her second cognac. "I guess because you were constantly surrounded by the fuckboy mafia. I figured that was more your scene."

"It *was* my scene," said Charlotte. "But only because nobody except you was out as a queer woman in that program. And you were obviously out of reach."

Had she really gone there?

"I didn't know you cared," Adrianna said with a glance over her reading glasses. She was clearly trying not to smile but when their eyes met she held Charlotte's gaze.

"Didn't you?"

Apparently, all Adrianna could do was laugh and look away. She'd been caught off guard twice in ten minutes. This wasn't like the Adrianna Charlotte knew. Or thought she knew.

"My people *c'est un bon métissage*," Charlotte said, knowing French was one of Adrianna's languages. "I identify as Creole. I don't feel the need to clarify beyond that. I'm not sure I *could* clarify enough for some people's requirements. I'm thinking about bringing Quadroon back."

Adrianna nodded. "I know what you mean, of course. Sometimes you want to say, so are we using the one-drop rule or the blood quantum? Just tell me which boxes you need checked."

She paused and they looked at each other intently. It felt to Charlotte as if they'd each suddenly recognized how rare it was to be talking to somebody who understood at a gut level that these difficult experiences add up. It was hard to believe they'd never been honest with each other like this in all that time together in New Haven, where they were two of maybe four or five women of color in the program—including the faculty.

But Charlotte had never seen herself as Adrianna's peer in those days. She'd occupied an elevated position in Charlotte's mind not only because of her advanced standing—widely recognized as superior for her glowing teaching evaluations and precocious publishing record—but in an almost ontological sense. It was as if she was made of different and better stuff than the rest of them. And she seemed not to need to bother much with those of Charlotte's ilk, who had yet to prove themselves as anything but standard-grade wannabes.

"But let's go back to the other thing," Adrianna said now, like a reporter who knows she's discovered a productive line of questioning. "So you were right there being queer all that time and I had no idea?"

"I was doing my damnedest," Charlotte said, thinking back. "I mean, of course, I was queer. Always have been. But I hadn't really figured out how to do that part of my life in the academy or whatever. Like, I'd see people at lectures or something and want to talk to them but then I'd think, what if they're not as much of a mess as I am at getting work done? Or what if they're smarter than me and I can't keep up with the conversation?"

"Charlotte Hilaire was insecure about her intellect?" Adrianna said, incredulous in the most flattering way. "I always thought one of the most attractive things about you was how modest you were about your brains. Never occurred to me that you didn't know how exceptional you were. You are."

Adrianna made a frustrated, almost dismissive, face and looked out the window. Perhaps because she had said more than she intended to, perhaps because she'd learned Charlotte felt that way all those years ago.

And she still did, truth be told. Especially now that she was face-to-face with someone she'd always thought so highly of. And had a thing for, let's just say it.

She realized Adrianna was looking at her again.

The expression in her serious eyes was hard to decipher. It wasn't, Charlotte was relieved to note, anything vaguely professorial, as if she was sizing up Charlotte's confession in any work-related, judgmental way. Rather, her gaze was soft. Soft, and kind, and a little reticent. She had, after all, just admitted to having found something attractive about Charlotte back in the day. Why did that feel like some incredible victory?

"Thank you," Charlotte said. "You know I always…"

No, no, no.

She began again. "You know, your opinion always meant something to me. Still does, of course."

Adrianna tipped back the last drops of tawny liquid remaining in her snifter. "Likewise, I'm sure, my dear," she said with a gentle, almost teasing, smile. "Shall we get out of here?"

Chapter Three

Last call in the bars and clubs usually came around 3:00 a.m. But in a tiny café on the night of what was shaping up to be a record-breaking blizzard, the girl making the drinks was eager to head home. Preferably before two, when the Metro stopped running. Adrianna and Charlotte were now the last customers. Adrianna signaled the server for the bill.

"So tomorrow, you're off the hook? The painting is uncrated and the eagle has landed or whatever they say that puts you in the clear?" Adrianna asked while they waited. Charlotte's cheeks were on fire. Adrianna was obviously trying to diminish the embarrassment Charlotte had caused herself with that last statement by circling back to the museum talk that had occupied them earlier that night.

Adrianna was acquainted with some of Charlotte's coworkers, good, bad and indifferent. It turned out she had been a docent for the museum's famed *Americas* show, several years back.

"I am indeed off the hook," Charlotte said. "The last I heard, James is going to try to get me out on Thursday."

It was only Monday. At a minimum, that would mean three more nights in Madrid. Could they possibly do more of exactly this? Charlotte wondered. Why else would Adrianna be asking?

Honestly, if Charlotte had found herself in a tell-all mode it was only because Adrianna was delightfully tipsy. It was thoroughly enjoyable to finally witness the notoriously aloof golden child who had taken herself so seriously back then let her hair down a little. Not that she had done so literally. They both evidently conformed to the unspoken academic code for long-haired women that called for buns and ponytails, so as not to seem too trendy or flirtatious. Neither could someone in their position run the risk of being misread as Jezebel, Jackie Brown, Carmen Miranda, or even a doppelganger for the Duchess of Sussex. Charlotte's cleavage already made it overly easy for people to cast her to type—hence the starched cotton shirt beneath her sweater, which had the effect of flattening, if only slightly, her buxom chest.

Curvaceous as Adrianna was, everything about her seemed similarly battened down, buttoned-up, and impervious to the wrong kind of prying eyes. Her nutmeg brown skin was as smooth and wrinkle-free as ever; Charlotte's own crow's feet were deeper. The streaks of silver in her dark hair and the air of gravitas that came with them had aged her somewhat since Charlotte's undergrad years—but in a way that she found appealing. Charlotte wouldn't mind at all seeing that hair loose—Adrianna's rough-textured, salt-and-pepper waves fanning around her shoulders while Charlotte gripped it in her fingers.

Adrianna paid and left an extra euro for the server, even though, as Charlotte had learned, tips were not expected in Spain. She gathered up Charlotte's coat and shook out the folds, holding it for her to put on. When Charlotte reached back to slip her arms into the sleeves, Adrianna moved in close behind her. Charlotte felt her warm, not unpleasantly boozy, breath at her neck as she hitched up the coat's collar to make sure it covered her shirt and settled just right on her shoulders. She thought about making a move—about turning around in that very moment and kissing Adrianna on her full red lips.

"It's going to be hard to get you a taxi in this," Adrianna

said before Charlotte could act, turning them both to look at the flurries swirling madly outside. She looked down at Charlotte's flats. "We can walk to my apartment from here, if we're careful. It's enormous. There's a pullout bed in the study. How does that sound?"

"Are you sure?" Charlotte asked. The invitation was exactly what she had hoped for, of course—except for the spare room part. And yet she was incredibly tired all of a sudden. Tired enough to collapse into Adrianna's arms right there.

"Now that I'm standing, I'm crashing pretty hard," she admitted. "Honestly, I don't know if I'd be able to stay awake long enough to wait here for a taxi."

"It's only a few blocks," Adrianna said gently. "We'll get you straight to bed and you can sleep in tomorrow. Can't imagine I won't be working from home if this keeps up."

"If you're really sure," Charlotte said. It was beginning to be a struggle just to keep her eyes open.

"Come on," Adrianna said.

She offered her arm to Charlotte and they made their way out of the café, down the street, around the corner, across a little plaza—where a pedestrian path through the snow had already formed—and into a plain but patrician four-story building. The three flights up to the apartment were slow going, with Charlotte sleepily leaning on Adrianna, but they made it.

A short time later, without knowing exactly what had happened, Charlotte found herself tucked into a comfortable sofa bed in a room whose only other furnishing was a massive desk stacked high with books, plastic binders, and unpacked boxes. Snow was falling steadily across a pyramid of lamplight outside the window. She drifted into sleep thinking about the way Adrianna had helped her out of her sweater and unbuttoned her shirt, for which Charlotte had been far more awake at the time than she let on.

★ ★ ★

The trick to avoiding bad jet lag is to immediately adapt yourself to the new time zone. If you take a night flight to Europe from the East Coast and get there in the morning, it's always best not to miss a beat. Once you get to the hotel, you simply have to force yourself to unpack. Walk. Eat. No naps. And definitely no flopping down on the first bed you see and waking up at God knows when.

Charlotte had this part down. Awakening the next morning to find that it was a respectable 9:30 Madrid time wasn't much of a surprise. She could survive on six hours of sleep but she could thrive on seven. Considering the red wine she had under her belt, she felt fit as a fiddle. Once the requisite where am I? how did I get here? what day is it? queries were mentally resolved, she stretched, sat up, and put her feet on the floor. The snow had stopped. Spanish snow. In Spain.

Wait, where was she again?

She rewound the events of the previous two days, what was essentially a marathon of laser-focused troubleshooting uninterrupted by any form of horizontality and then vacuum packed into 24 hours. But of all those hours, the only three she felt like replaying started and ended with Adrianna. In whose apartment she was apparently waking up. And whose Brooks Brothers nightshirt she was apparently now wearing. Lawd.

"Charlotte, are you among the living?" Adrianna's voice called from somewhere at the other end of the apartment. She must have heard her walk across the floor to the window.

"Something like that," Charlotte answered to the door.

"There's water and Advil on the desk if you want it," Adrianna said. "I haven't been up very long. Forgot about coffee until this minute. Will you have some if I make it?"

Forgot to make coffee? At 9:30? Downright diabolical.

"Oh, I'd love some, whenever you get to it," she said. "I'll be out in a few minutes, if that's alright."

The only response Charlotte could discern if she listened hard was the rapid-fire clickety-click of Adrianna's fingers on her computer keyboard; she was obviously working away while the intruder slept. This went on for several more minutes. The cessation of the typing was then followed by the sound of footfalls across creaking hardwood floors and the tinkle of bottles and jars that indicated the opening and closing of a refrigerator.

More creaking floors, then a soft knock.

"Who is it?" said Charlotte with mock formality.

Adrianna cracked the door and leaned in. She was still in pajamas. Actual pajamas, though partially unbuttoned ones, with red stripes and piping and a pocket. She proffered a bottle of cava in Charlotte's direction like meat before a lion.

"Of course, there's always the hair of the dog," she said. "It's an official day off in Madrid. They've closed the Biblioteca and the banks. This almost never happens. What say you to a taste of this?" As she waved the bottle back and forth, Charlotte glimpsed breasts as round and low as her own.

Yes, please, was her answer.

"Well, I don't see why not" was what she actually said. "But I also don't want to impose on you. I'm not sure how far we are from my hotel, but I bet they can send a car if you want to get rid of me before the snow starts to melt."

"We can cross that icy bridge when we come to it," Adrianna said. "Something tells me you'll want cava *and* coffee, not cava as a substitute for coffee, *verdad*?"

"Did we talk about coffee last night?" Charlotte asked. Otherwise, how could she know?

"No. But I seem to remember a certain travel mug being

more or less superglued to your hand for the duration of that seminar."

· "Damn," Charlotte said both in her mind and out loud. "You were paying attention, after all."

How glad was Adrianna that she had opted for the glamorous apartment. She'd barely let herself consider the possibility that she might, at some point in the year she'd spend there, have an overnight guest. But now that she did, it was good to be able to host her in a style approximating that to which Charlotte Hilaire was undoubtedly accustomed. Nothing wrong with treating yourself well when you worked as hard as she did, Adrianna reminded herself. Nothing wrong with taking a little time off for the good things in life.

The fellows in Adrianna's cohort were given the names of prominent scholars who would themselves be away on sabbaticals, usually in the US, and who might be willing to exchange their apartments for equivalent lodging in the States. Adrianna had found her sunny, quiet, tastefully decorated, unbelievably located Madrid apartment that way.

However, because she herself was funny about sharing space with strangers, she'd opted to leave her own place empty while she was gone. Fiscally speaking, this was a missed opportunity of mammoth proportions. The astounding rent she could charge for her sweet stucco house in Highland Park—purchased with money her mother had left her—would amount to at least two years' in-state tuition. To Adrianna, however, not needing to worry about even the most exemplary colleague rifling through her things, breaking something, or just generally sleeping (or what-have-you) in her bed, was priceless.

She didn't have anyone to send to college anyway.

She did, however, have Esther, her best friend and a professor at the law school, who was kind enough to check up on the house once a week. It was basically on the way from Pasadena, where she lived with her husband and nine-year-old son. Esther had written the previous night to say that all was well and that she hoped Adrianna was finally "getting busy" as she put it.

Not yet, Adrianna had texted back this morning. But I'm working on it.

The apartment's numerous kitchen cupboards seemed to contain every possible style of drinkware, from snifters to tiny etched liqueur glasses. But Adrianna couldn't find a champagne flute to save her life. Which was frustrating because her current plan was to summon Charlotte to the kitchen with the sound of a popping cork followed by the pouring of the sparkling wine into tall, suggestive containers of who-knows-what-might-happen-next. Wine glasses or tumblers just wouldn't have the same effect.

At any rate, something would need to be done soon because the kettle had whistled and the stovetop Italian Moka had just gurgled its last stream of espresso. The scent was sure to bring Charlotte in at any moment, salivating like a Pavlovian dog for the hot Americano she'd been promised.

"What is this fine French roast I smell?" she said, inhaling the aroma as she sauntered in. She was still wearing the borrowed nightshirt but she'd thrown her sweater over it in a show of modesty that Adrianna found incredibly cute, though not particularly effective as it only drew attention to a petite figure that was both athletic and voluptuous.

"Help yourself," Adrianna said. "I'm beginning to think my Spanish alter ego lacks champagne glasses. Very disappointing in an academic."

"Maybe they're so special he or she or they keep them in the dining room. Or maybe they get used so often—" Charlotte was perusing the kitchen as she spoke "—they stay out all the time." Her search complete, she walked over to a little wall-mounted shelf and plucked a plain pair of tall glasses from beside a hefty tome called *Historia de Champagne*.

"Voilà!" she said. And set them down next to the metal bowl Adrianna had filled with ice for the cava.

Just then, a phone pinged a ringtone Adrianna didn't recognize.

"Oh, that's me," said Charlotte. "I better make sure the museum is still standing." She walked quickly out of the room and headed back down the hall.

They better not call her in, Adrianna thought, feeling surprisingly anxious. Even a little possessive. Had she played it a little too cool by not attempting so much as the kiss they both seemed to be dancing around the previous night? It wasn't like her to miss out on an opportunity like that one.

When she reappeared a few minutes later, Charlotte looked both worried and confused.

"What's wrong?" Adrianna asked.

"That was the hotel. I'm supposed to check out today and they're booked for the holiday so they can't move me to another room. The woman at the front desk said she's been calling around all morning, but with the storm and Barajas shut down, she's not sure where to suggest. All the good hotels are full."

"I guess it's time to cross that bridge I mentioned," said Adrianna.

She wouldn't make the same mistake twice.

"Stay here. Have them send your things. I'll give you the address." She endeavored to make it sound like the single possible solution and a fait accompli. But beneath that veneer of calm detachment, it was unthinkable to her not to have

Charlotte for another night. And it was all Adrianna could do not to say so.

"Oh, no, I really cannot impose on you like that," Charlotte said firmly. She was standing in the frame of the doorway, one shapely leg crossed over the other like Raphael's Eve. "I've already interrupted your work. And I'm loath to make a nuisance of myself. Really. I'm sure there's somewhere completely fine for me to go. I just need to do a little searching."

This must be the inverse of Southern hospitality, for it was clearly Charlotte's decorous, old-fashioned code of conduct. Imposing on your host: the sin second only to pride. Adrianna could see her holing herself up in some gritty hostel in the *centro* just to avoid what she perceived as bad manners. But that would never do.

"And I am loath to send you out into a snowstorm," she said with as much conviction as she could provide without distracting herself from the more urgent business of opening the cava. "My work needs interrupting. I'm bored beyond words with this project. A day like this is a gift." She wrapped a dishcloth over the cork and effortlessly popped it. Say yes.

"Well, when you put it like that," Charlotte said, eyes brightening, "I can see it wouldn't be right to squander something so precious."

She walked over to where Adrianna was standing at the counter and leaned back against it next to her, crossing her arms over her breasts.

A peripheral glance revealed the full shape of her, angled like that with her ass out and her back slightly arched. The profile of Charlotte's beautiful features and the lovely chain of undulating curves from bust to waist to hips.

She caught Adrianna looking and smiled a dizzyingly wicked smile.

"You gonna pour that?"

"I don't want to be overhasty," Adrianna said, trying hard not to smile back. "There might be other ways to christen a snow day that I hadn't sufficiently considered."

"That makes one of us," Charlotte said, letting her arms drop to reveal her chest.

Adrianna let her eyes drop to Charlotte's nipples pressing hard against the nightshirt's thin cotton. Had she always been like this? Adrianna was beginning to sense the sand shifting beneath her feet, surprised to notice that she didn't mind feeling a little undone. Not one bit. Charlotte was demure. It was the best word Adrianna could think of to describe her. But there was something else beneath that unrehearsed refinement, something self-assured, almost cocky.

"So you've had other plans all along?" Adrianna said, putting down the bottle and trailing a finger up Charlotte's exposed thigh.

Charlotte smiled. "Oh, I'm always thinking ahead."

"Eyes on the prize?" said Adrianna in a voice that had dropped to a husky whisper.

"Eyes on the prize."

Chapter Four

In view of their longstanding relationship with Charlotte's museum, the hotel was indeed willing to ask someone in housekeeping to pack up the few things in her room and send them over to Adrianna's place. They'd even included a care package of extra toiletries.

The car arrived with the luggage while they were still flirting and deliberating in the kitchen, the cava as yet unpoured. Hearing the buzzer, Adrianna had reluctantly thrown on a robe and slippers and run down the three flights, leaving Charlotte still leaning on the counter to contemplate what came next.

"I'm putting your very nice suitcase in my room," a breathless Adrianna said as soon as she closed the apartment door behind her. "It won't fit in the study."

It would have fit in the study. But it fit a lot better in the bedroom.

"I'm out here," Charlotte informed her. She had taken the bottle and glasses and resituated herself on the living room sofa. If it had been in the States, the long, upholstered couch with its plethora of throw pillows would have sat smack-dab in front of a flat-screen TV. This one, by refreshing contrast, faced a wall of tall, arched casement windows looking onto mostly sky and a distant cityscape punctuated by the city's numerous church towers. Today the potted trees and summer furniture on the neighboring balconies were coated with an inch or two of velvety snow.

What sun there had been was already dimming.

Adrianna was surprised, but certainly not disappointed, to find Charlotte curled up at one end of said sofa, glass in hand, taking it all in just as she herself liked to do at sunset.

"It's beautiful," Charlotte said. "Doesn't look like any place else I've been."

"Sure doesn't." Adrianna sat down close beside Charlotte. Encouragingly close, she hoped.

Charlotte filled Adrianna's flute with pale bubbly and raised hers in a wordless toast. Their glasses clinked.

"What are we drinking to?" Adrianna asked.

"Bank closures and oversold hotels?" Charlotte replied with a laugh and a gulp. Her legs were folded under her and as she went to set down her glass, she slipped into Adrianna's shoulder, not seeming to mind at all when Adrianna leaned into her and caught her eye.

"If you'd have looked at me like that in school, I'm not sure what I would have done," Charlotte said.

"I can't promise I never did," Adrianna admitted. "Especially there at the end."

"You were definitely shopping around at one point, as I recall. Like a freshman for new classes," Charlotte said. "Least that's what it looked like from where I stood."

"I was a train wreck," Adrianna said solemnly. "My ex cheated on me with someone I cared about and I was worried to death I wouldn't get a job—and interviewing cross-country practically every week while I finished the last chapter of my diss. Those days seem incomparably easy, yet completely impossible when I look back. But I fucked things up with a lot of people and I hate thinking about it."

"Your heart was broken," Charlotte said, reaching for the

cava. She'd stopped looking at Adrianna but her voice conveyed empathy.

Had someone broken Charlotte's heart? Adrianna wanted badly to know.

"And I did that to others in return," she said.

"You are indeed a heartbreaker," Charlotte laughed.

"You're one to talk," Adrianna replied. "I can't believe you weren't dating your pretty little ass off—or seeing faculty on the sly at least. I don't think I do believe it."

"Well, you can believe it or not. I'm not saying I didn't sleep around some. But grads and faculty were off-limits. Not out of moral approbation. I just knew it would throw me off my game. I don't mind telling you I had tempting offers from both parties."

Good thing Adrianna wasn't one of those former suitors. It was so much better finding her again like this, now that they were both past the stage of perpetual heightened insecurity. Now that there was no history with Charlotte, only possibility.

Neither of them were drunk, just usefully relaxed, their inhibitions disarmed by the alcohol, their focus sharpened by the caffeine.

Adrianna set down her own near-empty glass and turned toward Charlotte.

"Let's toast to layovers instead."

"With what?"

"Come here," Adrianna said, just to see how Charlotte reacted to being told what to do.

"Make me," she replied, finishing what was left in her flute and starting to rise.

"Where are you going now?"

"I'm thirsty. Think I'll get a glass of water…"

"Fuck the water," Adrianna said. She pulled Charlotte back down to her for a deep, wet kiss that burned deliciously from the sparkling wine in her mouth and on their lips. Charlotte responded with a kind of unrestraint, immediately taking the lead. God did she. Adrianna suddenly seemed to feel her touch everywhere.

It was one of those moments when you don't realize how much you want something—*someone*—until she's within reach. She wasn't going to lose her second chance.

Charlotte was a bundle of delighted nerves. "Are you seeing anyone?" she asked, coming up for air after they'd been at it for several minutes. Adrianna, who was in the process of sliding her hands beneath Charlotte's nightshirt, momentarily stopped.

"Hardly," she answered, a layer of reserve creeping into her expression. "Are you?"

"Not even close," Charlotte said. "I have no idea why I asked that. Please don't stop. I'm sorry."

Adrianna turned her attentions to the nape of Charlotte's neck, hungrily kissing her there and below the ear before coming back to her lips. Charlotte felt chilled all over until Adrianna slid her hot hands over her waist. Her fingers momentarily surrounded her rib cage, then she began to palm Charlotte's nipples, gently kneading her breasts as she started—then stopped—kissing her. It was as if Adrianna sensed that Charlotte might be having second thoughts. But it wasn't that. Not exactly.

Adrianna sat back. "Sweet girl, I don't know what we're doing here," she said, in a voice that was new. "But I like you. Even more than I remembered. And I was having a very nice time just talking. So, if you want to take it slow…"

Like hell.

What Charlotte wanted was a guarantee that whatever was about to play out on Adrianna's sofa wouldn't ruin her for the rest of her single life. She was going to do this. There was no question. They were, after a fashion, going to fuck. And it would be everything she was prepared to admit she'd wanted from Adrianna for a very long time. But that felt terrifying. And not only in a YOLO kind of way. It felt terrifying in a once-might-never-be-enough kind of way. But once was better than never.

Wasn't it?

Charlotte cut off Adrianna's sweetly sensitive but profoundly off-base words with a long and very French kiss, laying them both down on the sofa.

When she cavalierly kicked off her lacy panties into the middle of the living room they both had to laugh. The kissing started again, building pleasure between her legs even before Adrianna touched her there. Charlotte hitched up her knee to show how much she wanted Adrianna, letting her bent leg fall open at her side. She could feel her own wetness.

Adrianna sat back again, this time to look. It was beyond hot to see her so turned on, briefly closing her eyes in appreciation, surely unconscious that she was licking her lips. She massaged Charlotte's thigh for a long moment before slipping her thumb just inside her.

"Oh, babe," Adrianna murmured, as if what she found was more than she expected. Given Charlotte's rough breathing she shouldn't have been surprised. Even so, Adrianna's voice got suddenly dreamy and low. "Fuck," she said. "You sweet, sweet thing."

"You see what you do to me," Charlotte responded matter-of-factly. As Adrianna's fingers moved over her, she let herself relax, feeling her body grow warm and receptive from the gentle motions over and around her clit.

Charlotte's nerves had briefly gotten the best of her, but this was what she wanted. She wanted Adrianna's attention—

and her hand—right where they were. Whatever came after would be what it was. But this amazing woman wanted her, too, not desperately or just for her body, but in a way that seemed grounded in getting to know her this time.

"Damn, you feel good, Charlotte," Adrianna said. And she dipped toward Charlotte for another kiss.

Charlotte let Adrianna kiss her for a few minutes, feeling the heavenly pressure of her breasts and the soft folds of her belly against her skin. But after that, she leaned forward to Adrianna and coaxed her down to the cushions, turning her on her side, positioning her top leg to reveal her own gorgeous sex.

It was just too hard to resist. Their bodies, their proportions, seemed made for doing just this and Charlotte suspected Adrianna would love it.

She moved into her, slowly brushing her own sex back and forth over Adrianna's until she groaned with pleasure. Charlotte braced herself against the fleshy part of Adrianna's taut brown thigh, slowly grinding against her. Looking down, Adrianna's face was in profile. But she was in obvious ecstasy, biting her lip and furrowing her brow. Charlotte bent over her giving harder, deeper strokes, and cupping Adrianna's breasts as she did.

"Yes, baby" was all Adrianna could manage, over and over and over.

Doing it this way took time. But they had time. Today at least. And Charlotte wanted to leave Adrianna with something she wouldn't soon forget.

She picked up the pace, roughly slapping against Adrianna so that their arousal was split between touching and parting, touching and parting. They were both feeling it deep now, both moving to increase the other's pleasure, which steadily climbed until Adrianna's moaning turned to dirty talk, then abruptly ceased, and she let go spectacularly, reaching back to grip Charlotte's ass and holding her there until she finished shaking and rocking.

Strong, capable Adrianna had let herself be taken and it felt so good to know she was the source of that beautiful release.

But Adrianna's gripping desire wasn't all Charlotte experienced in their strangely tender moment. She felt her own need and their connection, and she realized how long it had been since she'd negotiated the fine line between being in— and being out of—control.

They never made it into the bedroom that afternoon. But eventually, they did doze for a little while, with Adrianna spooning Charlotte under the sheets and blanket she had stolen from the guest bed in case things got…messy.

Despite her big talk, Charlotte was still exhausted from the flight and it was simply impossible for her not to fall fast asleep in Adrianna's arms. In fact, she hadn't even noticed when Adrianna gently extricated herself, padding off into the apartment at some point after the sun went down. When Charlotte awoke in a moonlit Spanish living room to the strains of Celia Cruz and the fragrance of something savory baking in the oven, she was filled with undiluted joy.

And unsatiated hunger; she was starving.

Adrianna appeared in the doorway. *"Muy buenas,"* she said. "Did you get a little rest?"

"I did," said Charlotte. "What in the name of all that's holy are you making out there?"

"Just a quiche," said Adrianna. "I don't make them very often. I had rough puff in the freezer and I must have New Orleans on my mind. It's the closest I can come to something Creole."

Charlotte had wrapped herself up in the sheet. "You came pretty close a little while ago," she said.

Adrianna gave a heavenward glance. "I did, didn't I? This'll be out in another forty-five or so if you want to take a quick—a very quick—shower. I waited just in case."

"Well, that sounds divine," Charlotte said. "Then I can help you in the kitchen."

"I thought I'd just make a little salad. And I have some bread, of course. And some wine," Adrianna said.

Charlotte liked that Adrianna was clearly also a planner. Were all academics that way? If she hadn't been hardwired to exist in a state of what-will-I-be-doing-a-year-from-now she'd have had to train herself into thinking ahead just to survive the museum. She was curious whether Adrianna had plotted out the success she enjoyed. It looked to Charlotte as if she'd moved seamlessly from triumph to triumph without so much as breaking a sweat; she found this both intriguing and intimidating.

"What are you thinking about?" Adrianna asked Charlotte, whose thoughts were migrating slowly but predictably toward the ways in which she had failed to achieve her own goals, personal and professional.

"I'm wondering how I managed to fall into this little corner of paradise," Charlotte said. "And thinking I better see if evil James has devised a way to pluck me from it."

She reached for her phone as Adrianna looked on with what Charlotte thought—what she hoped—was a wistful expression.

"Alors," she said. "Thursday. 1:19 p.m. Stopping in Detroit. Thence to Hartford. Terrible flight. Arriving at 10:30 at night. He says there was nothing direct. Boo."

"Boo, indeed," said Adrianna. "Get in the shower. I'll be in in five. Then we'll have twenty more minutes."

"What if we need twenty-*five* more minutes?" Charlotte teased her.

Adrianna flashed a sidelong glance. "We won't."

★ ★ ★

Dinner that night was perfection. First of all, it had been a long time since someone had cooked for Charlotte, who was no slouch in the kitchen herself. Second, being with Adrianna felt like winning a prize. Like something special made that much better for being completely unanticipated. Before she'd gone to the bar last night, Charlotte hadn't had time to worry herself into a state of abject anxiety about meeting someone new, as she had managed to do in advance of the two almost comedically bad setups she'd subjected herself to earlier that year.

Weirdly, perhaps, there was also some consolation in the fact that Adrianna had first met her now over a decade ago, even if as a closeted, tennis-playing, art history stress case. (Charlotte dearly hoped she didn't remember that version too well.) And there was their seminar, too, when Charlotte had learned from Adrianna how to talk back to a professor who speaks to you with racist or sexist undertones—without putting him on the defensive and turning it into a thing.

"*C'est parfait, chère,*" Charlotte said after the first bite of quiche—it was a Spanish take on the dish, with cubes of chorizo and a crusty layer of Manchego on top.

And she was an excellent cook. How could it be otherwise?

"Oh, good. I'm glad," Adrianna said. "So, will they need you at the museum tomorrow?"

"They shouldn't," Charlotte said indignantly. "As far as they know, I'm already back in Connecticut. They saw the Sargent portrait and signed off on it. I think tomorrow is another free day. James is under the impression, and I didn't tell him different, that I spent several hours today merely trying to get a roof over my head."

"I just don't want you to get into work trouble," Adrianna

said. She raised her eyebrows for confirmation before pouring her a glass of wine.

"Neither do I," said Charlotte. "But you know how Abigail is. Hot and cold. I think as soon as she knows the painting is OK, she forgets about me for a while. My God, this quiche is good!"

"So what's the deal with that asshole Grayson? He was the director when I was there. You said he was working against you. What does that mean? And how can I poison him without raising any suspicions?"

"No one would connect us as of this moment," said Charlotte, smiling. Surely it was a good thing that Adrianna's chivalrous side was showing.

She explained to Adrianna that Dr. Grayson had vetoed the past two shows she'd proposed, both of which used race and colonialism as central parts of the framework. The concept for the first show, which was to be about representations of black people in works by Winslow Homer and Sargent during and after the Civil War, had gotten her into particular hot water, with Grayson claiming Charlotte wanted to politicize the collection in a way that would damage the museum's reputation. Adrianna listened attentively, shaking her head in frustration as Charlotte related the circumstances around various slights she'd experienced.

"A few weeks ago, he actually said, 'I don't think of you as a woman of color, Ms. Hilaire'—he never calls me doctor—'and I'm sure I'm not alone in that appraisal. So why not make the best of a good situation?'"

Adrianna looked like her diamond studs might pop right off her ears. "He did not!"

"He did," Charlotte replied.

"You could sue him for that all by itself," Adrianna said,

putting her hand on Charlotte's from across the table. "I'm so sorry. What a fucking monster."

Charlotte hadn't told anyone about this. She was surprised at how terrible it made her feel to relate the story, to repeat those nasty dog-whistling words out loud. But she was also surprised how much better she felt when Adrianna understood. None of her white friends, and almost everyone at the museum was white, would have known what to say besides what they always said. *Are you sure? I think you may be overly sensitive to this stuff.* She'd stopped trying to explain after the first few months.

"He said, she said. I wish I had recorded it, but I didn't."

"What happened next?"

Charlotte appreciated that Adrianna was careful not to ask her what she did or said, as if there was a correct way to handle that kind of shitty situation.

"I just stood there saying nothing for a minute. Honestly, I tried to think what you would do. I've always remembered how you dealt with Dr. Vandewater when he said any of the endlessly fucked-up things he said in our class. I think I told him he had no right to talk to me that way and just walked back to my office. It's been a while now."

"I think about how I dealt with F.X. Vandewater sometimes, too," Adrianna said. "Not forcefully enough, more often than not. But at least he stopped talking about 'the subjugation of the negress' by the end of the term."

"Did he ever ask you out?" Charlotte inquired.

Adrianna shook her head, as if even the notion was beyond considering.

"Please don't tell me," she said when Charlotte remained silent.

"Not in so many words, of course," Charlotte said. He was retired now and she hadn't thought about this for years. "Some horseshit about coming over to his house after a night class to pick up review copies of Pollock—or maybe it was Grigsby— he'd been saving for 'the right student.'"

"What a piece of garbage."

"I never took him up on that." Charlotte neatly set her fork down on the edge of her plate. "But those books showed up in somebody's carrel a few weeks later, and I knew exactly where she got them."

Chapter Five

When Charlotte woke up the next day, not on the pullout in the study but buried in the feathery duvet on Adrianna's bed, she could see the sun low and mellow in a sky tinged with the palest hint of blue. This biggest of the bedrooms was spare but comfortable with a few antiques, simple, expensive linens, and arched windows that matched the ones in the living room.

She closed her eyes again, instantly aware of a hard lump growing in her throat starting at her collarbone. Was it there because, the night before, Adrianna had focused on that very spot, covering her neck with kisses before she traveled up to her mouth or down to her cunt? Charlotte felt emotional. She could tell herself it was jet lag or hormones or even too much coffee and cava, but she had a sinking, dizzying feeling it was starting to be something else.

The quiet all around her made it too easy to be alone with such thoughts. In fact, Adrianna's apartment building was disconcertingly tomblike. Barely any street noise. No evidence of other tenants. Even now on a weekday morning, the only sound was the strains of some kind of classical music that had traveled from another quarter of the immense three-bedroom to the hallway outside her door. Certainly, the music was nothing she knew; profane rather than sacred but still solemn-sounding. More Bach than Mozart, softened by rich female voices. She struggled to hear the words. What she got instead, beneath the cellos and harpsichords, was the percussive patter of Adrianna working; she was undoubtedly out there writing something original and field-changing hours before lunchtime. The knot in Charlotte's throat tightened.

Her phone informed her that it wasn't yet 10:00 a.m.

She wondered how long Adrianna had been at it; whether she had thought to stay in bed with Charlotte or had quickly reverted to study mode after their late night of endless sex. She wondered whether she was rested. Whether she needed rest. Or if Adrianna might belong to some not-entirely human species that survived on wine, women, and work alone.

Just then the bedroom door creaked open and, still facing the window, Charlotte heard but didn't see Adrianna come in. She was stealthy as a cat. Charlotte turned her head at the last second, half expecting to see the kind of supernatural creature she had been contemplating.

Bathed in the pale sunlight streaming in, Adrianna did look a bit otherworldly as she stood gazing down at the woman whose name she had repeatedly cried out just a few hours earlier. She stood beside the bed in today's choice of pajamas, crisp white cotton, blue piping, sheer enough to reveal her brown skin underneath. Charlotte looked on silently as Adrianna began slowly unbuttoning the shirt, inviting her to watch, leaving it open when she was done, giving Charlotte a full view of her softly muscular torso. Adrianna untied her pants and, once they dropped to the floor, stepped out, naked below the waist.

"What are you getting up to in here?" she asked.

Charlotte didn't want to say that she was retracing the steps of the past few years, wondering where she'd gone wrong. So instead, she flipped back the duvet, leaving the top sheet clinging to her body. She felt unsettled under Adrianna's gaze even though Adrianna was the nearly naked one.

"Am I meant to unveil you like a nymph?" Adrianna asked playfully. "Or unwrap you like a present?"

Charlotte lay there still and quiet. She wanted to be playful. But she suddenly felt strangely sad and a little scared. Embarrassingly so. Adrianna had graciously stretched the most mind-blowing one-night stand into three nights and all she was getting in return was a little girl in her feelings who couldn't just roll with it. Why was she such a hot mess?

"Ay, mi amor," Adrianna said soothingly. "What's wrong? Did I upset you?" She sat down on the bed and took Charlotte's hand in both of hers.

"Hardly," Charlotte said. It was all she could muster.

Adrianna smiled at her in a sweet, knowing way. She slipped off the pajama top and laid it at the foot of the bed. Then she lifted up the sheet and pulled the heavy feather comforter over both of them, drawing Charlotte close.

When Charlotte looked at her like that—brown eyes shining from what Adrianna figured must have been crying, maybe upon finding herself alone in the bed of a woman almost ten years her senior in a labyrinthine apartment in Madrid—she wanted one thing. She wanted Charlotte to feel safe. Adrianna wanted to hold Charlotte so that Charlotte would hear her heart galloping, and she would know that, for now at least, she was right where she should be.

Charlotte seemed to relax with Adrianna's arms around her. They lay like that for several minutes listening to each other breathe. But then Charlotte's lips started to move across her chest. She might be delicate in certain respects but as Adrianna was learning, she was no prude. Nor did Charlotte expect, or even prefer, to be topped.

What she was doing now, burying her face in Adrianna's tits, drawing her whole tongue over her nipples, back and forth, was making her crazy. Sometimes Charlotte held her breasts and bit or sucked loudly, sometimes Adrianna could feel her skin against the roof of Charlotte's mouth as if she might swallow her whole.

Adrianna couldn't help rising to her as she felt herself opening to Charlotte's touch. Charlotte stopped licking and sucking. She came up and leaned over her, brushing Adrianna's lips with her own beautiful breasts. They were alike that way, both with large, plum-colored areolas, though Charlotte's nipples were naturally harder and more thimble-like than her own.

Charlotte had her on the edge now, all from this calculated foreplay. She seemed happy to be in control, fully at ease running things. Adrianna badly wanted it this way; she had been in control for forty-two years and she needed it to stop once in a while.

Even so, it shocked her a little that she felt ready on this particular Wednesday morning in December to give herself completely to this smart, funny, and drop-dead gorgeous younger woman she hadn't seen in years.

When Charlotte came in close to kiss her, Adrianna pivoted and put her lips beside her ear.

"Fuck me, Charlotte," she whispered as demandingly as she could.

Charlotte sat up.

How could that smile retain its shyness even now?

"Is that what you want?" she asked calmly, reaching back between Adrianna's legs. "Hmmm, yes. I think you should be fucked."

Charlotte braced herself on her forearm and straddled Adrianna's thigh, her own sex warm and wet against her partner's skin. They kissed for a few minutes while Charlotte rubbed Adrianna's clit in firm circles; steady but sloppy, failing to establish a rhythm, leaving her unsure what was coming next. Adrianna threw her gaze at the ceiling:

"Neighbors," she whispered between gasps. "We have to be quiet."

"Don't worry, darlin'. I don't think you're ready yet," Charlotte said, as Adrianna frowned her frustration. "Too distracted." Charlotte went a little harder and faster and Adrianna moaned quietly into the pillow, giving her a pleading look.

"Fuck me, honey," she begged.

Charlotte was a vixen. She knew how much Adrianna wanted her but had no qualms about making her wait.

Her pretty hands were small and she was inside Adrianna before either of them knew it. Adrianna's hips began to thrust in response as she tried to get her mouth to Charlotte's bouncing tits. It was as if she had already gained expert knowledge of her body, knowing just where to brush her fingers or place a kiss.

Charlotte coaxed her slowly, deep inside, fingers on her clit until Adrianna felt herself tighten and release. She was almost there but she didn't want to give in because it was so very good. Charlotte was so very good. She was out of her mind with, fuck, what was it?

When Charlotte bent low to listen to her she felt herself break apart and dissolve. Adrianna astonished herself: she wasn't going to *cry*. Was she?

"Damn, damn, damn," Charlotte purred, looking down at her. "You are so fucking beautiful."

Hearing that voice say those words, Adrianna couldn't not pull her back for a kiss.

"You're the beautiful one," she said. For some reason, knowing that Charlotte would see the tears in her eyes didn't matter to her one bit.

Chapter Six

The next day came too soon. Especially because they'd agreed that Charlotte should get to the airport, which was inexplicably nightmarish even when it hadn't been closed for two days, well ahead of the prescribed window. This meant she'd need to leave the apartment fairly early in the morning, probably right after breakfast. It also meant they'd have a shorter long goodbye.

Following yesterday's categorically sublime afternoon sex, Charlotte had taken advantage of their post-siesta hours when the obvious choices were a) shower/bath and more drinking b) more sex or c) change of scenery. The latter was the only real option because she knew that Adrianna would want to, or at least feel compelled to, work. Like any other pre-tenured academic in her shoes, scarcely a day went by when she didn't write.

Charlotte's excuse to leave the house was therefore grocery shopping, for which Adrianna unwillingly surrendered her to the Carrefour store in the basement of an office building about two blocks away.

While out she had picked up several ounces of *pata negra*, the pricey and silken *jamón ibérico* that she could rarely find in New Haven, even at the local Spanish bistro—to go with some of her favorite Spanish cheeses, a nutty Idiazabal and creamy Leonora for tapas on their last night. But the main purpose

of the errand was to find the evaporated milk and yeast she'd
need for beignets. Because, New Orleans cliché or not, who
doesn't love a steaming hot, powder sugared pillow of freshly
fried dough first thing in the morning?

She could make beignets—and had—under virtually any
conditions, as long as she had a thermometer and a deep
enough pan for frying, which any kitchen where churros and
tortilla had ever been made was sure to keep on hand. And
while the recipe was not difficult, she knew the time required
to make the dough that night and roll and cut it the next day
would keep her mind helpfully occupied.

When the alarm went off at sunrise, Charlotte saw that her
plan was working. For although the first thing to run through
her head was: *When will I see her again?* this was quickly followed by: *Best start frying up that dough.*

Touchingly, Adrianna was still in bed with her. In fact,
Charlotte woke up the way she'd fallen asleep, with the in-
describable feeling of Adrianna's breasts pushed against her
bare back. She snoozed the alarm but promised herself she'd
get up before it went off again.

If Adrianna was asleep she was remarkably silent. If she
wasn't asleep, Charlotte almost didn't want her to say anything,
knowing the sound of her voice was likely to make her cry.

"Noooooo," Adrianna wailed theatrically when the alarm
chimed away a few minutes later. *"Todavía no. Pas encore."* She
began kissing Charlotte's back in a dozen places.

"Time to make the doughnuts," Charlotte said, gravely.

Adrianna laughed. "I'm not sure whether even your beignets are worth less time in bed with you. How long do we
have again?" Although currently her hand was draped over
Charlotte's hip, it showed definite signs of heading either
north or south.

"Not long enough for that. Sadly," Charlotte said, her voice catching, "I should get up. Before I can't get up and I miss my flight and I lose my job and have to come back here and stay with you."

"Sounds perfect to me," Adrianna said.

When Charlotte said nothing in response, Adrianna rubbed her shoulder. "Kiss me good morning?"

Charlotte took a deep, deep breath. "I don't think I can," she said. "I know I'm being silly. But…"

"Just turn around, babe," Adrianna said. She took back her arm.

Charlotte was fully aware what would happen if she looked Adrianna in the eye, knowing what she'd felt for her these past three days and having no idea what the future might—or might not—hold. But she did as instructed anyway.

"Since you ask so nicely," she said, shifting to her other side.

Adrianna kissed her hand. "You know, don't you, this has been sheer bliss and I cannot imagine not seeing you again." Her brown eyes were bright but she looked a little blue.

"And I can't imagine not being seen," Charlotte said. But even her attempts at lightheartedness couldn't stop her from tearing up. "I'm just not sure how to think about all this."

"How do you want to think about it?"

"I guess I don't want to think about it at all," Charlotte said. "I want to be here longer. I don't want to miss you like I know I'm about to miss you and not know if I'm going to see you again. Or when."

Adrianna didn't immediately reply.

What could she say?

"How does a month sound?" she asked a few moments later.

Charlotte looked up, suddenly feeling as if she might be able to avoid liquefying into a pool of longing and despair.

"Like a gift from above."

"Good. What are you doing New Year's?"

Charlotte let go a tentative smile. "Nothing I can't undo. Who's asking?"

"I'm making a short New York trip after Christmas," Adrianna said. "There's actually some stuff I need at the Hispanic Society and a friend of mine has a studio in Brooklyn she's not using. Madrid is depressing AF over the holidays. It's like a ghost town here. So I've been planning to bounce. But just for a few days. You won't be in New Orleans, will you?"

Charlotte was too overwhelmed by the idea of spending New Year's with Adrianna to think about Christmas. Which she had only spent in New Orleans once since her father died four years ago. She shook her head.

"You and me in Brooklyn for the New Year. Yes?"

"Yes." Hell yes.

The frying of the beignets occupied Charlotte for most of their remaining time together, as Adrianna suspected it was intended to do. This was a protective strategy of some sort, Adrianna surmised. A way for Charlotte to compartmentalize her feelings by giving her hands something to do. It was the opposite of Adrianna's approach. She would have thrown herself into reading or translating something needlessly difficult in an attempt to get one side of her brain to overtake the other with intellectual puzzles rather than emotional ones.

But Charlotte was a physical person. She knew her body; she seemed to revel in it. And she certainly was good with her hands.

A little less than an hour before the car was scheduled to arrive, they'd sat down in the kitchen to a plate of impeccably browned little squares whose white sugar coating had transformed into a melted glaze in the most impressive way. They had coffee. They talked for the first time about Adrianna's book-in-progress and Charlotte's next, disturbingly Anglocentric, exhibition. And in this way they began to ease themselves out of the temporary reverie in which they'd been dwelling.

It was time to wake up.

Adrianna wondered who found it harder. On the surface, Charlotte was surprisingly upbeat about their farewell to the past three days of complete devotion to each other. Knowing the specific date they'd see each other again seemed to help. But Adrianna could also tell she was putting on a brave face; acting as if she had no fears or regrets even as tears threatened to burst from the corners of her lovely coffee-colored eyes for the entirety of the morning. It was all Adrianna could do not to hold Charlotte tight until she let herself cry, pressing her tears away with her thumbs and kissing her hard when she got it out of her system, so that she wouldn't be embarrassed. So she'd know Adrianna understood.

But stoical Charlotte had kept it together and Adrianna didn't want to make things worse. Traveling while emotional can turn a person into an airport sideshow all too easily. Crying in public was something Adrianna simply could not abide from herself—and she didn't like to think of Charlotte breaking down in some Barajas ticket line, either.

When the moment finally came to say goodbye it was with a quick touch of her lips to Charlotte's perfumed cheek. Adrianna had whispered "It won't be long, sweet girl" in Charlotte's ear. Charlotte had given her hand a tight squeeze barely eking out an "I know, I know." And then she was gone.

Adrianna then stood at the living room window tracking Charlotte's hired car as it pumped its brakes down the narrow street. She breathed a heavy sigh full of the relief that comes from knowing the act of separation is over even if the missing is just about to kick in. For all her sexual passion, lovely Charlotte was embarrassed by the strength of her emotions; by the sure knowledge they'd started something that might, if

they let it, make them both into something new. It was thrilling and it was terrifying. And as Adrianna was now forced to
admit, Charlotte wasn't the only one who felt that way.

Adrianna received Charlotte's first text, after the requested
updates about her delayed flight status and eventual take-offs
and landings, the next day when she arrived at her apartment
in New Haven.

Home, she had written. xxoxx.

Adrianna had been here before.

She and Vera had begun seeing each other when they both
lived in Chicago. Adrianna had moved back there to try
to get a museum job after finishing her undergrad years at
Penn. When Adrianna was admitted to a super-competitive
Ivy League PhD program, they'd begun a disastrous long-
distance relationship. The back-and-forth had been costly—in
so many ways—and even though Charlotte's first transatlantic
text filled Adrianna with delight and pleasure, she couldn't
help remembering all the things that could go wrong when
two people were in their situation.

She knew Charlotte would be beyond spent, as much from
the flight as from their time together. And she wanted to give
her space to relax and recover. But, and she knew this from
being the younger one in the past, Charlotte might also be
feeling a little needy. She was funny that way; equal parts
demonstrative and reserved. Adrianna liked that Charlotte
seemed self-aware enough to be at least somewhat comfortable with her vulnerabilities. She hadn't been nearly so capable
of expressing her needs to a romantic—or a sexual—partner
when she was in her early thirties. She wasn't especially good
at it now.

It was exciting to feel constantly aware of another person's
feelings for her again. And scary, too. Although she hadn't

really admitted it to herself Adrianna knew something inside her had shut down after her breakup with Vera; in her most private moments, she'd told herself she didn't need anything but her professional life and her friends. But after only a few days with Charlotte, she could see that this was merely a way of protecting herself from the possibility that she'd never meet anyone as brilliant and as captivating as Charlotte was. She was younger and sweeter—and certainly more privileged in her upbringing—but she was every bit her intellectual equal. There's nothing sexier than a woman who gives you a run for your money in the streets *and* the sheets.

Which brought her to Charlotte in the bedroom. Never in her wildest dreams would Adrianna have figured this proper-seeming Southern femme for a power bottom—if not an out-right top. Never. Yet this was a role Charlotte assumed with few discernible inhibitions, visible aplomb, and complete technical facility. Complete. Technical. Facility. Sweet Jesus did she know how to get a girl off.

It was 8:30 in the morning. Adrianna was showered and ready to walk out the door. This was her normal departure time, leaving a few extra minutes for the usual quick coffee at El Jardin before she resumed her post in the archives, patiently copying out the often surprisingly uneventful diary of an aristocratic, art-loving baroque nun.

Today that routine task seemed unimaginable. The idea that her mornings would start this way for the next three weeks filled her with a disconcerting ache. It wasn't objectively long, she knew. In the calculus of Long-Distance Relationships (LDRs) anything less than a month is not considered worth mentioning. But right now to Adrianna, twenty-two days waking up without that gorgeous little body by her side seemed like forever, if only in terms of her ability to maintain anything resembling a focus on what she needed to accomplish. For her promotion. For her job. In Los Angeles.

On the other side of the North American continent from New Haven.

With three hours' time difference. Not to mention the promise of: expensive and energy-sapping cross-country flights. Endless reconciliations of one institutional calendar to the other. Late nights out and missed texts. Inappropriate colleagues. Drunken department parties and museum openings. Grad students in too-short shorts and exposed midriffs.

Unable to make it to the door, Adrianna took off her coat and walked despondently back into the kitchen.

The ancient refrigerator was intrepidly humming away. On top, safely out of reach, sat the Spanish version of a Tupperware container. Adrianna retrieved the plastic box, set it in the middle of the table, and stared at it for a good five minutes. That battle of will lost, she popped off the ill-fitting lid and grabbed one of a handful of the remaining beignets. Although the little pastry was room temperature and by now a little tough, she tore through it, and the others, too, as if she hadn't eaten in days.

Chapter Seven

Charlotte didn't have any queer girlfriends, as in queer friends who were female-identified, in New Haven. Of her wokest straight friends, only Natalie, who worked in conservation, would likely grasp the significance of what had happened to her in Madrid. The rest of the ladies would want to think of her three days in the apartment of an amorous former crush as the extended version of a hookup—what Charlotte had assured herself it was before she'd started falling, or falling again, for Adrianna.

And then there was James. James was male, it was true. But he was gay—he didn't hold with "queer"—and as a readable queen who'd been out since roughly kindergarten, he definitely knew a thing or two about difficult relationships and relationship difficulties of the homosexual kind. Charlotte hadn't quite decided who to talk to first when she returned to work. But she knew it would need to be someone.

The decision was effectively made for her.

Natalie hadn't been at her customary easel in the paintings lab when Charlotte poked her head in. But James had practically tractor-beamed her out of the hallway after she approached his glass-walled office on the third floor and, seeing that he was talking with someone from accounting, had kept on walking.

"Yes, good. Good. Understood. I hear you loud and clear,"

he said rather rudely to the numbers-cruncher, rushing him out of the office with the prior week's reimbursement spreadsheets.

"Mademoiselle Hilaire," he then shouted after Charlotte as she disappeared down the corridor.

"Tout de suite. Get back here, you!"

"Sooooo," said James, after she had occupied her favorite of his chairs. "How was Madrid? Three extra nights and no request for approval at the Ritz. You missed your chance. Did you sleep on the Metro? I've heard of depending on the kindness of strangers, but I worry, you know. Do tell, missy."

She did feel a little guilty for not cluing James in. He almost certainly would have understood, if not aided and abetted her in securing another day if Charlotte had had the presence of mind to ask for it. Now that she was back she could hardly believe she'd basically been incommunicado for three business days. That was new behavior to be sure. *Being abroad.* The words alone brought back the bliss of lying next to Adrianna. Her soft sheets. Her views of the city. Adrianna's wandering hands in the early morning; her mouth; kissing the tidy little hip scar from her teenage appendectomy.

After Charlotte sketched the scenario in broad strokes, James was quiet for a few seconds, shutting his eyes as if he was doing a math problem in his head.

"Three little words," he said. "Happy hour. Wednesday."

Things started to pick up midweek at One Fifty-Five, which was the only happy hour James would be caught dead patronizing. There were some quite excellent bars in the city but for confidential-ish conversations about matters of the queer heart, One Fifty-Five had definite benefits. It wasn't, for example, the kind of place Charlotte might run into any of her supervisors and/or gossipy female coworkers, who tended to smell a scandal faster than white on rice, as they said where Charlotte came from.

James had ushered them to his favorite table in the depths of the less popular side room, which still afforded an excellent view of the door for easy monitoring of the incoming and outgoing.

"And this is Adrianna Coates of the Krauss prize a few years back? I remember her from the *Americas* show. Even I could tell *she* was a hottie," James said. "Moderate height, dark, and as I recall, she didn't suffer fools."

"No," Charlotte said. "I would have thought not."

"So how did you leave things? Is what I see unfolding before me the first act of a torrid long-distance dalliance or the cooling embers of a scorching—or should I say, scorched earth—one-off?"

It was bracing to hear her circumstances boiled down to two such contrary possibilities, neither of which, and certainly not the latter, fit the way Charlotte wanted to see things.

"What you see before you is a big ball of confusion. I'm living an out of body experience. When I left I was perfectly fine being here, being single. And now I can barely get up in the morning without her lying next to me. And all it took for me to get this way was three days. I feel crazy."

"Three days of chess? Three days of Netflix binging? Three days of yoga?" James asked, mischievously.

"Three days of the best sex I've ever had. Probably the best sex I ever will have. And I don't mind telling you, I've had some good sex."

"Pleased to hear it. Also, pleased we're not in the breakroom right now," James said. "I guess what I'm getting at is what do you want from this, from her, and what do you plan to do about it?"

"I know exactly what I want," Charlotte said almost without realizing it. "But I'm not going to reveal that at this stage."

"Let me guess. Because you might not get it?" James chided. "You don't have to tell her right now. In fact, probably better not to. Yet. But could you tell me if you had to? And if not me, your therapist? Now's the time to think about what this means to you. Now, before anyone gets hurt."

James was a wise old bird.

"*You* are my therapist," Charlotte said. "And this round's on me."

When Charlotte got home that night she felt a little inebriated and a lot better. It was, again, just nice to be heard by someone who understood what she was going through. James had had his share of long-distance romances, bipartisan, bisexual, and even bi-coastal, mostly with men he'd met in the course of his twice-yearly trips to various queer-inundated cities around the world.

His parting words were easier heard than adhered to: try not to cease living your life in anticipation of the next encounter with the love object; keep yourself busy with things that matter to you personally; don't put anything on hold or give up an opportunity based on what you think might happen. And of course, the hardest of all, no matter what comes up, be honest with each other.

By the time she'd gotten ready for bed it was almost eleven, which meant it was almost five in the morning in Madrid.

Tonight, when she badly wanted to hear Adrianna's voice before she closed her eyes, all Charlotte could feel was the thousands of miles between them. This part was hard. They'd texted off and on at all hours since she'd been back. Charlotte had tried to let Adrianna take the lead as far as frequency of contact. Above all, she didn't want to seem—didn't want to be—needy.

Adrianna seemed to want to be in touch. She wasn't one to play games, thank God, but not surprisingly, she appeared to prefer a schedule of sorts. Like most people, she was more of a daytime texter than a caller. But she had a thing for talking on the phone, or its audio-only FaceTime equivalent, at night. She liked to hear what she called Charlotte's indescribably sexy voice—and let her imagination do the rest.

For going on a week, they had spoken at some point each twenty-four hours. It helped that Adrianna, as Charlotte well-knew, was both an early riser and a night owl—she was usually up tinkering with some article or piece of research until at least midnight. If Charlotte got home fast enough from work, she could catch her then.

At the other end of the day, they seemed to be falling into a pattern where Charlotte would awaken to find a text waiting from Adrianna, usually sent when she broke for an early-afternoon lunch at the library.

This is what had happened the next day.

Adrianna: Good morning, sweet bird. How was the happy hour?

Charlotte: Good morning ♥ ♥ ♥! James is such a nice man when you peel away the cattiness. He's good to me. How's tricks in the convent? ☺ Sealing my fate with that one.

Adrianna offered a few tidbits from the day's diary entries, which Charlotte seemed to find more fascinating than she did at present. As Adrianna had explained it, not having much else to do, the nuns kept meticulous and exhaustive records. It seemed as if they must have spent most of their lives writing letters and keeping track of what seemed truly insignificant to many a modern reader. Who gave an orange or a needle or a feathered fan to whom, for example. On the hunch that there was more to these transactions than it seemed, Adrianna had been tracking gifts exchanged between the pampered nuns of the royal convent just beyond the center of Madrid and its sister Order in the Spanish colonies that were Mexico.

After the research update, they'd discussed their plans for the (rest of the) day.

Adrianna: If you want, txt me when you get home, I'll prob be up since this proposal is due tomorrow.

Charlotte: What's it for?

Adrianna: To extend sabbatical a term here. Stay through next fall.

Adrianna's breezy response hit her like a stomach punch. Here she'd been thinking all she needed to do was make it through the spring term. In four months, Adrianna was supposed to come back from Spain. Charlotte knew she planned to go back to LA for the summer. But back to Madrid again next fall? She couldn't stand the thought of being so far away for so long.

But apparently it was fine with Adrianna.

Charlotte didn't know what to say. She could see that Adrianna was writing something back. Rather than reacting in a way she'd wish she hadn't, she waited for the next blow of bad news.

I'd still come back to the States for the summer, Adrianna

wrote. Part of the deal. Summer school teaching. Just one class.

Like that was any better? They'd still be separated by thousands of miles and at least three hours' time difference. Who cares whether it was an ocean or ten states? Clearly, Charlotte had gotten ahead of herself. And besides, it was time to finish getting ready for work.

Ah. I see, she typed. Not so bad, then. Well, those ptgs won't catalogue themselves. Good luck with the nuns xx.

Txt when home? I miss you. Maybe we can talk? xxx Adrianna wrote back.

And that, in a nutshell, was what absolutely sucked about all this. For the first time, Charlotte felt a tinge of genuine regret about what happened in Madrid.

Objectively, of course, her life had not exactly been fulfilling before.

Yes, she was lonely, if you got right down to it. She hadn't had a second date in over a year. But things were doable. She was in control of her feelings, her schedule, work. How was it that she'd offered herself so fully to this woman she barely knew? Humiliation washed over her thinking of the hidden parts of herself she'd shown to Adrianna. From the minute Adrianna had put her arms around her, Charlotte felt safe, cared for. She had trusted that, going with her intuition the way she usually did.

But what were they really to each other?

Some of the qualities she would have said she most admired about Adrianna now taunted her as red flags. Adrianna was driven. In order to achieve what she'd achieved, a prestigious position at a top school, a hyper-competitive sabbatical fellowship, a book contract, a house, it couldn't be otherwise. Especially for a queer woman of color. Why should she put her sabbatical extension on hold for someone she'd slept with for a few days? Why should Charlotte expect her to?

Charlotte was glad she hadn't responded with a show of disappointment or surprise when Adrianna had the grace to inform her that she was submitting the request to return to Spain. In some ways, she had to admit, there wasn't much of a difference between being in two different countries and being in two different states.

And anyway, it wasn't as if they were in a relationship.

This wasn't exactly the best start to the day. The out-of-body feeling was back; Charlotte couldn't properly concentrate on much of anything. This time, however, the sensation was less pleasantly delirious and more hopelessly deflated. She was so preoccupied, in fact, that she'd let the shuttle pass right by her and had to run to the next stop to catch the express bus. It was ear-burningly cold and the snow heaped beside the curbs was the same dirty, salty gray sludge she'd left behind on her trip.

Since grad school she had lived in East Rock, a faculty and grad-heavy neighborhood of verdant streets and big old Victorian houses, many of them divided into apartments like hers, a couple of miles from the museum.

It was only a fifteen-minute bus ride downtown. On her way to work during the week, she usually scrolled through various artworld blogs or read a few pages of a novel on her tablet. Today she took out her phone and pulled up her earlier conversation with Adrianna. Rereading their exchange, a sickening feeling of sadness rose in her. So much so that Charlotte thought she might actually lose it on the crowded Yale shuttle, surrounded by cramming undergrads and pretentiously opining doctoral candidates who would wonder how she, a graduate of their fine institution, could let her feelings get the best of her in so public a manner.

If only she could put Adrianna's comfortingly strong embrace out of her mind, Charlotte thought; if only she could forget what it felt like to be kissed by her, she could get on with her uneventful but mercifully un-emotionally-attached former life. But no such luck. Instead, she was being forced to admit that her progress toward the life she wanted, where the woman she was with considered her feelings before she made decisions that would affect them both, had come to a screeching halt. And she hadn't even had her coffee yet.

Chapter Eight

Adrianna was about four sheets into the diary entries for the week of January 23, 1645, and something was finally happening. For almost a decade, beginning in 1636, the subject of her research, the illegitimate sister of the most powerful duke in Spain, known as Sor Epiphania Hilaria Luisa, had sent various trinkets to a prioress in the "New World." She might send one gift a month or ten every six months but regardless, she recorded the date of the parcel's departure from her own convent and the date it was received and opened according to (now lost) letters she had evidently been sent from the gifts' *criolla*, or Creole, recipient, cloistered at the convent of the Incarnation in Valladolid, Mexico.

It had taken Adrianna the better part of a year to get to the mid-1640s, knowing the diary entries would stop altogether in 1648, when the author died at the age of seventy-two. But until today, nothing of real art-historical significance had appeared in the personal papers of a woman who was thought to be among the most acquisitive and sophisticated collectors of her distinguished noble circle.

Archival study is not for the impatient. Ask any scholar who has spent months or years in a research library. There, hunkered down daily among a batch of letters or common-place books, it could take months to just get accustomed to the writer's penmanship. To decode the idiosyncrasies of a written hand and its singularly inked flourishes and ampersands. The nearly identical f's and s's. The words strung together like beads on a string, uninterrupted by the knots or clasps of punctuation.

Ask this same scholar about the "big" score or the eureka moment. They're almost certain to tell you they had all but lost hope, or run out of time or money or a visa, immediately before they struck gold and found what they didn't even know they were looking for.

In other words, the best discoveries often occur on the last day. So the timeliness of Adrianna's discovery was not lost on her. Her proposal for permission to return was due in less than six hours. So far, she had basically bullshitted her way through it, singling out the tiniest, most inconsequential passages as somehow significant to our understanding of transatlantic patronage and gift-giving between royal nuns. In reality, as she knew, there was precious little there, there.

But the words on the page in front of her would change all that; this new passage was a bona fide find. The new translation would get her the sabbatical extension—if not lead her to the El Dorado of job security in the form of tenure itself.

For Adrianna, wanting to share news like this with someone was an unfamiliar sensation. She badly wanted to text Charlotte, but it was still too early—not even close to dawn in New Haven. This was the part she hadn't missed. You could convince yourself and other people that you were in a romantic relationship with someone on the other side of the world or the country, but too much was lost in real time for that to be or feel like truly being together. Hours from now, by the time she and Charlotte talked that night, all sorts of things might have happened to either of them.

Adrianna went back to the diaries. They were bound in a nondescript green morocco leather with the family's heraldic emblem, a phoenix with an arrow in one talon, stamped in gold on each cover. She wondered about the device—a bird that rises from the ashes to fight again—or something like that, she imagined. The diary was currently resting on one of the red velour cradle pillows the library required readers to use for the protection of such items, its pages held open like butterfly wings with small fabric-covered weights.

The words on the right page jumped out, now that she knew their significance:

> *Today, a painting of fruit with a squirrel, sent to her love in Valladolid. The best thing of its kind we have here and unlike anything she will have seen in her city.*

Charlotte's day had only gotten worse. She was surprised she'd made it home in one piece. As bad luck would have it, the express shuttle had a flat tire, forcing all its riders to wait for the next one or walk the remaining few blocks downtown. The walk had made Charlotte both bone-chillingly cold and late. So late, she'd had the misfortune to miss the first few minutes of an all-staff meeting led by Grayson, the subject of which was budget cuts and possible staff reductions. James had attempted to console her after: *You're the best courier we've ever had*, he'd said. *Museums love you. I think you're safe from the chopping block for now.*

The best courier we ever had.

It sounded like an epitaph for someone she never wanted to be. Seven years of grad school all to become a glorified delivery girl. Not only had her time with Adrianna made Charlotte want to be with her; it made her want to be where she was professionally. She'd never felt less successful.

The rest of the day was spent running down paintings in storage for the museum's upcoming *British in New England* show about which Charlotte couldn't give fewer fucks. She'd forgotten to take lunch, torn a small hole in her blouse, and started to feel headachy from the mold as she almost always did after prolonged time in the basement. Five o'clock could not have come soon enough. She couldn't wait to get home.

She'd just settled down on the love seat with her shoes off and a glass of wine when Adrianna texted to ask if it was a good time to call.

She sounded excited. It was after midnight in Madrid and Charlotte could picture her sitting at the desk in the study accompanied by some period-appropriate oratorio as she banged out an invaluable translation until she realized that some courier in Connecticut was probably expecting her to call.

"Hi, baby," Adrianna said. "How are you?"

More and more Charlotte felt like she didn't want to answer that question when asked.

"Good," she said. "Well, cold—it's freezing here. And you? Did you get your proposal in?"

"Just in time," Adrianna said brightly, as if it were a great thing for both of them. "And by some miracle I actually had something to back my rationale. I only found it today."

"Wow," Charlotte said, her heart dive-bombing her stomach like a flock of swallows. "That's fantastic. Tell me."

"Charlotte," Adrianna said in what Charlotte now recognized as her come-to-Jesus voice.

"Hmmm?"

"You sound sad. Is everything alright? Tell me about today."

This was all it took. It appeared Adrianna now had the power to completely alter her mood simply by being so damned understanding. And it made Charlotte supremely uncomfortable to think how much she suddenly seemed to need something that only this particular woman could provide. She had meant to end the story with the flat-tired shuttle. But before long, she'd gotten as far as catching her sleeve on the metal railings in storage and James's backhanded compliment.

"Sweet bird," Adrianna said in a voice both sexy and calming. "That sounds like a horrible day. But you must know you're so much more to them than a good courier."

"I'm a pretty decent cataloguer, too," she said. "But that might not fit on my gravestone."

They both laughed. "Is the show as bad as it sounds?" Adrianna asked.

"It's worse in a way. The curatorial proposal we saw is basically all about evidence of eighteenth-century academic painting in nineteenth-century American painting. Mostly portraiture. And mostly men."

"Of course," said Adrianna. "Well, the job market's still in play. Maybe this will be your year to get out of that place. They don't deserve you and any good school would be lucky to have you on their faculty."

"I'm the lucky one," Charlotte said. Adrianna didn't need to know that she hadn't applied for any of the disappointing half dozen positions posted so far this year, all in fourth-tier programs where she'd teach "art appreciation." She'd rather stay at the museum than take on a grueling course load somewhere she'd never been, introduced to the department as the latest "diversity hire."

"I miss you," Adrianna responded kindly. "Two more weeks and I'm going to lock you up in that studio and throw away the key."

Didn't that sound nice. Clearly Adrianna was imagining their get-together as another three-day sexcapade. She had to smile to herself just thinking about that. Adrianna Coates wanted to spend New Year's making love to her and maybe not even leaving the apartment. Again. But was it really making love when you weren't officially lovers? Or even girlfriends? Not that they could get that figured out if Adrianna was willing to suddenly up and change the rules of a game they'd only just begun to play.

Charlotte wanted to spend the rest of her evening warmed by the glow of Adrianna's affection. To be her sweet bird and think of being thought about that way. But already it wasn't as easy as that. Adrianna was infinitely caring, but she clearly had her own life and her own agenda, too. And tonight it felt like that agenda didn't necessarily include Charlotte coming along for the ride.

Fueled by the day's earlier discovery, Adrianna was full of energy. She'd even arranged to talk to her friend Esther after the late-night call with Charlotte. It would still be early afternoon in LA, on a day when Esther had, as usual, no one scheduled for her scheduled office hours. She prided herself on intimidating her law students into feeling they could only avail themselves of her time in the event of the employment law equivalent of a life-or-death situation: "I am (only) at your disposal should you get fired or fail to get hired," as it said on her syllabus.

"So tell me everything," Esther said. "One minute you're a candidate for one of those convents you study so tirelessly and the next you're the villain in a Diderot novel."

"You are way too widely read for an attorney," Adrianna said. "But one thing leads to another, apparently. Is this what a midlife crisis feels like?"

"I'll let you know when I get there," said Esther, who was only a year younger than Adrianna. "Let's see. Have you bought a red sports car recently? Oh, that's right, you already have one. So avant-garde."

"If you're finished," Adrianna laughed. "It's almost last call over here."

Talking with Esther sometimes felt like doing a stand-up duet. She had the quickest, driest wit Adrianna had ever encountered—not exactly what you'd expect from a graduate of Harvard Law. After they'd first met, at a new faculty thing the year they both started, she'd developed a very brief, and really rather platonic, attraction to Esther, who would turn out to be not only the funniest person she'd met but quite possibly the straightest. The attraction quickly evaporated, but their friendship was the one she cared most about. They'd grown even closer when Esther had a close call with cancer the previous year. Thank God, she was totally in the clear now.

"Guh-head," Esther said, sounding like the Jersey girl she was. "I assume you slept together?"

"Boy did we," Adrianna said. "I think I'm in trouble."

"Did you use protection?"

Adrianna couldn't help laughing. "You know what I mean."

"I've heard stories," Esther said. "OK. Real talk since, shockingly, I have a live one in a few minutes. Some eager beaverette who didn't read the syllabus, apparently. But back to you. This is someone you knew from Yale, right? Is she a good person? Is she worth shaking things up for?"

"She's a very good person," Adrianna said. She wasn't sure how she knew this with certainty, but she knew she did. "I can't remember the last time I felt like this. I mean, I've dated people in LA. As you know. But this is like another order of magnitude. I'm pretty crazy about her."

"You sound happy," Esther said. "I think she's making you happy. It's either that or the paid sabbatical or the archival jackpot."

"I know," Adrianna said. "I'm not living in the real world right now. My real world. I'm not sure I'm capable of making good decisions when I'm not living in my own house or doing my real job. But I'm fucking smitten. We're spending New Year's together."

"In Spain?"

"Brooklyn."

"I see."

"Any advice?"

"Get preapproved and bring cash to the deal?" Esther chuckled at her own joke. "I think at our age you just trust it. It's not like she's a complete stranger so there's no due diligence. You just let things go where they go. It's scary for you and it's scary for her. And that's why they call it falling."

Esther's office hours attendee had shown up shortly after she'd left Adrianna with this typically Estherian summation of her situation, complete with analysis and recommendations.

At our age, she had said, as if they were in their sunset years when they'd barely tiptoed into their forties, good looks firmly in tow. But yes. At her age, Adrianna thought, she had in fact learned a few things about women. And relationships. It was whether she'd learned *from* the past that was up for debate.

But wasn't it all moot in the first place?

Sure, you ask your friends for advice, but is anything they say going to stop you once you've started lucid dreaming of kissing someone's silky soft inner thighs?

You just trust it, she had said. Trust what? That because you looked up the cost of buying a business class ticket for someone you're going to see in two weeks, everything's going so well?

And that's why they call it falling. Well, that part was almost right. Adrianna had felt herself rising more than falling; her heart leaping when she got a text from Charlotte or when Charlotte's voice answered her call. There was falling, too, when they'd said goodbye in Madrid and when she suspected she'd hurt Charlotte with the sabbatical proposal news—which she still hadn't found a way to bring up again. The stability of her previous life seemed greatly overrated, Adrianna thought, now that even the falling was countered with sky-highs.

Chapter Nine

Charlotte had only been at work for about an hour on Monday when she was summoned into the office of Abigail Foley, the primly volatile head registrar and associate director of the museum. Normally, she wouldn't have given it a second thought. But since Grayson's ominous warning about possible budget cuts, and by implication, layoffs or worse, she steeled herself before knocking on the door.

Abigail was never very readable. She began the conversation with a question about the status of Charlotte's recent cataloguing odyssey—had she found any double portraits from around the American Revolution that might fit the framework of "The British Are Coming" as she had taken to referring to their next big show—and did she think she'd be done with her latest batch of entries by this Thursday?

Charlotte provided thoughtful and confident answers to these and other questions. But she was right to be suspicious of the last one.

"We need you to courier a Benjamin West out to the Huntington before Christmas. Can you do that? It's a three-day trip—barring bad weather of course. You'd be back on the 23rd."

Charlotte's heart sped up. Adrianna wasn't coming to New York until the 29th. But somehow the notion of traveling days before her arrival made her ridiculously nervous—what if something happened? What if there was a delay? But also: the Huntington!

"I've never actually been to the Huntington. Isn't that in San Marino?"

"It's about twenty minutes outside of LA. We'd put you in Pasadena, though. Not downtown."

Who'd have thunk it?

"Sure," Charlotte said. "Happy to do that. I just need to be back for Christmas."

Abigail asked her if she was going home—where was that again? And Charlotte told her she'd be spending the holidays in New Haven with friends. James was her friend, so that part was only a mild exaggeration.

When she was home for Thanksgiving, Charlotte's mother had artlessly struggled to ask Charlotte about the possibility of going on a Christmas cruise this year with one of her also-widowed bridge club cronies. Though it was framed as a question, she'd clearly already booked the ticket. She and her mother weren't close, but Charlotte had hoped they might spend Christmas together this year and start to change that a little. Since the double whammy of her father's unexpected death and the coming out that only narrowly preceded it, they'd never had a real conversation about Charlotte's (sex) life—what her mother now heavy-handedly referred to as "her way."

His death had provided a useful excuse not to revisit her coming out, and whenever Charlotte brought it up even indirectly, her mother asked her not to make her relive those difficult days. But now, perhaps by her mother's design there would be no reliving of anything this year and for Charlotte, no going home for the holidays, either.

She'd never had a chance to introduce either of her parents to anyone she was dating. Her father had almost died thinking, he claimed, that she was straight. Charlotte wondered what her mother would make of Adrianna. And the other way around, of course. If that meeting ever did take place, it would have to be on their—likely highly lubricated—terms. Something told her if anyone could hold her own with Mrs. Mandeville La Fresnoy Hilaire, it was Dr. Adrianna Coates. There was even, Charlotte had to acknowledge, something fairly appealing about the idea.

But for now she'd merely told her mother the cruise sounded like a fine idea. They would see each other in the New Year, maybe Easter. Bon voyage!

That afternoon Charlotte went straight home. If she caught the bus instead of walking like she used to, she could be settled in time to catch Adrianna before she went to bed.

"The Huntington?" Adrianna said. "You're kidding. That's hysterical."

"I can't believe I'll see LA for the first time without you."

"I know. I'm not sure how I feel about that. What if it snows and you have to find an old friend to stay with?"

"Anything can happen on these trips," Charlotte said.

"Let's hope not."

Charlotte sensed that they were testing each other in some not entirely unserious way.

"No," she said. "Not anything. I just wish you could be there. But I guess Pasadena isn't LA proper, right?"

"No. It's a bit like the Short Hills of LA. But you'll literally be fifteen minutes from my house in Highland Park. Less, if I were driving you. I was really looking forward to taking you to the Huntington. Their cactus garden is one of my favorite places."

"They schedule me so tightly, I probably won't have time

to see anything. And even if I do, I promise to save the succulents for when you can show them to me."

"Don't you always? Hey, would you want to have dinner or a drink with my friend Esther? She lives in Pasadena. Her house is quite something. And her husband is kind of a dick. But her son is very cute. Anyway, I'm sure she'd love to meet you."

Adrianna hadn't talked about her family much but she had talked a lot about Esther, who seemed closer to a best friend to her than anyone Charlotte could currently think of in her own life.

It might be strange meeting Adrianna's confidante without Adrianna there to mediate. But it seemed like an awfully nice idea. And in a funny way she'd never admit to anyone but herself, Charlotte wondered if it wasn't a bit like being invited to meet Adrianna's family. Esther was a friend, but Adrianna obviously thought of her almost like a sister. A sister from another mister for sure, given what she described as their totally different backgrounds, but a soul sister nonetheless.

"That would be nice," Charlotte said. "If she has time."

"Oh, she will."

They'd spent the rest of the conversation on a funny interaction Adrianna had had with an elderly neighbor in the apartment building and the free coffees that were sometimes coming her way from the lesbian owners of El Jardin, now that they knew she played for their team. As midnight approached, Adrianna had to stifle her yawns and Charlotte's stomach started growling, so they said their goodbyes.

A couple of hours went by.

Charlotte streamed her shows, drank some wine, got into pj's, and moved her computer to the bedroom for a little late email catch-up before she called it a night. She was coming back from the kitchen with a glass of water when both her phone and her computer chimed simultaneously.

It was Adrianna. Her heart skipped. They'd already talked and it was so late now. What could be wrong?

"Are you in bed?" asked the voice on the other end.

Charlotte set down the water and got back under the covers.

"I am now," she said.

"I wish you were fucking me."

"I wish I were fucking you, too," Charlotte said. "Hold on, I have to take my panties off. There. I'm so wet just hearing your voice."

Adrianna sighed. "I can't wait to kiss you again, Charlotte."

"Do you think about me fucking you, honey?"

"God, yes."

"Do you think about me rubbing your clit nice and slow? Getting you all wet and ready for me. With your big brown tits in my mouth, so I can bite them and suck them?"

Adrianna moaned.

"Aw, that's right. Rubbing your clit so hard. So good like you like it."

"Fuck, Charlotte. You're so fucking hot. I don't want to come yet."

"I know, honey mine, that's why I stopped. That's why I took my hand away for a minute to hear what you're gonna to do to me."

"I want my lips on your hard little nipples," Adrianna said. "And I want to slap your ass when you ride me. And I want you to feel my hot tongue when my face is buried in your pretty, pretty pussy."

When Charlotte finally clicked off, after getting off, she was very nearly as delirious as she'd been that first time in Madrid. Somehow, she and Adrianna had been so focused on being together, and so present for what they were doing, Charlotte half couldn't believe Adrianna wasn't there beside her when she came down from the magnificently unhinged orgasm she'd fought to muffle, at least a little, while lying there between the not especially thick walls of her East Rock bedroom.

She was alone. But it didn't feel that way. Adrianna had been every bit as into it as she was. She was the one who started it. And, though she was by nature just a tad bit more restrained than Charlotte, she'd found her rhythm soon enough and brought Charlotte to a physical and emotional place she'd never gone "on her own" in the way she had mere minutes before.

Listening to Adrianna call her name when she came was the sexiest thing she knew, or had known, in maybe ever. Lying there on the edge of dreaming, it was those sounds and the words that went with them, *It's all for you, Charlotte*, that she would fall asleep to. And not only tonight.

Two days later Charlotte was in an Uber on her way to Pasadena. The flight was long but uneventful—one thing about the museum, it was probably to do with insurance, was that they never skimped on courier travel. She'd certainly never had any trouble sleeping in business class. Eight hours later, she even felt something resembling rested.

No wonder she was the best courier they had.

And Los Angeles, for goodness' sake. She'd been to San Francisco and Seattle and Portland but never sunny southern California where the current sixty-eight degrees in December felt a little like a cruel joke. The freeways alone were astonishing to her, like a tangle of spaghetti.

They'd sped past what she assumed was the city's skyline at one point, but before she could get a good look they were off on another exit blurring another expanse of strip malls with a greenish suburb in the distance. After a while, the air became clearer and the landscape blue and mountainous. Pretty, she thought. If not as lush as New Orleans, it was still far more tropical than Connecticut.

They took another looping exit, cut over five lanes in as many seconds, and, two turns later, emerged on a wide boulevard ornamented with palm trees and massive Mediterranean villas. Movie star homes. With tidy emerald lawns, pool-concealing hedges, and Ferraris parked in their circle drives. Another right and they'd pulled up at the gate of a giant fenced estate of some kind that turned out to be the grand old Huntington museum and gardens.

As always, it was a good thing Charlotte got a look at the place in daylight because by the time she finally emerged from the depths of storage it would almost surely be dark.

Both so much and so little would happen prior to that.

The Huntington's receiving area, deluxe by most standards, seemed very California to her. The people were easygoing and nice. The temperature was perfect. And there were views of the surrounding gardens—Japanese, Chinese, camellia, rose—through actual windows. With all this lush beauty so close and yet so far, it was even more painful to be stuck in a holding area reading email and filling in spreadsheets for hours on end. When she'd parked herself there at noon, it was already 9:00 p.m. in Madrid.

Owing to James's careful planning, her passenger flight had beaten the freighter plane carrying the painting to LAX. Once that arrived, Charlotte had been on the tarmac to watch as the pallet was forklifted out of the nose and de-palletized. She'd then made sure her crate was carefully loaded onto a truck. Now, she was waiting for the truck to arrive at the Huntington's receiving dock, where she'd then eagle-eye their handlers as they offloaded the crate to storage. Tomorrow, she'd be back for the uncrating and inspection of the painting. After that, she'd go back to the hotel for dinner and get up in the dark for her redeye back to Hartford the next day.

The truck finally pulled in around five and everything from there was very anticlimactic. Just the way she liked it. The crate was intact under all its plastic sheeting and the professionals deftly took over, carting off a rare double portrait by Benjamin West to a climate-controlled room somewhere on the premises. It was only at this point that the museum's associate registrar, a young guy in skinny jeans and a half-tucked button-down—a Duke grad, as she might easily have guessed—made an appearance. Although he'd rather smoothly invited Charlotte to drinks, she'd politely told him that she had other plans, much to his apparent dismay.

James had put her up in an over-the-top resort hotel nestled, as people there liked to say, against what were evidently the San Gabriel Mountains. She didn't have much time to enjoy her absurdly large room, however, because Esther was coming almost any minute to meet her in the lobby bar for a drink. That Adrianna's BFF had been cagey about confirming dinner plans, Charlotte respected—there was nothing worse than facing an entire evening with someone you've just met and don't especially want to get to know.

"She's more like you than me," Adrianna had said. "If you're ten minutes late, she'll text you and be bitchy until she's halfway through her first drink. So do with that what you will."

Aside from revealing something about how Adrianna viewed her own assiduous punctuality, this made perfect sense to Charlotte. She was sure to be sitting at a good table in the hotel's stylish Art Deco bar at the crack of six o'clock.

It was always fun to people watch in a new city. Here in temperate California people were staggeringly good looking by conventional standards. She found their rehearsed casualness somewhat silly, being of the mind that a little ironing never hurt anyone. It was a relatively diverse crowd by New England standards. Certainly, the kind of hotel her mother would have liked, with rafts of gleaming exotic woods, tufted booths, and towering flower arrangements. She kept thinking the tan and petite women coming her way with their Bottega bags and sweater sets might be Esther but they merely looked through her and continued walking past her table to their own.

Then, just as Charlotte was feeling a bit bitchy herself, a very attractive, neatly suited woman with wavy shoulder-length brown hair and the brightest lapis blue eyes came up beside her.

"If I were you and this was a first date," she said, sitting down at Charlotte's table without even confirming who she was. "I'd have left five minutes ago."

Charlotte laughed and awkwardly extended her hand now that they were sitting across from each other. Esther was probably about Adrianna's age. She was tan but not overly so and her toned legs suggested tennis rather than yoga. She wore a breathtakingly large diamond solitaire on her left hand and when she looked at you with her piercing gaze it felt as if there were nowhere to hide—not that you'd want to.

"Luckily for me it's not. In LA, as you will soon, we hope, learn," said the woman who was Esther, "traffic and driving are continually invoked to cover a multitude of sins. So much so that nobody ever believes you when you say, for example, that you got rear-ended on the way to meet them unless they can see your car for proof or, at least, as evidence. Which, when we leave, I invite you to do. Though you won't know for sure when what I show you happened actually did, in fact, occur."

"Oh, I take your word for it," Charlotte said simply but full of concern. "But, good Lord, that's rough as a cob. Are you alright? Is your car?"

Esther beamed. "Oh, I'm completely undone already. You're lovely. I bless your union unequivocally. And yes, I'm fine. And the car will live to see another bumper replacement, I'm sure. What do you make of Pasadena?"

Charlotte could see in an instant how much one could learn about the law from Esther Adler, who must be a mesmerizing lecturer for those who could keep up and an absolute terror for those who couldn't. She explained to Esther in brief what her job had been up to that point in the day and that, sadly, she hadn't seen much of anything besides the streets between the highway and the Huntington and this hotel.

They ordered Manhattans. Esther then asked her about her dissertation and her feelings about teaching and whether she had been in New Orleans for Katrina, which she hadn't as it was her freshman year at Yale and she had left in mid-August to spend a few days getting to know the East Coast before orientation. It felt a bit like an interview for a job whose description she'd never seen. After they'd both gotten to the point of eating their craft maraschino cherries, Esther suggested they move on to dinner.

Chapter Ten

After the first Manhattan Esther's personality was not appreciably altered, at least not in a way Charlotte could perceive. She said she didn't usually have more than one of anything at dinner but that she was feeling inclined to do so tonight if Charlotte agreed, which she did, and so they ordered another round.

"This way I can take an Uber home and have the repair guys pick up my verifiably rear-ended vehicle here tomorrow. It's closer to the shop anyway."

A planner. Just like Adrianna.

"And your husband, he's not a lawyer too, is he?"

"Of course he is," Esther said. "Also on the faculty at the UC. And a judge. Which is the height of annoying in an argument."

"Undoubtedly," Charlotte said. "Does he make you approach the bench?"

Esther laughed wryly. "He bangs his gavel," she said. And then, under her breath and definitely not to Charlotte, "And apparently that's not all he bangs."

It was the kind of moment when you can't believe you heard what you heard but you're also absolutely certain you heard it. Charlotte realized she really should let it pass. But for some reason she didn't want to. It wasn't only that being with someone so close to Adrianna made her feel closer to Adrianna, she liked Esther so far and thought she was lovely, too.

"Are you saying what I think you're saying?" Charlotte asked her.

"I'm sorry," Esther said, continuing to look elsewhere as she spoke. "I had absolutely no right to do that. Hence the one Manhattan rule. Please just forget it. And please, I beg of you, don't say anything to Addie."

First of all: "Addie"!

And second, how awful to have to meet your best friend's younger lover when you've (just?) learned your husband is cheating on you with one of his own. What a dick, indeed.

"No, of course not," Charlotte said. "I will have to tease her about that nickname, though."

"Oh, no. That's almost (but not quite) as bad. Et tu bourbon!" Esther took a sip. "Which provides a nice segue to: Adrianna is an incredible woman, as you know. She's also terrible at letting her guard down and even worse at what the kids like to call work-life balance. Whatever you're doing seems to be helping and I'm so grateful for that. Advice from counsel is not to let her put work before your relationship. She'll try. It's a distancing thing. And further, not to put *her* before your work just because you're younger and still looking for the right fit professionally. You'll find it and she'll just have to go along for the ride. Speaking of which, learn how to drive a stick shift."

Charlotte was touched by this. Getting pretty drunk but definitely touched. She wanted to hug Esther, but she was pretty sure that would be a dealbreaker.

"I wish I had a friend like you," she said instead. "Addie," she laughed, "drew the right bull, as my daddy used to say. And I've known how to drive a stick since I was fifteen."

★ ★ ★

The next day at the museum was devoted to the inspection, which went well. The crate was in great shape and the painting inside it was perfectly fine, too. The Huntington staff were even impressed by the packing strategies employed by their East Coast counterparts. By midafternoon, Charlotte had officially done what she came for and was off the clock. Just in time to take a brief stroll through the acres and acres of flowers and trees for which the place was justifiably famous. But not the mysterious cactus gardens, whose prickly specimens she had glimpsed from the restaurant. She'd save those for Adrianna.

Charlotte had just returned to the hotel when a local number popped up on her phone. Fearing it was someone from the museum with a fire to put out, she answered immediately. It was Esther.

"How would you feel about taking a little drive to see a local liberal arts college?" she asked, apropos of nothing. "I've got my husband's car while the other one's in the shop, and I feel like getting out of Dodge."

It seemed about as random as could be. But she really did want to see more—or at least something—of southern California, and she liked the idea of seeing Esther again, too. If only to make sure they'd gotten past the previous night's weird hiccup about her cheating husband.

Esther picked her up in a very flashy black BMW convertible with paper plates still attached. An 8 Series, no less. Charlotte couldn't remember the last time she'd ridden in a car without a top that wasn't her own—they were simply stupid to own in New England where you might have only a few good weeks a year for going without. Esther, in another version of last night's understated skirt suit, her hair presumably pulled back to counter the wind, looked amusingly mismatched with what was practically a Formula One racecar—like a dominatrix masquerading as a, well, law professor. Esther's requisite giant California sunglasses helped her cause, but it was still funny to see her at the wheel of such an ostentatiously bad boy ride.

They drove for about half an hour through a landscape that Charlotte surveyed as it went from historic and attractive to unsightly suburban sprawl and happily back again. Through places called Monrovia and Azusa to a final destination that turned out to be the Piedmont Colleges. Esther pulled into a parking lot in the middle of the massive city of red-tiled roofs and mission-style buildings. It felt to Charlotte like a movie lot, or what she imagined a movie lot might look like—the complete opposite of Yale's pseudo-British Deco-Gothic architecture and New Haven's comparatively diverse urban setting.

"So this is the Piedmont Colleges. Since you said you missed teaching, I thought you might like to see a California campus that wasn't UCLA or USC," Esther said, in full tour guide mode. "One of these is even a fine and performing arts college."

"Right," Charlotte said. "Lyttleton-Hawes. I had a friend in grad school who went here. It's really beautiful."

"Let's walk," Esther said. She started off in the direction of a charming white stuccoed building with a pair of grand-looking carved wood doors that seemed to be surrounded by astrological signs. When they were only a few steps from the stairs a tall suntanned man in a blue suit emerged from the building and began walking toward them.

"Peter," Esther said collegially, when he arrived. "You *are* here. Good, good. I want to introduce you to my friend Dr. Charlotte Hilaire, assistant curator at the Woodley Center for American Art—she's doing a courier trip to the Huntington with a..." She turned to Charlotte. "What was it?"

Charlotte took the cue without missing a step. "It's a double portrait of Benjamin West and an unidentified child," she said, going into just the right amount of pertinent detail.

"Peter is the dean of the colleges," Esther said. "First among his great achievements is the expansion of the museums."

They talked for a few more minutes, Dean Peter asking Charlotte questions ranging from plainly polite to weirdly specific—the kinds of budgets an assistant curator might reasonably manage, for example. Then, he was off, and Esther continued walking them down the path until, a few minutes later, she turned to look behind them.

"Good, he's gone," she said. "Let's go back to that bar."

Charlotte wasn't at all sure what had just happened, though she had an idea. Was her ersatz sister-in-law craftily moving the pieces around on the dusty chessboard of her career? She didn't dare ask Esther directly. But the coincidence of "running into" the dean who headed up the museum's initiatives and other art-related things seemed a little too good to be happenstance.

And it wasn't exactly kosher, either.

But then, that was academia. And that was art history for sure. Connections, or the lack of them, were so often responsible for one's not getting on in the world. People liked to act as if it was mainly about the quality of your program—sure, so-and-so got the Brown job because she came out of Berkeley, or Columbia, or NYU or Yale. But it took more than that. A good word from a former school chum at one of these schools or a nod from an advisor's long-ago student on the search committee. Or a random encounter surreptitiously facilitated by the best friend of the woman you cannot get out of your mind.

Charlotte was delighted to be back at the bar at the hotel—it was warm enough today they might even sit outside. But she was a little sad about the timing, which meant she'd probably finish too late to call Adrianna. As they were walking toward the parking lot, Charlotte caught sight of Mr. Esther's bimmer.

"So, twin turbo inline six, eh? I bet that's fun."

Esther looked as if Charlotte had uttered some unthinkable profanity. "I don't know what you just said but it took me right back to Shitty Husband Land so I'll thank you to stop."

Charlotte's smile vanished.

Esther guffawed. "Heh. Gotcha," she said. "But really. I have no idea what language that was. Don't tell me you're a car person."

"For a split second when you picked me up in that, I thought I knew what you meant about driving a standard," Charlotte said.

"As if," said Esther. "Stephen wouldn't know how to drive a stick if you pulled one out of his ass. Which would be an improvement for both parties. There I go again." She opened her door. "I know what. Will you take a picture of me in the driver's seat for Addie? She'll like that."

Adrianna had indeed liked the picture when it was sent by Charlotte a few minutes later. It was a good time to let her know that they were only now heading back to the hotel and would be having a quick drink before she likely took something back to the room for dinner. The car to LAX was scheduled to pick her up at 4:00 a.m.

Esther had considerately ensured that their drink was an abbreviated one. Just a glass of white wine each this time. They'd bid a fond farewell—Esther had no doubt she'd see Charlotte again sometime soon. She said it as if she believed it but of course Charlotte wasn't sure what that would or could mean.

She texted Adrianna from the elevator to see if she was still awake.

How was the beach? Adrianna replied.

L. Next time. Esther is the best.

Isn't she though?

My turn to ask if you're in bed.

I'm waiting for you.

Take your clothes off. And give me 10.

Charlotte took a very fast shower before she slid naked under the covers of her king-sized bed. They hadn't done this for a while. And she couldn't wait. When they were both at home, they liked to hear each other's voices. But here at the hotel, Charlotte thought sexting would be more discreet.

Adrianna wrote: Sometimes during the day I stop and picture you leaning over me the way you did in Madrid. Your gorgeous tits.

You sucking my tits. Making my nipples hard.

You putting your hand between my legs. Rubbing my...

Just then an errant notification from the airline eclipsed the rest of Adrianna's response. Charlotte couldn't avoid it:
Fuck, fuck, fuck she wrote.

You *are* hot, babe. I didn't know you were so close

No. Fuck this fucking weather, Charlotte typed. My flight's been delayed. There's apparently a huge storm coming up the east coast.

She wanted to cry.

Damn. It'll be OK, baby. What are you most worried about?

I don't want to spend Christmas in the airport. Tomorrow's Xmas eve eve

I bet they'll get it figured out. Will you still go to LAX early?

Probably

I know you don't want to think about it, but I'm 100% sure Esther and Stephen would be thrilled to have you for Chinese food and champagne. She adores you like I knew she would. Can I run that by her? Just in case

You know how I hate to impose. It's getting to be a habit

I promise she won't see it that way

You're very sweet to me

You're very sweet. I can almost taste you

Hmmm...fuck. I want you so badly right now

Soon. I'm counting the days

Are you?

You know I am

It was late, too late to take things any further, though Charlotte easily would have. Tonight it wasn't the sex, or only the sex, she wanted. It was the intimacy. Traveling, being on the other side of the country, it was like the increased distance made a hard thing even harder. She was—and felt—farther away from Adrianna when, being out of her comfort zone, she needed to feel closer.

And now the possibility of bad weather keeping them apart on New Year's Eve.

Charlotte began crying. There on her island of a king bed in her superior junior suite, she simply started sobbing like a baby. It wasn't tonight. It wasn't anything Adrianna had done. God knows, she'd actually said she was counting the days. Which Charlotte had needily questioned. To which this astounding saint of a woman had again said just the right thing.

It wasn't Adrianna. Who was perfect. Who seemed completely comfortable with the way things were going. With the distance. With being apart for weeks—or even months. With all of it.

Charlotte was the one who couldn't stomach—she was feeling genuinely sick—the idea that she might not see Adrianna at New Year's if this storm intervened. She was nearly in a state of panic now. And it wasn't the first time. With Adrianna, something so minor as a missed text could immediately surface all her insecurities; the littlest thing, an ambiguous or delayed response, could ruin her day, which she knew was bad. Bad, and not true to the independent woman she had become long before she met Adrianna. Again.

Eventually Charlotte was all cried out. She had bottled up

her feelings for long enough. A classic blubbering, red-eyed catharsis like this had been in the cards for a while.

She went into the bathroom, blew her nose, and splashed cold water over her face, feeling at least provisionally ready for whatever came her way. She would see Adrianna some-how. She would feel her arms around her and they would be together again. She just needed to keep it together.

Chapter Eleven

Adrianna wrote to Esther almost immediately after Charlotte told her she thought she might be stuck in LA for Christmas. She was, as she had been told more than once, a fixer. It was natural to her to want to find a solution for a problem, in this case, Charlotte being stranded for the holidays with nowhere to stay.

Yet she detected something besides the usual impulse this time—something beyond what she knew was sometimes an essentially selfish desire to prophylactically resolve a problem and get back to what she needed to do. This wasn't that. This was coming out of her feelings for Charlotte. This was the heartbreakingly vivid picture of her girl, her beautiful, brilliant girl, lonely and out of options at LAX. Wanting to fix this didn't scare her, but it did surprise her. Adrianna hadn't given herself many opportunities to take care of someone who wasn't a student or a family member or a friend in need.

Charlotte's strength was real and she didn't need saving, that was for sure. But Adrianna was finding something very appealing, and honestly, kind of hot, about assuming a new kind of role with a younger woman. She wanted to be there for Charlotte, she wanted to do whatever she could to keep her from being upset, or hurt, or sad. And that felt good.

She was hoping Esther, who had already told her how much she liked Charlotte, would spontaneously offer to invite her to the house without being encouraged to do so. Instead, she detected something in the tone of Esther's email that made her want to hear her voice in person. So they scheduled a check-in call.

"And that accent," Esther said. "She is absolutely the most charming—and she's funny, too. You did not tell me she was so young, though. I'm not sure I've ever had a body like that. She had me at *y'all*."

Adrianna laughed. "She looks younger than she is. I'm glad you liked each other. She thinks you're the best. And she covets Stephen's car. As do I. I don't know whether to attribute it to debutante fragility or what, but she has a nervous side under that quiet confidence. She's pretty upset about getting stuck there for Christmas. Who wouldn't be?"

"Jews. Muslims. But also Buddhists. Hindus might not care."

"Yes, obviously. Forgive my shiksa misstep. Though I think our own Hindu friends would definitely care about sleeping at LAX, just ask them."

"So, you want me to invite her to stay with us?" Esther said. "And I would like nothing better under normal circumstances. But these are not those."

"What's going on?" Adrianna said, suddenly agitated. "You're not sick, are you?"

"No, no. God no, Addie," Esther said, seeming to register the level of concern from someone who had been at her side for the whole ordeal. "Something invasive is once again fucking with my life, but this time it's not cancer."

"So it's Stephen, isn't it?"

"I mean, some would say, 'At least the guy waits until his wife is out of the woods to have an affair with a student.' If remission following a single mastectomy is what you mean by 'out of the woods.' But I prefer, 'What a colossal fucking asswipe, how could he do that just when his wife is being considered for a Superior Court judgeship?'"

"First, holy shit, congratulations, that's fantastic, I knew this was coming! You're such a baller. And second, that fucking motherfucker. Is he fucking a student?"

Adrianna was not completely surprised about the judicial thing—she'd heard from mutual friends that Esther was on the governor's radar—but she was surprised, in a conventional sort of way, about the cheating. Esther was pretty extraordinary. And while she wasn't Adrianna's type, as it turned out—or vice versa—she was an amazing woman married to a superficially successful but profoundly, and worse, smugly, mediocre man. He was the kind of guy who looked over your shoulder for someone more important while he shook your hand. Who pretended to have read the book you mentioned when you both knew he hadn't. And who had shown his true colors after Esther's reconstructive surgery, when, as she had painfully confessed to Adrianna, he could no longer seem to have sex with her.

"Remember when I said I had a genuine office hours appointment a while back? That was actually her, if you can believe it. She decided, no, *they* decided, that it was time to tell me about them and she was the one to do it. At my office, no less."

"No," said Adrianna, incredulous. "He sent his student to tell his wife they're having an affair?"

"And that they're going away for Christmas—she's Presbyterian, don't you know—to figure out what she called *next steps*. Which is why it's not the best time for a houseguest. Fisher's simultaneously furious and blaming himself, of course. His friends are finishing Hanukkah and wrapping presents and he's getting divorce hints from his deadbeat dad and ice cream every day from his mom, who can't figure out what else to do for him."

"Wow," said Adrianna. "I'm so sorry, E.A. I wish I could be there myself. Distraction is what you both probably need."

"Wow, right back," Esther said icily. "Don't spin me, Addie. Even for the sake of your cute little stranded girlfriend."

Fair enough. She hadn't exactly meant to do that. But she hadn't not meant to do it, either.

"You're right, I'm sorry again," she said. "In my defense, you're my best friend and she's, well, she's someone I care about, so you can't exactly blame me for wanting to make both of you a little less miserable. And I do think having her there would make you less miserable. She makes killer beignets."

"Well shit," said Esther. "You buried the lede on that one. Alright, alright. If she makes the beignets and I don't have to pick her up at the airport, she can stay here. Tell her to call me when she's on her way."

Adrianna would have felt the tiniest bit guilty if it hadn't been made abundantly clear to her that nobody played Esther Adler. She was doing Adrianna a favor and they both knew that now. It was a kindness. But one that Adrianna had a feeling Esther would nonetheless be glad about with Stephen away and charming Charlotte there to keep her company.

If you have to spend the day at an airport, Charlotte thought you could do worse than LAX, which was bigger and cleaner than Newark or LaGuardia, with better restaurants. And more importantly, with a better airline club, access to which was another perk of Charlotte's museum job. And where thanking heaven for small mercies was concerned, it was also lucky she'd already delivered the painting. If she'd been delayed on the front end, while the art was in transit, what started as a mere compressed cross-country trip would have quickly become a stress-fest of epic proportions, with Charlotte babysitting the crate as they figured out how to keep it safe between delays.

As it was, Charlotte didn't need to worry about anything but herself and her carryon, and this she counted as a blessing. Still, it's not necessarily a good thing to have free drinks at your behest beginning at five in the morning. Until the day's first delay of her already delayed flight, Charlotte had limited herself to the time-tested daytime go-to of Baileys and coffee. But around noon, when an alert flashed on her phone that the departure previously pushed back to 3:47 was now delayed until 7:38, she decided she deserved a real drink.

Why can't airlines just tell the truth?

Which, in this case, would probably look something like: *Good evening Hartford-bound passengers, just so you know, like an inveterate casino gigolo, we're going to string you along for the next several hours, then, at about midnight, when the truth is evident but all the restaurants are closed and the good hotels are sold out, you'll have no choice but to shuttle to the local shithole we've booked for you and do all this again tomorrow, which, by the way, is Christmas Eve after a full day of canceled flights, so you might want to kiss midnight mass, and your awaiting friends and relatives goodbye this year. But we'll be sure to update you… JK. We're really just gonna get your hopes up and leave you stranded at the last minute.*

Fool me once, Charlotte thought and texted Adrianna with the news. As promised, she had been in touch with wonderful Esther, who had, according to Adrianna, offered her guest room to Charlotte as soon as she could get there and was looking forward to seeing her again and introducing her to her son.

Did she tell you? Charlotte texted.

Tell me what?

Charlotte waited, hoping Adrianna would see where she was headed. She couldn't imagine Esther wouldn't tell her about whatever the dickish Stephen was currently up to, es-

pecially knowing that Charlotte had put two and two together at dinner.

About Stephen? Adrianna finally typed back.

I'm sure the last thing she wants is company right now. Will
he be there?

Oh, good. I'm glad you know. She said she thought you got
the picture. He won't be there. Going to Bermuda with the
student. Unbelievable.

What an asshole. I feel terrible for her. But it's not like I really
know her enough to be any help at a time like this

Indeed, it wasn't like Charlotte knew Adrianna all that well,
either. And now she'd be staying with her friend at a really
terrible time in her life, just so she wouldn't be alone for a
holiday that Esther didn't even celebrate. And then there was
James. She had written to him earlier in the day to let him
know about the trip issues, but also to prepare him for her
inability to attend his very fun orphans-only all-day brunch
event on Christmas day.

I know, Adrianna wrote.

Must be strange to be there. Wish I'd been able to change my
ticket and spend Christmas with you in BK.

I just hope we can both get there by New Year's Eve ☹ But
thank you for arranging things with Esther. I feel terrible going
but I guess I'm also feeling sorry enough for myself to not want
to be alone in a hotel room. Or an airport

I fly out in four days. That's a long time from now. I'll get to New York. Don't worry, sweet bird.

Dying to see you, Charlotte answered.

Me, too, more than I can say. Full disclosure: Promised Est. you'd make beignets to seal the deal

Hah. Done and done.

The sun was low in the sky when Charlotte finally located the Lyft driver outside the terminal and tossed her luggage in the popped trunk. The driver was a woman, which tended to surprise her; it still seemed very much a man's business and not very safe for all the usual reasons. But this woman looked like she could handle herself. She was probably a few years younger and Charlotte would have bet the museum's collection that she was queer even before the driver started chatting her up.

"So, how was your flight?" From the hint of an accent, Charlotte guessed she might be a Spanish speaker.

"Canceled," Charlotte said, making an exasperated face in the rearview mirror.

"Oh, dude. That sucks," said the driver. "So you're from here?"

"Connecticut. I got here a few days ago and I'm trying to get back."

"For the holidays?"

"That was the idea."

"Shit. So you're missing Christmas. If you celebrate Christmas. Not saying that you should or anything."

Charlotte smiled at her. "No, I do. But luckily I have a friend out here who's going to take me in. Well, my girlfriend has a friend who's going to take me in."

The driver couldn't help but react to that. They both grinned.

"Nice. Is your girlfriend in Connecticut, too?"

"Spain. For now. But she lives here."

"Shit again. Your life sounds complicated."

"Whose isn't, right?"

"Truth. I was seeing this girl from Arizona for a while. But we just couldn't make it work. It's like, she was always in a different mental space and she was also hundreds of miles away. And I'm an actor, so, I'm all over the place even when I'm here, you know?"

She did know. And it had been like that with them sometimes, too. Adrianna was always deep into her research and Charlotte was often dealing with work. And they still hadn't had a real second date. Not the kind where you see each other the next day or week after you first slept together—where you go out to dinner and wonder what's next. What if they couldn't make it work from a distance, either?

"Like stage or screen or TV?" Charlotte asked, forcing her thoughts to the present. It was the first time she'd met someone who fit the stereotype. Not the starlet stereotype, though this woman was anything but unattractive, but the hoping-to-get-discovered stereotype. Charlotte realized that the driver might think she was in the industry somehow. Maybe that was a Pasadena thing.

"Mostly TV so far. I've done a couple of commercials. The usual stuff. Hoping for my big break. You know how it is."

"I work for a museum," Charlotte said. "I have no earthly idea how it is. But that sounds good. Does being queer make it harder?"

"Right now? No. If you want to play a queer. And there are actually some queers to play right now. But if you want to do anything else, forget it. Being Mexican makes it harder than being queer right now. And being a Mexican queer. Shit, we need our own Lena Waithe."

There was just enough sun left for Charlotte to make out a few of the strip malls and mountain ranges she had seen the first time, just before the car took the snaking turn off to the foothills of Pasadena. Los Angeles was pretty at night, too. All the sparkling lights and the fuchsias and blues of the sunset and the dark outlines of the palms. It was the furthest thing from Christmas she could imagine. But somehow that felt OK.

Chapter Twelve

Christmas day at Esther's started with Charlotte's beignets. The three of them were in the kitchen and Fisher, Esther's taller-than-average blue-eyed boy, was stationed at Charlotte's side carefully monitoring the process. Fisher had something of an interest in cooking, Charlotte learned, and he was thrilled to be a part of deep-frying, with all the attendant dangers that hot oil might bring to a kitchen in which the microwave and the convection oven were king.

"I think that one is ready for flipping," he said.

"I think you're right," Charlotte answered. "Should I do it?"

"I got it," Fisher said, as if they were strategizing a deep-sea rescue. "I just need to move that other one over a little, then I can turn it."

They'd almost finished the last of the dozen or so squares Fisher had helped Charlotte roll out and cut up, watching her every move along the way. Esther was in her library at the other end of the gigantic house, supposedly working on something legal. Charlotte was a little surprised, but flattered, that Esther had left her third-grader alone with an only child who had never really taken to babysitting.

But she liked Fisher. He was disarmingly serious in the same way she had been at that age—and the way Charlotte suspected Esther had likely been, too.

They were draining the last of the beignets, browned to a

perfect golden crisp, when Esther came in and sat down at one of the chrome stools alongside her vast, marble-topped island.

"How's it feel to be a real sous chef, Fish?" she asked her son, who was decked out in his mother's striped commercial apron.

"A sewer chef?" he answered, feigning misunderstanding.

"Funny," said Esther.

"I had some concerns about the oil at first," Fisher said. The phrase was obviously something he had picked up from one or the other of his parents. Charlotte figured it was Stephen. "But Charlotte showed me how. After that I pretty much did the rest. It was fun. Now it's time for the powdery stuff."

"Don't sugarcoat them on my account," Esther said, winking at Charlotte.

"It's not just for you, Mom," said Fisher, immediately frustrated in the way only a nine-year-old can get. "It's what the recipe calls for. I wish Addie was here for this. She's my sous chef."

Charlotte and Esther laughed.

"I wish she was here, too," Charlotte said.

More than she could say. And she'd been doing such a good job putting Adrianna out of her head until she heard her name. Addie. The other Adrianna. The one she'd never seen in this West Coast existence. Something in her expression must have given her away since Esther made an obvious effort to get Fisher's attention, perhaps before he began to put one and one together and wonder if they were a couple like his mom and dad.

"So show me how you do this," she said.

Charlotte had filled a paper bag with powdered sugar and she now gave Fisher a demonstration of how the magic happened, dropping a beignet in and shaking it gently before she removed it and set it on one of Esther's exquisite floral platters, peacock blue with gold trim. That she had brought out the Sèvres for the occasion made an impression on Charlotte, who had the highest esteem for fine French porcelain.

"I should make more coffee," Esther said. "Something tells me it's obligatory for this delicacy."

"Bonne idée," Charlotte said.

Esther smiled at her warmly. Then she asked her in perfect Parisian French if she had grown up speaking the language.

Charlotte answered, also in French, that she hadn't. But that she'd spent a Fulbright year in Paris and, being Creole in New Orleans, grew up around that version of French culture.

"What are you guys saying, anyway?" Fisher asked after a few more exchanges.

"I was saying that you're about the best beignet sugarer I've seen," Charlotte said. "But I said it in French so you wouldn't get a big head about it."

Fisher laughed, returning to his paper bag with renewed focus.

Adrianna's Christmas was pretty much a day like any other. Just the way she needed it to be. She had a book review for *Art Monitor* due the first week of January and she knew that if she didn't send it to the editor before she left for New York, she might not get it done. At least not the way she should. There were book reviews and then there were book reviews. This was the kind that might make a person's career—a long, painstakingly footnoted, critical but defensible account of another scholar's work on Spanish baroque convent art. The only way to do it justice was to set aside a good-sized block of uninterrupted time, just like this, to give it her full attention.

She'd grown up in a house where Christmas wasn't a particularly religious holiday, so that part of not celebrating it felt OK. She remembered the year, she must have been eleven or twelve, when her parents had simply stopped taking them to church, even on Easter and Christmas. She'd now come to the conclusion that it might have had something to do with her parents' correct suspicion that their only daughter was, and would soon declare herself to be, a lesbian. That to her father, a man who prided himself on his strict moral code, the hypocrisy of taking a gay kid to a homophobic house of worship just hadn't sat right with him, whether he himself could accept this essential aspect of his daughter's being (he could) or not. But she was always conflicted over whether or not to call her brother, a cardiologist with a practice in St. Louis. Their relationship had grown increasingly distant after she came out to him in college. He could always call her if he wanted. But she didn't think he would.

A reminder notification went off and Adrianna jumped in her chair. Charlotte—and Esther—would be calling in ten minutes from Los Angeles. It had been nice to think of them spending the day together.

You just never knew what life had in store.

If someone had told her last year at this time that this was what her Christmas would look like, she'd have called their bluff. She didn't dare think what next year might bring, though she could hope.

Which brought her to Charlotte. What had she gotten herself into there? Before they'd met, everything was going so well. Professionally at least, she'd felt more on track than she ever had. And now what? Her first thoughts in the morning and her last thoughts at night were of this woman in another country, who she was coming back to be with when what she should be doing, if she knew what was good for her career, was working on publishing these new archival finds. Getting ahead. Making her name. It seemed so much harder now, and more terrifyingly—less important—with her thoughts perpetually drifting to Charlotte's smile. Or the soft curves of her hips. Or the way she said "might could" without realizing it.

Adrianna minimized the review draft document. She needed to get her head out of writing for a few minutes before she talked to the girls. It would be great to hear both their voices. It would be wonderful to see Charlotte and to wish her a Merry Christmas. The cursor blinked back at her judgmentally; she hadn't really been concentrating on her work to begin with.

Charlotte's beignets were making their second appearance after dinner. This time Esther paired them with chocolate ice cream, the rationale being that they were celebrating Christmas and Hanukkah together with beignets instead of jelly doughnuts for the latter. The three of them ate and played cards until Fisher, wound up from the sugar and the excitement of having a houseguest, combined with his father's inexplicable absence, had finally crashed and reluctantly gone to bed.

It was nice FaceTiming with Adrianna, though to Charlotte she seemed almost disturbingly content in her scholarly confinement. She was on deadline, she reminded them, the better to enjoy her time in New York just days away.

"I warned you about the work thing," Esther said after.

They were sitting in her study, a good-sized corner of the front of the house with floor-to-ceiling bookshelves, Eames chairs, and a comfortable sofa. They'd done the call to Spain from there, with Fisher running in and out to show Adrianna various drawings and schoolwork—and beignets—he thought might be of interest. As Esther explained, the two of them had a history of furtive tête-à-têtes about his "illustrations" as Fisher called them.

"You did warn me," Charlotte said, swirling the viscous,

black cherry liquid in her balloon glass. Esther had excavated some excellent red wines from Stephen's cellar.

"The fact that she's getting the work done before she comes to see you is a big deal."

"I get that, but if I'd known she was staying there for Christmas just to do work," said Charlotte after a big sip. "By herself. I'm just surprised, I guess."

"That she didn't want to come back to be with you sooner?"

"Maybe. But she already had the ticket."

"And you had a courier trip. As it turns out."

Charlotte looked up and caught—was that the word? Let's say *saw*—Esther looking at her in a way that she wasn't ready for. The thought crossed her mind that Esther, the straightest woman in the world, might not be.

"Did you always know you were gay?" Esther asked, uncannily.

"I think I did," Charlotte said. "When I look back on it, women were always at the center of my universe. Teachers, relatives, friends. It's just the way I'm made. Men don't do a thing for me. And women are a constant source of fascination."

"All women?" said Esther.

Charlotte gave her the sternest look she could. "No. Of course not."

"I think…" Esther said hesitantly. "I think Adrianna once had a crush on me. I've always been straight. Nothing else was within the realm of possibility. But she's my best friend, someone I can't imagine not having in my life. You're both very lucky."

At first Charlotte had worried that Esther might actually be flirting with her. There was some kind of chemistry between them, and they both knew it. But she'd fervently hoped this was that not-unusual thing that happens between straight women and lesbians where they can be friends, even close friends, knowing it might be otherwise in a parallel universe but that this is not, nor would it ever be, that universe. It's easy enough when they're happily married; a bit more challenging when they're not.

Charlotte wasn't sure what was on Esther's mind. But she knew she'd been through a lot so she gave her the benefit of a doubt.

"Adrianna is amazing," she said. "And I do feel incredibly lucky that we found each other again," she said, stilling Esther's eye with a firm glance. "And you are kind and talented and beautiful. Maybe you should expand your notion of the possible. People do change."

Esther only smirked a tiny smirk in response, before taking a gulp of her wine.

The day after Christmas, LAX was running more or less on schedule and Charlotte was able to catch a flight back to Hartford, where the storm had dumped a mere foot of snow. In the end, the storm to end all storms had underperformed, and it hadn't been difficult to get a car to New Haven that night.

It was good to be back in her own bed, though Esther's Italian sheets were like cashmere and Charlotte could have gotten used to drinking rare, stratospherically high-priced red wines on a daily basis, merely to piss off Esther's husband.

Tomorrow was the day before Adrianna would be back in the States. And with that long-anticipated date fast approaching Charlotte was (predictably) getting nervous. As she looked around her apartment, at the worn Ikea sofa and the grandmotherly bibelots—mostly inherited from her actual grandmother—and the rose-colored walls in exchange for which she'd paid an extra deposit, Charlotte wondered what Adrianna would think of the way she lived.

After all, neither of them had any idea what the other's life truly looked like. Charlotte had only seen Adrianna in a borrowed habitat, nor would Adrianna see this apartment, since they were meeting in yet another location to which neither of them had a direct connection.

For now, she was beyond excited about the rendezvous in Brooklyn and she had the haircut, and facial, and waxing to prove it. They had joked that it sounded like the least romantic plan imaginable—or like a lost Neil Simon play. But Charlotte couldn't think of being anywhere with Adrianna as less than romantic. Just the thought of sitting next to her made Charlotte long for them to be together.

She'd texted Adrianna at the various stages of her journey and now that she was home, it was too late to talk. However, Charlotte suddenly remembered that she had Esther to update, too. She quickly fired off a text to thank her again and let her know she was safe and sound and contemplating a good night's sleep in her comparatively burlap-like linens. Somewhat to her surprise, Esther wrote back immediately.

Fisher is already asking when you'll be back

Oh! He is just the sweetest. Loved meeting him Charlotte replied.

Nice having you here. Apologies for bad behavior.

Charlotte wondered what Esther's idea of bad behavior might be. Was it the way she allowed herself to look at Charlotte? Now that they were apart, Charlotte could more readily admit to herself that she'd felt Esther's eyes on her more than once. But only when they'd been drinking. She wanted to believe Esther's bad behavior was somewhat beyond her control; straight women who find themselves inexplicably

attracted to other women are notorious for acting inappro-
priately or impulsively, at least at the beginning—as if it was
someone else's fault. She was just glad Esther hadn't turned it
back on her or pretended it never happened.

Not myself right now in many ways. You gave me a lot to
think about, Esther added a few seconds later.

Now she really wondered what was going on in the future judge's head. Esther was a looker. A legal genius, one
inferred. So funny. And yet. She knew beyond question that
her feelings were so strong for Adrianna that even if Esther
had pushed past whatever it was and hit on her, she wouldn't
have been even remotely tempted to reciprocate. And thank
God Esther hadn't.

Give my love to Addie—can't wait to see her!

And thank God for that, too. For surely this was as good
as typing: *Mea culpa! I am mortified that I almost made a move
on the woman my best friend is seeing and I promise I will never do
anything like that again.*

Charlotte dearly hoped not.

What a strange few days it had been. Certainly a Christmas
like no other. But now it was like a page had been turned.
Charlotte loved the week leading up to New Year's Eve. Aside
from the vacation days, it was usually a time when, with the
stresses of Christmas with her family behind her, she could
enjoy herself with people like James and take stock of the past
twelve months newly infused with clean-slate optimism.

New Year, new life.

Charlotte had learned a lot in Pasadena. She'd learned that
Adrianna was thinking about her even from Madrid. Enough
to save her Christmas. Enough to want her to spend time with
her best friend even when Adrianna couldn't be there. And

she'd learned that she wasn't especially great at living in a state of indeterminacy. However much Charlotte prided herself on being fun and flexible, what she wanted in her heart of hearts looked more like security and stability.

It was too soon for all that, but it was good to know just the same.

Chapter Thirteen

Adrianna's flight was delayed. Her own disappointment coupled with Charlotte's was the last thing she wanted to contend with. And it made both of them every bit as unhappy as she knew it would. What she didn't expect was for Charlotte to get philosophical.

Whenever you get here, I'll be ecstatic

Adrianna could tell Charlotte was making a courageous effort not to turn the situation into high drama. And her attempt was welcome. Nothing could be said that would offset the anguish of worrying they'd miss New Year's together.

But then, Barajas being Barajas, the departures board was reset and her takeoff was scheduled a mere hour from now. Adrianna knew better than to confirm this with Charlotte. Not yet. She waited until she was on the plane and the highly gelled flight attendant was wagging his finger at her for continuing to text after the doors had closed.

She was on her way to see the woman who might be the love of her life. *Por fin!*

The love of her life? And what did that mean exactly? Adrianna had dated a lot in her life. She had slept with what could probably be labeled a significant number of women. And she had had two long-term relationships, both of which ended with her spouse at the time cheating on her for reasons she would still rather not admit, even to herself.

The love of one's life was theoretically the ONE. At this point in her life, however, it seemed pretty clear to Adrianna that you can never know so early in the game if this one is THE ONE. Wanting Charlotte to be THE love of her life was already a bit insincere since she had already had other loves of her life, even other ONES. Some of them were amazing women, but women who were just not right for her for forever. What she felt for Charlotte didn't need to be unlike anything she'd ever experienced before. But it did need to feel like the real thing. And it did. It had.

But that was then. The first time seeing each other since they'd said their near-tearful goodbyes in Madrid would be here within hours. And while she'd told herself not to put too much pressure on that much-anticipated point of reentry, she had already rehearsed some of the things she might want to tell Charlotte as soon as she saw her. They'd talked so much—and other things—in the interim, she felt she knew Charlotte a lot better than when they parted. But she was nervous anyway. Nervous. Adrianna laughed to herself. How long had it been?

Once they landed, she'd almost made it through customs, when she was ushered away from the rest of the passengers. Adrianna and a couple of other people of color, two of whom were presumably Arab, were shunted off into a smaller room for light grilling with a side of no explanation. What had she been doing in Spain for the past five months? Why was she going back? What was the nature of her so-called research?

When she started explaining about Sor Epiphania's diaries she could see the agents' eyes glaze over, which helped convince them she was merely a boring academic. And after she showed them her ID for the Biblioteca they were satisfied enough to let her proceed. Then it was straight to the baggage claim and out into the wintry evening air of the state of New York. It was good to be back.

They'd initially planned to meet at the apartment, a true pied-à-terre in the sense that it afforded a person, maybe two, a foothold in Brooklyn. A few blocks from the park, it was eight floors up in one of the few prewar buildings in the borough— a nice Roosevelt-era co-op with a few small apartments, like the studio her friend had bought right after the crash, inter-mixed among the bigger ones on each floor. A violinist by occupation, the studio's owner played with the Philharmonic and had another apartment in the Marais and a girlfriend in London, which was where she was for the holidays. Adrianna had stayed there before but never with anyone else.

Her Uber driver was neither a talker nor a listener to music, so they had settled into companionable silence for the forty-minute trip from the airport. After sleepy Madrid, it was per-versely heartening to see New York doing what it does so well at the end of December. Being a big unapologetically capitalist American city gearing up for the New Year, its streets thick with post-Christmas shoppers and lights still strung on the trees and buildings. Madrid's sister metropolis felt decidedly more worldly and diverse. It was a city of snow and tourists and whole communities of people who didn't give Christmas a second thought. She had missed the way she always felt in New York: anonymous, in the heart of things, on a mission. But now that mission was Charlotte. After seeing her there in just a few minutes, Adrianna knew the city would never be the same.

Few things are better than knowing your lover, who you haven't seen in far too long, is on the plane, on their way, com-ing right at you like a ninety-mile-an-hour ace, with nothing to stop them. Once Charlotte had confirmed that Adrianna's

Iberia flight was out of the gate she was free to enjoy the waiting. Free to shave her legs again. Free to repack her suitcase.
Free to fantasize about waking up to Adrianna's kiss—and in
all likelihood, her typing.

She got a car to Union Station and took the train to Grand
Central. From there, she'd decided to Uber to Brooklyn instead of the subway, which would probably have been faster.
The argument she made to herself was that it was bitter cold
and there was still snow everywhere. She didn't want to feel
hassled. Or get her gorgeous boots salt-stained. She wanted
to be irresistible in her long coat and hot Yves Saint Laurent
dress. Adrianna could see casual Charlotte later.

She was in the car to Fort Greene when Adrianna texted
her.

Soooo sorry mi amor. A bit of a customs prob. Profiling, anyone?

Taking a car from LaGuardia now. If you beat me. Meet me at
the cafe down the street from apt. It's Walter's. Soon! xoxoxo

Again, the fates conspired to heighten her already heightened anticipation, Charlotte thought. Now she would be the
kind of person who brings her luggage into a place of business.

When she arrived, there was only one table available at the
little restaurant called Walter's and it was just inside the door,
too close to the cold to allow Charlotte to take off her coat,
in fact, since the frigid air outside was reintroduced into the
packed little space with every customer's entrance or exit. She
went ahead and ordered a glass of wine. Best to start slow.
Who knew if Adrianna would want to stay for cocktails or
dinner or what? Charlotte hadn't eaten since breakfast—these
past few days, she'd suddenly started feeling more conscious

of her weight than usual. Her stomach was growling, though whether from butterflies or intermittent fasting, she couldn't be sure.

The wine settled her nerves. A little. But still, Charlotte was agonizing—what if things were different between them? What if they realized trying it again was a mistake? What if the feelings she'd had since their three days together were based on something she'd merely imagined? Adrianna had a full and impressive life of her own. What could Charlotte add to that?

Now Adrianna's car was moving through recognizable streets and subway stops, past the park itself. She could feel her heart racing and her head swimming in a kind of confusion, all of it prompted by the realization that she'd be seeing Charlotte in the flesh, within minutes. She'd be feeling the person attached to the voice and the words that had stood in for her for almost a month. Her body, her touch. Adrianna smiled, frankly delighted by the almost teenage eagerness she was feeling.

Hadn't they only just met up at a bar in Madrid? Hadn't she just woken with Charlotte in her bed in someone else's apartment? It was both yesterday and forever ago. Would they fall easily into their give-and-take, into the shifting exchange of power that was one of the many things that made being with Charlotte so exciting for Adrianna? The car stopped and the driver asked her if this was the place.

When Adrianna came through the door her eyes went straight to Charlotte, who appeared to be joking with the server refilling her water glass. She was heartstoppingly attractive—friendly and funny and so perfectly herself. She was wearing a woolly dark brown coat. Her pearl and diamond earrings and the pale pink pashmina looped around her neck set off her freckled, golden skin in a way that made Adrianna feel as if she'd never seen her before. Not like this.

She would gladly have stayed there looking on for longer—there was nowhere to go but forward. Adrianna turned to maneuver her suitcase around the shoes and toes in its way and when she glanced up again Charlotte was looking right at her, smiling that smile.

She stood up beside her table and Adrianna practically ran to her, not entirely conscious of what she was doing.

"Hi, baby," she said, pulling Charlotte in.

"You're here," Charlotte said. "You're really here."

Out of politeness to the restaurant, they stayed for one drink. But immediately after the last sip, they were out on the sidewalk, where Adrianna made them stop for a minute before they embarked on what she assured Charlotte was no more than a block and a half walk to the apartment—which Charlotte already knew since she'd already had to double back to Walter's from her original drop-off.

She herded Charlotte off to the side between a couple of tall potted spruce trees and put her hands on her waist. Charlotte put her arms around Adrianna, who was wearing her own long and very beautiful black coat and a patterned silk scarf under her shirt. Charlotte thought Adrianna's eyes looked tired but no less expectant and her crimson lipstick was dauntingly fresh. But Charlotte couldn't stop herself. When she tipped her head up, Adrianna's lips immediately answered her, kiss for kiss.

"Did I mention I missed you?" Adrianna said.

"If this is the part where you tell me your apartment's just a block away, I'm not really that kind of girl," Charlotte said.

"This is the part," Adrianna laughed. "And I'm pretty sure you are."

There was more errantly lipsticked kissing on the elevator. Until a man in a suit got on and pretended not to see the red smeared across both their faces.

The apartment was intimidatingly clean in the way that many New Yorkers find necessary when their spaces are small. One got the impression that the owner would immediately notice if a throw pillow were wrongly knifed or a teaspoon ended up where the soupspoons go.

"She's astoundingly anal, as you can see," Adrianna said. "But after we leave, her awesome crime scene cleaning service will come in and it will look as if we were never here. It's part of the arrangement. So go crazy within reason. As long as we don't spill red wine, we're fine. As a rule, I only drink clear liquids when I'm here. Way too stressful otherwise."

"Good thing I brought cava," Charlotte said. She had found some very good Spanish bubbly at her favorite wine store in New Haven. It took up half of the room in her luggage, but it was worth it.

"Great minds," Adrianna said. "I bet you're hungry. I'm absolutely ravenous. I figured we'd order in."

It was nice that it wasn't New Year's Eve yet. This took the burden of having an extraordinary night off their shoulders, which made it even more likely they would. Adrianna had a Thai place in mind, and they ordered all their favorites— tom kha gai and wide noodles and curry. While they waited the required hour, they took a shower together, remembering each other's bodies and letting go of the worry and anxiety that had been a part of the day so far.

There was no longer any need to worry about what it would be like to see each other for the first time after they'd said goodbye in Madrid. That was over now and things were going exactly as they'd hoped.

The shower was actually a deep cast-iron bathtub ringed in waffled white curtains. There was no way not to be inti- mate. As soon as she got in, Adrianna began to soap Charlotte's breasts and belly, gently rubbing her back with the rather coarse washcloths the violinist preferred. When she was properly rinsed, Charlotte kissed her under the warm water, pressing their breasts together.

"You feel amazing," Adrianna said. "But have you been eating, *mi amor*? We'll have to have some good meals while we're here. I know I'm ready for everything that is not *tortilla y jamón*."

During their phone conversations, though she'd immediately regretted it, Charlotte had let it slip once or twice that her mother almost constantly nagged her about her weight, even when she was in the leanest shape of her life, playing varsity tennis. Adrianna's subtle words almost broke Charlotte's heart. If she'd gotten it into her head that Adrianna hoped she would be other than she was in Spain when she was at her more typical weight, she now knew this was something she'd imagined—and that it didn't matter.

"Not that I'm saying anything about anything either way," Adrianna said now, trying to correct herself. "You're everything I've ever…"

"Thank you, honey," Charlotte smiled, turning Adrianna around to help rinse her back.

There was a lot they could have done that they didn't do. Neither of them seemed inclined to yet. Charlotte needed their first night together to last as long as possible and that wish allowed her to hold back when what she really wanted was to slide her hand between Adrianna's legs and hear her moan her name.

Adrianna turned off the tap, as if she'd read Charlotte's mind.

"Just in time," Charlotte said.

"For what?" Adrianna handed Charlotte a towel and took

one for herself, stepping over the tub and onto the mat as Charlotte followed.

"For me not to do what you know I want to do to you. Before dinner," said Charlotte, wrapping herself up.

Adrianna was toweling her dark hair. She looked younger without her makeup. Charlotte wondered if she detected a slight melancholy there; it wasn't the first time she sensed something of the sort. They dried off and got into their pajamas—Charlotte had brought a nightshirt of her own this time.

"We're disciplined. I'll give us that," Adrianna said.

"Delayed gratification is a way of life for me," said Charlotte.

"I'm not so crazy about the delays," Adrianna said before kissing Charlotte hotly on the mouth. "But I'll take the gratification, every time."

Chapter Fourteen

The delivery finally arrived and they ate and drank cava on the love seat against the long wall of the studio—across from its tidy and truly shiplike galley kitchen, which had a fantastic assemblage of mirrors hand-cut by a local artist mounted across the wall. There was plenty to talk about. Charlotte wanted all the details about the discoveries Adrianna had made in Sor Epiphania's diary. Adrianna grilled Charlotte on Esther's state of mind after—and during—asshole Stephen's infidelities.

It was a relief to Charlotte that she felt so much less nervous with Adrianna than she had the last time they'd sat side by side like this. *Those* nerves had never been about the sex, though. And now, with the showers and the reconnecting behind them, Charlotte felt almost incapable of concentrating on the carefully constructed sentences flowing from Adrianna's animated mouth, however engaging they were.

She removed the lacquered tray between them, which was piled with food containers, placing it on the vintage Lucite coffee table. Then, instead of sitting down again, she slid off her panties and straddled Adrianna. As their lips met and their tongues started to find each other, Charlotte unbuttoned Adrianna's pajama top. Her breasts were still warm from the heat of the shower. Charlotte grazed her dark nipples with the backs of her hands until they wrinkled and stiffened.

Adrianna breathed hard through their kisses. Her hands

were all over Charlotte. Waist, hips, breasts, but Charlotte's silk top still formed a barrier between Adrianna's fingers and her own skin.

After teasing her this way for what felt like forever, Adrianna lifted the nightshirt over Charlotte's head. They sat looking at each other and Charlotte noted the same slightly pained expression in Adrianna's eyes. She leaned forward and kissed her between her breasts.

"You look a little sad, hon," Charlotte said, not entirely sure she wanted to learn why this might be so.

"Not sad," said Adrianna. "Painfully happy."

"Is that really all?"

"All? It's everything. You're so fucking… I mean, it almost hurts, Charlotte. I'm not kidding. I knew I wanted to see you again but, honestly, I don't think I'd let myself realize how much. I'm just trying to be in the moment. It doesn't come naturally to me."

"I know it doesn't," Charlotte said. "You're a freaking extraordinary planner. But there's nothing to plan right now." She leaned forward again, enough to whisper in Adrianna's ear, "Just touch me."

They stayed on the love seat for most of the night, only getting up for a glass of water or to recover for a few minutes. When the sky started to brighten with the first signs of dawn, Adrianna suggested they move into the bedroom.

The little alcove off the main room was technically just that. Its double bed almost completely filled the space, one wall of which was taken up by a tall, mullioned window with an unobstructed view over the brownstones across the street. The violinist kept jades and echeverias on the sill and they looked happy there, even in winter, likely owing to the bright southern exposure.

"I saw the outskirts of the cactus garden," Charlotte said when they had settled in. "But I didn't go any farther. It looked like another planet, like science fiction. I wonder if that's what Louisiana looks like to y'all."

"I guess you'll find out one of these days," Adrianna said. "Have you heard of the art fair called Prospect New Orleans? I don't know anything about contemporary art, but people say it's a great way to see the city. And it's mostly POC artists, I gather."

"And you say you're ignorant about anything after 1750," Charlotte said. She was always impressed when someone could associate New Orleans with something other than Mardi Gras and Tennessee Williams, bless his heart. Or even beignets or Beyoncé, for that matter.

"I went to the last Prospect," she said. "And it was really good. I think you'd like it. And I know you'd love New Orleans. When I take you there—and I will *take* you there—we'll go to happy hour in the best food hall on God's green earth. St. Roch Market. And we'll eat dollar oysters and drink bourbon and then I'll bring you back to whatever Airbnb we have to stay in because my mama is such a vacuous harpy, and I'll fuck you 'til you scream."

"You think you can make me scream?"

Charlotte was already kissing her way down Adrianna's stomach. "Honey, I know I can make you scream."

Considering how much they both liked to strategize, there was very little structure to their three days in Brooklyn. Adrianna had tried to determine from afar whether Charlotte would want to be in or out on New Year's Eve. Charlotte continued to demur, saying she'd be happy eating pizza and watching whatever version there was of Dick Clark or Guy Lombardo, as her grandparents always had, with no need to go anywhere.

This was exactly how Adrianna felt, although her parents and her family in general were more the types to go dancing than stay at home to watch the ball drop.

They were both women who loved to dress, however. And it seemed a shame to Adrianna to miss an opportunity to see Charlotte in a date-night outfit, though she really couldn't imagine her looking any more beautiful than she had sitting at her table at Walter's.

Just in case, she'd made a reservation the day after Charlotte left Madrid. It wasn't a particularly hip or famous restaurant, just that exemplary type of hidden gem, very New York kind of place. Nothing special on the outside but pure romance within. Tinkling chandeliers, tiny lamps with tiny shades on the tables. An old queen at a grand piano playing, and occasionally singing, all the best standards. It was said that Mel Tormé and Bobby Short had sat in there on occasion, back in the day.

When, at about four o'clock that afternoon, Adrianna informed Charlotte that they had a 9:00 p.m. dinner reservation, she could tell from the response that she'd made the right decision.

"How did you know I'd bring something to wear?" Charlotte practically shrieked with excitement.

"I just did. But also. It's New York and looking like you do, jeans, heels, and a white button-down would have worked just fine."

"I call your jeans and white shirt," Charlotte scoffed. "And raise you a Balmain dress and Manolos."

"I fold," Adrianna laughed. "And don't mock. I may go that jeans route myself. A little Anne Fontaine. A little Chanel. I hope I won't embarrass you."

Charlotte made the sound of a growling jaguar.

★ ★ ★

Charlotte couldn't have chosen a more perfect restaurant. Every course was exceptional, from the pâté to the frisée, and they were treated very well by everyone. The one thing that wasn't as expected was the piano player, who happened to be a masculine-of-center lesbian with pomaded hair and a white tuxedo. She sang the standards. But once she got her eye on Charlotte and Adrianna she threw in a little raunchy Bessie Smith and Gladys Bentley. By the time they left, half the restaurant was singing along or dancing. It was a dream of a night.

After dinner, although it was barely above freezing outside, they walked the several blocks home just to wake themselves up. The restaurant was booked, of course, so they'd had to give up their table before midnight. It was still a few minutes shy of 11:00 and champagne was virtually running through their veins. But as they'd been drinking and eating in proper measure, it hadn't gotten the best of them. Along with the wine, they'd had coffee, water, and a superior crème brûlée even by Charlotte's standards. The two of them were practically floating by the time they got into to the apartment.

No sooner had they closed the door than they were kicking off their heels and making out like fiends. Adrianna tried to steer them to the sofa. But Charlotte took her hand and led her into the bedroom, where she proceeded to strip Adrianna down to nothing but her white satin bra. She sat her at the edge of the bed and stood between her legs, still fully dressed.

Adrianna reached up to undo the loose bow that was Charlotte's belt. The jersey dress fell open to reveal her black lace push-up bra, and lower down, the sleek black Wolford garter belt that had been holding up her seamed stockings so far that night. Charlotte let her dress drop to the floor.

"Fuck," Adrianna said reverently.

"Oh, we will," Charlotte said. She hadn't yet thought how she wanted this to go, but with Adrianna sitting there looking at her that like that, certain trajectories came to mind.

"Undo those, will you?" she said, stiffening her stance.

Adrianna had already begun to run her fingers under the satin straps of the garters, snapping them against the cool flesh of Charlotte's ass.

"If I must," she said, releasing the little ribboned clasps until the thick black bands of Charlotte's sheer stockings loosened ever so slightly around her thighs.

"Now," Charlotte said, placing her palm on Adrianna's chest and giving her a slight push backward. "Heels up."

"Shit, girl. What are we doing?" Adrianna asked. Her face was glowing and she looked, for her, even the tiniest bit confused.

"You're not doing anything," Charlotte said, climbing onto the bed to meet Adrianna, who was sliding back on the mattress toward the pillows. "And I'm doing you."

She knelt beside Adrianna, holding her legs behind the knee with one arm so that she could stroke her for a little while, making sure—as if there were any need—she was good and wet before she put herself there.

But for a little "Mmmmm"-ing, Adrianna was quiet at first, rocking her hips, and caressing Charlotte's leg, the only part of her body she could reach.

"Kiss me, baby," she finally said. "Or else I'm gonna come right now."

Charlotte let Adrianna's bent knees fall open and climbed through them, lowering herself onto Adrianna's belly and nuzzling her erect nipples through the satin, naughtily leaving traces of her lipstick there.

Adrianna Coates was lying there willingly exposed and so eager, waiting for Charlotte to take over. Waiting for Charlotte to make love to her. Seeing her like that had Charlotte dizzy with desire. She could tell just how much Adrianna wanted her. But more than that she could sense how much she trusted her. The sweetly admiring expression in Adrianna's deep brown eyes, the hoarse yearning in her voice, and her hands—clutching at the edges of the bed—made Charlotte feel like there was nothing she couldn't do. Nothing she wouldn't do—for Adrianna.

She anchored her knees behind Adrianna's raised thighs and pressed against her, feeling her own clit throb. She was as wet and just as impatient as Adrianna.

As soon as they touched, Adrianna jerked forward to meet her, fitting their bodies in place.

Charlotte leaned down and kissed her, the friction of her movement setting off the exchange of pleasure between them. It happened again when she moved back onto her heels, dragging herself with deliberate care against Adrianna, feeling and hearing the resistance as she brushed back and forth.

Adrianna reached for Charlotte's breasts, squeezing them with feverish enthusiasm, like a schoolboy—or girl—finally permitted to touch.

She was out of her mind, head whipping from one side to the other, murmuring all sorts of things along the way.

Charlotte continued to rub and graze her clit on Adrianna's until she had them both scarcely able to take another pass. She leaned down once more for a kiss.

"Yeah, baby, yeah. Fuck, Charlotte, I'm gonna come."

"I'm right there, honey."

And then they did come, impressively together, their fingers laced against the bedsheets as they shook and shuddered against each other for hours. At least it felt like that.

At last, if only to give her trembling glutes a needed rest,

Charlotte pushed herself away from Adrianna, who swung a leg over to make a protective crook with her knees.

"Charlotte," Adrianna cooed, looking blissful and grateful and bleary-eyed. "My darling, darling Charlotte..."

As her voice trailed off, Charlotte smiled at her, not so shyly this time. "Happy New Year," she said. "Addie."

Even Adrianna slept in late the next day; almost until noon. She was as shocked by this as she was by their shared clearhead-edness. Neither of them was the least bit hungover. Though they were definitely hungry.

"I'd say we should go to brunch, but there's no way that's going to happen without a reservation made a year ago. At least we have leftover noodles," Adrianna said.

Now look who was being philosophical.

"And yet, we're out of bubbly," said Charlotte.

"I'm sensing you have something in mind," Adrianna said. She was getting wound up merely from the sound of Charlotte's voice.

Charlotte started kissing her shoulders.

"I do," she said. "Have something in mind. But you'll have to run to the store while I execute the first stages."

"Sounds complicated. What am I getting?"

"Anything clear. As long as it has bubbles."

Adrianna got back into jeans and the sweater she had worn on the plane. There was a good corner store about a block away that never seemed to close and this was her destination.

Some streets were predictably quiet. And their block, which was completely residential, felt like a stage set. On Fulton, people were out and the bars and restaurants were packed with the brunchtime crowd, considerable even on a non-holiday. Adrianna wondered what in the world Charlotte was up to.

She hoped it would have something to do with food. Now she was really starving.

Inside the corner store there was a long line for the one cashier. People's hands were full of everything from handles of vodka to day-old carnations to Rice-A-Roni. She was glad to see that there was still champagne to be had. If, and as soon as, the blonde commandeering the cooler would make a goddamned choice and close the door. Adrianna came up behind her a little closer than she normally would have, in an effort to vibe her into acting more quickly. To no avail. The woman simply glanced behind her momentarily, noting Adrianna's presence, she felt sure, before returning to whatever deliberation she was in the middle of.

A middle-aged woman in a long fur-trimmed down coat queued up behind Adrianna.

"You'd think it was life or death," she said in a stage voice.

"Maybe it's a meet the parents scenario," Adrianna responded quietly. She was feeling unusually generous.

"That's easy. Moët," said the woman louder still. "Not too cheap, not too pricey, just tasteful. Easy choice."

"That's what I was planning to go with. Provided I get the chance."

"At this rate, there'll be nothing left to celebrate."

If the blonde was listening to them, her pretense of not giving a shit was truly believable. Eventually she reached for a bottle behind a bottle. From what Adrianna could see, it was the last of the Moët. The glass door slammed closed with a double bounce and she turned around, greeted by one moderately sour and one extra-sour expression.

"Adrianna!" she screamed.

Chapter Fifteen

Charlotte had had this in mind from the beginning. At some point during their three days, she would want to cook for Adrianna, and when that time came, she would make her another sexy signature dish. Frozen shrimp and bacon were the only challenges in terms of transport. But the weather helped and the ice packs provided peace of mind. The grits were dry, of course, and the other ingredients had all made it unharmed or unthawed, to be hidden away in the fridge at the first opportunity after their arrival.

The recipe had the advantage of being simple and fast. And it smelled heavenly. Not too heavenly, she hoped, for the meticulous violinist.

By the time she heard Adrianna's key in the lock she had fried up the bacon and peeled the shrimp. The grits were bubbling away in all their creamy cheddared glory. The garlic was minced and the scallions were sliced. And of course she'd brought along her Cajun spices.

"Oh my God," Adrianna said.

Charlotte smiled but didn't turn around.

"You will never believe who I just ran into," Adrianna continued, rhetorically it would seem. "Hadley Fairweather. From Yale. Remember her?"

Charlotte remembered.

"Golly," she said, faking detachment as best she could. "What's she doing in Brooklyn?"

Besides living here, of course. Hadley never let anyone forget her parents had moved to Williamsburg from the Upper West—before it was such a cliché. So much grittier. More real.

"She grew up here, remember? Or in New York, anyway. Her parents live in Williamsburg and she was grabbing champagne for brunch—I guess her brother lives around here—and she invited us to a party tonight. I haven't thought of her for years. You two knew each other, didn't you? She's a trip. Does nineteenth-century, right?"

"We knew each other," Charlotte said, petulantly tossing the shrimp into a sizzling skillet. "She was a year ahead of me and she finished early. And never let me or anyone else forget it. She's a trip alright."

Adrianna set down the bottles on the counter and came up behind Charlotte, wrapping her arms around her waist.

"What in the world are you making, my darling one? It smells incredible. How did you manage all this?"

Charlotte was soothed somewhat by Adrianna's appreciation. It wasn't her fault, exactly, if she'd been taken in by the connivance of scheming Hadley Fairweather, also known by Charlotte's boys as the "blonde bomb shelter."

"I brought some things from New Haven. I knew we'd get tired of takeout. And I wanted to cook for you."

Adrianna kissed her neck.

"I'm the luckiest woman in the world," she said.

"What time is the party? Sounds like you want to go?"

"She said any time after nine. So we'd be long done with brunch and even the first round of dessert—" she winked "—by then. But I'm sensing she's not exactly your favorite person. Hadley is definitely high-maintenance. And not especially self-aware, if memory, and seeing her in a public place, can be trusted. Did you guys come to blows or something? How bad was it?"

"I didn't care enough about her for that," Charlotte said. "She was always unhumble-bragging about some commissioned essay or declined fellowship or adoring professor, all male, of course."

"Okay, you really don't like her. My bad. I think because I was further along and older, she was vaguely respectful. Which I might have mistaken for not being an asshole. All clear now. We can stay in and eat this wondrous meal and they can have Williamsburg. This was so thoughtful, baby."

Charlotte loved it when Adrianna got solicitous. So far, it didn't happen too often outside the bedroom. But she could be very sweet when she was eager to please.

"Hand me that hot sauce, will you?" Charlotte said, plating the grits. "And can you sprinkle on the scallions while I grab the biscuits?"

"Biscuits? You are fucking kidding me. Am I in paradise?"

"Made them yesterday. I hope they aren't stale. They're hot, so watch out."

"You. Are divine."

Charlotte was, in fact. Her cheesy grits were about as close to good sex as food can come. And Adrianna showed her gratitude accordingly and in kind. With good sex.

After they finished eating at the little table by the window, they'd moved to the kitchen counter. And from there to the bedroom. And as they lay there deliriously catching their breath for the umpteenth time in forty-eight hours it occurred to them both that being out in the world together would only make it more fun to come home again.

"I guess we can go to your stinky old party," Charlotte said. "Just don't expect me to fawn all over her ladyship. But are we going to be out to them. I mean, as a couple?"

"Well, I'm certainly not planning to introduce you as my fellow art historian. Would you prefer lover or paramour?"

Charlotte laughed. But it was a sincere question. They hadn't exactly established their relationship status. And this wasn't helping. But Adrianna knew that.

"I'm sorry, babe. I'm being squirrely. I'm still getting used to this. It's been a long time. Really, it's never been like this at all for me. As I told Esther, I'm pretty crazy about you."

Charlotte felt her face flush. She wished she could replay that statement again. And again. Adrianna hadn't said *the* words and that was alright. Other women had told Charlotte they loved her on the second or third date. And look where that had gotten them.

But she was pretty crazy about Adrianna, too.

"Can I introduce you as my girlfriend?" Adrianna asked. "That's how I think of you."

"Sure," Charlotte said, trying to play it cool. "Just don't introduce me as the Woodley's best courier."

"I promise."

Of course the party wasn't just any Williamsburg party. Of course it was hosted by Hadley's parents in their tricked-out town house, replete with Calder mobiles and Jean Prouvé furniture and, Charlotte was fairly certain, a Degas sketch on the wall of the library that was most visible to the casual passerby.

It was a catered hors d'oeuvres kind of deal. With a bartender in a black shirt. And lots and lots of people. Including numerous art history faculty members and grads from their old program. Charlotte's single source of solace was that she had brought a second, fairly incendiary, open-backed, date-night dress and she had had the good sense to wear it. Adrianna had gone with jeans, a fitted shirt, flats, and some very good jewelry—which Charlotte feared might have a once-romantic backstory. She looked amazing. But she always looked amazing. Just as she always made Charlotte feel amazing.

"You know," she said under her breath as they stood in the drinks line. "Now that I know what's underneath that dress, I'm ruined. At some point tonight, I will absolutely try to get you to come with me into a bathroom. Easy access or not, do not let me do that. Remind me that we cannot do that in a house full of Yale people. Do you promise?"

"I promise." Charlotte rolled her eyes though she realized it was a necessary precaution.

Hadley was pretty. She knew it, Adrianna knew it and, more to the point, she knew that Charlotte knew it. One might be tempted to say she was pretty "if you liked that type" because she was a textbook example. Some would call her a classic beauty, by which they would mean a WASP par excellence. Dishwater blonde, cool blue eyes, petite angular features, slim shoulders, a rather "boyish" physique. High breasts. Rosy cheeks. Straight teeth, if a little on the horsey side.

She looked, Adrianna thought, a little more than the thirty-three or so she must be. And she definitely looked older than Charlotte, who, like Adrianna, had the benefit of melanin working on her behalf. Even with her au courant little black dress and bleached smile, Hadley couldn't avoid looking tired. But all of them looked tired if you got too close. From playing, from working, from both. All of them stayed up too late trying to beat each other to the next journal acceptance or fellowship. And the vast majority of them drank too much—or worse—to feel they'd temporarily escaped from stresses that nobody anywhere except them would recognize as real or justified—how hard was it to look at art all day?

When Adrianna and Charlotte arrived the guests had apparently reached critical mass. Almost as soon as they got their drinks and found themselves absorbed into a circle of interested former peers, a man who was evidently Hadley's father starting rapping his glass with a spoon to get their attention.

"Friends, I want to wish you the very happiest of New Years," he said, as his sun-burnished, Hublot-wearing wrist emerged from an artfully rolled-up sleeve to raise a flute. "And I want to thank you for joining us to celebrate our youngest, Hadley, as she prepares to leave New York for that city by the sea, Los Angeles, to accept the prestigious position of assistant professor of art history at USC. We wish you all the success you deserve, my brilliant daughter."

"Hear, hear," came the replies. "To Hadley!"

Adrianna felt her heart jump for reasons she dared not acknowledge. She looked to Charlotte beside her, who smiled back with a serenely catlike expression that felt about as sincere as Hadley's having "forgotten" to mention the purpose of the party when they met at the corner store.

"I had no idea," Adrianna leaned over to whisper in Charlotte's ear.

"She didn't tell you that this was a celebration of her new job?"

"No!" Adrianna said it about as firmly as she'd responded to anything since they met. "She was in a hurry. She just said come to a party tonight and gave me the address. No mention of USC or LA. Are you kidding me? Of course I would have told you that. We wouldn't be here if I had known."

But of course Adrianna never would have told Charlotte about any of it. She would never in a million years have told her that this obnoxiously entitled scholar had snagged a sought-after job in Charlotte's field in her own city. A job she was fairly certain Charlotte had also applied for.

Within minutes, Hadley had inserted herself in their group.

"Well, this is fun," she said. "You two. So hot. I guess Charlotte and I had more in common than I knew."

"Meaning?" said Charlotte in a voice just south of menacing.

"Meaning, I wasn't exactly *out* at Yale, either. We can't all be as butch and brave as Adrianna."

Adrianna let out a sort of muffled gasp.

"So you're saying you're queer?" said Charlotte.

"I identify as bi, yeah," said Hadley. "And, unrelatedly, really, I'll be affiliated with Feminist, Queer, and Gender Studies at USC in addition to Art History."

"Really," said Adrianna.

"But Adrianna, you're in LA, too, right? I just remembered," Hadley said.

"Really," said Charlotte.

"We'll have to get together. Where do you live?"

"Highland Park," Adrianna said as drily as possible.

"Perfect. I'm renting in Silver Lake. But I'd love to find something in Highland Park."

"It's a great neighborhood. Very diverse, though it's gentrified as fuck these days. Reminds me of what happened here."

Adrianna watched Charlotte straighten up in affirmation as she said this. But she could tell she wasn't happy. What a mess. This girl would clearly be nothing but trouble. And now, trouble in her own backyard.

"Have you been out yet, Charlotte?" Hadley asked. "It's so different from New York. The museums don't compare, of course, but that's what airplanes are for."

"I was just there, actually," Charlotte said without further elaboration.

"Nice," Hadley said. "Next time you visit we should go to bars. I never believed what they said about California girls until I saw them en masse. But it's all true. How's art history at UCLA?"

Adrianna looked more surprised with every word. "It's good," she said. "Lots of good people. Strong students. I'm very happy there."

"And yet, you're where, Charlotte? Still in New Haven, right?"

"Charlotte's at the Woodley," Adrianna said without thinking. She felt Charlotte bristle.

"Yes," Charlotte said. "The Woodley. But Adrianna's doing a sabbatical in Madrid this year so, guess what? We're even farther apart than you imagined."

Adrianna put a proprietary hand on Charlotte's deliciously bare back, hoping she would feel her support and yes, her claim. But Charlotte stepped away, grabbing another glass of champagne from the passing server.

"Well, that sucks," said Hadley. "If you need a shoulder to cry on, you know where to find me when you get back."

"That's nice of you," Adrianna said, sounding like it wasn't. "Happily, I don't have anything to cry about. After your first year on the tenure track at USC you might be doing some crying of your own, though."

"Well, maybe I'll come do it on your shoulder, then," Hadley said, brazen as could be.

Charlotte was plainly glaring at her. But being a pretty blonde surrounded by adoring fans in the comfort of her parents' ten-million-dollar town house, Hadley didn't seem to care.

Chapter Sixteen

Charlotte was drunk. Adrianna must be, too. But she wasn't showing it. At least Charlotte was feeling drunk enough that Adrianna's potential drunkenness wasn't obvious to her. If she was indeed drunk, that is. They might not have stumbled had the apartment—and the location of the light switches—been more familiar to them. It hadn't been a problem before. Tonight, however, it was the unmemorized furniture placement that literally tripped them up.

"Shit, shit, shit," hissed Charlotte as she banged her shin on the coffee table.

"Are you OK?" Adrianna asked, sounding a little annoyed, Charlotte thought.

"I'm fine," she said.

"Do you want the bathroom first or should I?"

"You go. I'll get us water," Charlotte said.

"Great," said Adrianna. Again with the curtness.

"Something wrong?" Charlotte asked her.

"No, babe. Just tired. I'll be out soon."

It was their last night and Charlotte didn't want it to be like this. She took the two glasses of water to the love seat. The toilet flushed, then the sink faucet ran. Then there was silence for what seemed like a very long time. She got more water. The hydration was starting to clear her head. They'd stopped drinking a while ago, barely speaking in the car.

Finally Adrianna came out. She was wearing her pajamas and they were buttoned up tight. Well, that couldn't be good.

She came over and sat next to Charlotte, who offered her a glass.

"Thanks," she said and downed it in one go.

"How are you doing?" she asked in a way that made Charlotte feel as if she had turned into collateral of some kind.

"Just as fine as can be. All things considered."

"She's a bitch," Adrianna said.

"Just like I told you," said Charlotte.

"Yes, you did," she said. "I'm exhausted. Can we go to bed?"

"We can," Charlotte said. And she stood up and went into the bathroom.

A few minutes later, when Charlotte got into bed, Adrianna was breathing hard, clearly asleep. It was only a double mattress, so there was no way not to touch her. But Charlotte kept to her side, not wanting to make things worse. She wasn't sure what was going on. But she intuited that Adrianna was irked with her. Which in that moment, seemed unfair. Charlotte was the one who'd had to stand there while this Williamsburg ho openly flirted with her girlfriend. Who she would now be sharing the same city with.

Adrianna suddenly reached back behind her and laid her hand on Charlotte's hip.

"Come here," she said, not very sweetly.

Charlotte scooted closer, fitting herself into the curve of Adrianna's ass, her face pressed tight against her back. When she let her arm fall over Adrianna's side, just below her breasts, Adrianna took her hand and pulled it up to her heart.

"You're the one, Charlotte," she said sleepily. "Nobody else matters."

The next day, Adrianna had to get into the city for a couple of hours before her overnight flight. Her stop at the Hispanic

Society was, officially, the whole purpose of this brief respite from a foreign residency that did not permit out-of-country absences of more than five consecutive days. She recognized this familiar feeling of malaise, the word that best captured her sadness that morning.

They'd woken up in each other's arms, as if some of their tensions had been magically worked out during the night while they slept. From the bed, the day looked gray and mood-matching. It was quite cold in the apartment despite the optimistic clanks and hisses of the radiators.

"I hate this part," Charlotte said.

"I know." Adrianna pulled her in a little tighter. "I hate it, too."

"I'm so glad you came back," Charlotte said. "It was the best New Year's I've ever had. I'll never forget it."

She seemed intent to focus on the positive, which Adrianna appreciated. For whatever reason the reality of returning to Madrid was hitting her hard. She breathed in Charlotte's citrus scent, kissing the top of her head. These are the feelings people claim they want to experience. The intense dread as the minutes tick by. The questions about what it all means for the future. The impending jealousy and misunderstandings related to separation and time zone differences and work. The pain of being apart. People actually prayed for this shit.

"I'll never forget it, either," she said. "But as good as you looked that night, I will also never forget seeing you the minute I walked into the restaurant. In your coat and scarf, making that guy with the water laugh about something. Fucking thrilling."

There was no verbal response. In a few seconds, however, Adrianna felt her chest moisten with Charlotte's warm tears. In a few more seconds, Charlotte started to sniff a little. And then, when Adrianna gave her a good squeeze, she let it all out. Adrianna was beginning to realize that Charlotte's way was to keep her emotions in check basically until she broke like a dam. And she was willing to be vulnerable that way with Adrianna, who knew Charlotte's butch side—and there was no question she had a butch side—even though she also hated that she let herself seem so fragile.

"Oh, baby," Adrianna said. "You know how much I'll miss you."

"I know," Charlotte said. "I'm just being silly again. It's your fault. You say such lovely things. How can I not cry?"

"Let's make a plan right now for when we'll see each other again," Adrianna said. The idea of where had just come to her.

"Really?"

"Of course, really. How about CAA?"

Awful CAA. The College Art Association conference was like the culmination of March madness for art historians—except that it took place at the very worst time of the year for travel, in mid-February. Publicly presenting one's research in the form of a twenty-minute "talk" was an important feather in a junior scholar's cap—and at the other end, senior people with legendary careers were typically feted there. But what gave the conference its widely acknowledged atmosphere of hopes abandoned, dreams deferred, and fortunes lost (mainly at the hotel bars) was its darker purpose, as the site of semifinal interviews for the year's tiny number of open art history positions at the nation's colleges and universities. To double down on the dismal, the conference alternated between two of the coldest American art cities, namely, New York and Chicago.

Her place well assured in the world, Adrianna hadn't submitted a proposal and wouldn't be giving a paper this year. But she could easily convince the fellowship people she needed to be there for professional reasons.

"I *am* going to CAA, actually. In your very own hometown," Charlotte said, immediately brightening. "I'm giving a paper on Brer Rabbit and Jim Crow."

"Well, that sounds like something I need to hear," Adrianna said, fully serious. "Valentine's Day in Chicago. Yes?"

"Yes," Charlotte said. "Hell yes."

With this plan in place it was a little easier to go through the motions of packing and preparing to say goodbye. But only a little. Charlotte still felt her heart very much in plain sight on the very edge of her sleeve. During the last hour she could hardly look at Adrianna.

They decided that Adrianna would leave first so that Charlotte could get herself together and maybe even take a car to Grand Central if she was feeling especially effusive. Adrianna would take the train into the city to document the paintings they'd pulled for her and get a look in person at an enameled religious pendant that may have originally been sent by Sor Epiphania to her prioress in Mexico.

Charlotte badly wanted to ask Adrianna if she could come with her; figuring she could sneak off to see the rest of the museum on her own, with no one knowing they'd arrived together. They might even be able to have lunch.

She knew Adrianna would have a hard time denying her request, which gave her the strength not to put her in that difficult position. She needed to focus on her work—which had made it possible for them to see each other in the first place—and Charlotte would respect that.

She did respect it. But as she stood at the window watching the small black form that was Adrianna roll her suitcase toward the corner and disappear into the January day, she felt a little hopeless in spite of herself.

Charlotte finished drinking her coffee, washed the cup three times, and replaced it in the cabinet, carefully orienting its handle in the direction of the others. Once she had gathered all her things, double-checking for renegade thongs or earrings between the sofa cushions, Charlotte zipped up her suitcase and gave herself a final look in the bathroom mirror. Then she closed the door behind her and headed to the train. With Adrianna safely on her way, she was feeling more herself. And now she had Valentine's Day to look forward to.

Part Two

Chapter Seventeen

April may be cruel, but it's got nothing on a New England February. Whereas April at least offers the promise of spring, February brings nothing to the party.

Except maybe more of the same. So far, the weather in this new year had been relentlessly cold, with blizzard after blizzard dumping new snow on old. Two things were keeping Charlotte going at this point. The first was seeing Adrianna in three days. The second was an unanticipated job interview at the conference.

Almost immediately after she'd returned from New York with Adrianna, an open position had been posted by the Piedmont Colleges. Of all places. It was a hybrid job divided between the art museum and art history department and it would require teaching duties as well as curation. Charlotte had become so accustomed to clicking on the webpage where everyone went to find out what jobs there were—only to find nothing for which she might remotely qualify—that she had to refresh the page a few times to believe what she was seeing.

Of course it had traces of Esther's handiwork all over it. Not that she could be sure. If, Charlotte reasoned, Esther had somehow managed to informally introduce her to the search chair, which seemed to be the role Esther's dean friend, Peter, was playing, the best thing would be for her to pretend she was none the wiser. She didn't want to put Esther in the position of telling her one way or the other. Nor did she want her to know she'd thrown her hat in.

Nor, truthfully, did she want to be back in touch with Esther so relatively soon after the awkward quasi-flirtation that had gone down at her house. It was tricky. Letting Adrianna know she was applying was as good as letting Esther know. At least this was the excuse Charlotte gave herself for not telling Adrianna she had applied for a job at a school within an hour of her house in LA.

Charlotte and James had installed themselves at what they thought of as their table in the back room at One Fifty-Five. It was a happy hour featuring seasonal mulled wine, with cloves and cinnamon and oranges. Charlotte warmed both hands on the steaming glass mug in front of her.

"So the woman you're going to see in two days knows nothing about the results of your job search?" James said, his gray eyebrows raised.

"That is correct," Charlotte said. "As of now, it's the only interview I have. I can't believe I even have one. You know how it's been. If I tell her about this and she thinks I'm pressuring her and then I don't get it… I just don't think it's worth the humiliation. You're the one who said it's probably better not to declare my intentions yet."

"I did say that. Two months ago," James said. "What if you do get the offer? Did you think you'd just spring it on her? I don't like the sound of that at all."

"Your idea is that I tell her at CAA?" Charlotte frowned. "I haven't seen her in over a month. And you know how stressed I'll be. I just want to enjoy being together."

"Can you imagine moving to California for her?"

"I can imagine moving to California for the weather," Charlotte said.

"Point taken," said James. "Now answer."

"I think so?" she said. "It's not like I've never left my comfort zone, you know. Coming up here from the South was no small thing where I'm from. Nobody in my family has gone anywhere but Tulane, Sewanee, Spelman, or, in a true show of rebelliousness, Ole Miss. For generations. I think I can move from one Yankee coast to the other for the person I love."

"Aha!" said James. "So you do call us Yankees!"

They both laughed.

"In all seriousness, old thing," he said, a wistful look flashing across his handsome, weathered features. "At your age, one often imagines these chances will always be there for the taking. I can tell you, in my case anyway, they're more like bronze pennies. Theoretically they're out there but also very, very rare, and very, very valuable, and you can easily let them slip through your fingers without knowing it."

"I haven't gotten the job yet."

"No. But if the offer is made, wouldn't it be wonderful to be able to share the good news with Adrianna rather than putting her into a pressure cooker? And if, by some unfathomable injustice, you don't get it, wouldn't it be nice if she were there for you then, as well? Most importantly, she'd know you're serious enough about a future together to include her in your thinking."

"What if it scares her off?"

"Then you'll know the two of you are in very different places. And you can decide with that in mind."

"You make it sound so easy," said Charlotte. She felt like the wind had been knocked out of her sails, as her father might have put it.

"Hard now, easy—or easier—later beats the hell out of the other way around."

Charlotte didn't want to think about any option that didn't mean being closer for longer to Adrianna. They all sounded hard to her.

Adrianna had mixed feelings about going back to Chicago. She hadn't had any desire to go to this year's conference before it occurred to her that she might use it to see Charlotte. It wasn't that she wouldn't always have a place in her heart for the Second City, with its incredible buildings and food and cultures. But Chicago was full of memories, not all of which were pleasant, of course, whether of girlfriends past or loss and family dramas of the ongoing sort. For her, a business trip "home" always required clipping the emotional strings attached.

The one mitigating factor was the location of the conference hotel—near the Loop, about ten blocks south of the Art Institute—in the heart of the business district where many Chicagoans spent very little time. She'd grown up north of that part of the city, in one half of an architecturally significant graystone—the typically larger, Midwestern equivalent of a New York brownstone—in Logan Park. Several miles from downtown, the green and rather drowsy neighborhood of Adrianna's youth was ethnically diverse even for Chicago. Most of her first friends at St. Brigid's, the Catholic elementary school she attended, were some combination of Polish, Irish, Puerto Rican, or Afro-Cuban like her mother's side of the family—but there were Asian and white kids, too. She hadn't realized how special the mix was until she hit Penn.

Lately, if she went back to Logan Square, it was usually to try a new restaurant. But Adrianna knew it would be hard to keep Charlotte off her old block. She'd want to see where Adrianna grew up, where she came from, especially given how little Adrianna had to say about those years. There was hardly anyone left to introduce her to at this point. She wouldn't mind showing Charlotte her old neighborhood; but the weather would probably make it difficult.

It was the fantastic diversity of architecture that got her thinking about all this, as the Uber car from O'Hare stopped and started on the Dan Ryan. On a slow drive into the city one couldn't ignore the distinctive cupolas and steeples of enormous Catholic churches and cathedrals—Orthodox, Polish, Irish, Italian, Mexican—each with its own style, that popped up picturesquely among the much shorter apartment houses and old department stores. The city struck her this time as happily different from staid and relatively homogenous Madrid. And so unlike New York in its spread-out vastness. About the same square miles, but if you factored in Chicagoland's housing projects and six-flats, and bungalows, and factories, and parks, it seemed to go on forever in three directions, with only the endless icy lake putting a stop to the sprawl.

She loved it.

About ten minutes out from the hotel, her phone pinged with the news that Charlotte was in the room. *Isn't that a lovely image* was Adrianna's first thought. *Here we go again* was her second.

It wasn't exactly a piece of cake, emotionally, this new life. Three encounters in as many months. Today was already the culmination of their second countdown to the next opportunity to be together. Their parting in another three nights would constitute their third almost-certain-to-be-tearful and probably angst-ridden goodbye. But the time together, and increasingly, the time apart, made it worth it. Adrianna was every bit as excited to see Charlotte as she had been in Brooklyn. Maybe even more.

Although Charlotte had practiced the lecture she would deliver half a dozen times, she thought this last window of time before Adrianna arrived would give her one more chance before she became as distracted as she knew she would be just by having Adrianna so close by. The interview was mercifully the next day at 12:45 and the talk was in a session that started at four o'clock. Tomorrow was likely to be pretty brutal. But when it was over, her official duties would be, too. And she'd have two more days away from the conference with Adrianna instead of stewing in the viper pit at the Hilton.

Adrianna never stayed at the Hilton. She preferred the more urbane, and more expensive, Blackstone across the street and she'd booked a room for them there. Even from the opposite sidewalk, where she waited for the insistent bellman to quite unnecessarily help her with her luggage, the CAA stress was palpable to Charlotte. The Hilton seemed to exude an air of fear and loathing from each of its dozens of revolving doors— it clung to the new overcoats, J.Crew skirt suits, and annoying hoodies of those to be interviewed just as it radiated from the bespoke blazers, flowing, internationally purchased shawls, and soft black turtlenecks of those who would do the grilling. Lanyards with plasticized name tags were as ubiquitous as the fat flakes of snow that had recently started to fall.

The room was on a high floor, but hadn't much of a view, which Charlotte feared would displease Adrianna. It was large by New York standards, with expanses of white marble in the bathroom and two club chairs and a desk. The bed, piled high with pillows clad in Egyptian cotton, looked obscenely comfortable. Charlotte approved of its firmness as she perched on the end of the mattress stretching out her tired feet.

Adrianna would be there soon. She would be there soon and what would Charlotte tell her she had to do the next day at 12:45? Not that Adrianna would be suspicious a claim to want to stop in on some session or other relevant to French painting or race or the nineteenth century. But she didn't, she wouldn't, keep the truth from her. That much she had promised herself.

It was early afternoon outside but in the room, with its lack of view and low lighting, it felt like the middle of the night. Charlotte tapped the bottom edges of her printed-out double-spaced ten pages on the dresser top and replaced them in the manila envelope marked "CAA talk—4pm; Roosevelt Room."

There was nothing more to do now but read it to the seven or eight people who would probably show up. Any topic on race was asking to be ignored in this crowd, and that much more so if it pertained to race in America. Still, it was good to be back in the game. Having an interview made her feel like she might be someone worth hiring in a way she hadn't for a while. And in reworking the paper from a chapter of her dissertation she'd been surprised to find that it held up, these years later, and was actually, though she'd never openly say so, much better than she'd remembered.

Adrianna hadn't read any of Charlotte's recent work—at least as far as she knew—so the idea of having her there in the audience only raised the stakes. It reminded Charlotte of their seminar, and she had tried to make the most of her desire if not to impress Adrianna, then to be her best self, doing what she did, as she put the talk together. She was ready for Adrianna to see her in another light.

Chapter Eighteen

Without explanation, Charlotte had texted Adrianna to pick up a key card at the desk when she got there. It was odd. If she were in the room as she said she was, surely she could just let Adrianna in herself. Then again, Charlotte had a thing for surprises; she was Adrianna's polar opposite in that way. Based on their previous rendezvous, she could be out shopping or picking up dinner or concocting something else to make their time together even more memorable and exciting.

The room was on the eleventh floor with a lake view; she'd thought Charlotte should see the aspect of the city that made it so special to live in. Right now its shores would be thick with colliding shards of ice that made the beach look as if it was made of rock crystal. To her, Lake Michigan in winter—when you could actually hear the ice floes whining and creaking—had always been far and away more enchanting than even the thawed-out, true blue water in summer.

Adrianna was about to knock at the door when she realized the soft music she heard was coming from inside. She smiled a secret smile and took a breath before inserting the key card.

The lights were ridiculously low. The music was Etta James's "At Last." What little glow there was in the space originated from the bathroom. Adrianna wheeled the suitcase to an empty corner. She took off her coat and patiently hung it. She took off her boots and lined them up in the closet. And then she went in.

There were candles. There was a champagne stand. And there was Charlotte. In a high tub full-to-brimming with bubbles.

Charlotte flashed her a dazzling smile, letting the music do the talking. That look. Could she ever get tired of it? It was a look that made her occasional second-guessing of Charlotte's feelings for her—or hers for Charlotte—disappear into the ether. It made everything worthwhile to be looked at like that.

She took off her blazer. She unbuttoned her blouse. She unzipped her wool trousers, Charlotte's eyes on her as she got naked.

When she stepped into the hot, hot bath they still hadn't said a word to each other—though when the playlist moved on to "Dance for You," Adrianna cracked up.

After a little maneuvering and sudsing they nested themselves so that Charlotte was leaning back against Adrianna's chest. They stayed like that for a while, eventually talking about their trips and Charlotte's impressions of Chicago, which she had visited twice before but only for other conferences.

"Should we go out to dinner? Or stay in?" Adrianna asked.

"It's so cold," Charlotte said. "Can we stay in? Room service is always so ridiculously expensive but maybe we could have something delivered."

"Room service is very good here," Adrianna said. "You're worth it, believe me. Besides, tomorrow or the next day we will definitely be eating at the chicken place around the corner, sort of a less upmarket Popeyes. Their spicy two-piece and fries will make room service a distant memory."

"I do like it spicy," Charlotte said.

"You see why they say the only things to do in the Midwest are eat, fuck, and drink beer. It's either disgustingly hot or dangerously cold."

"I'm down for all of it," Charlotte said. "Though I might want to switch up the order."

Adrianna was feeling profligate. One advantage of only see-ing your girlfriend every month was living it up when you fi-nally did. They had steak with truffle butter, they had shirred brussels sprouts, buttermilk potatoes, and very good red wine sans the fear of spilling it on the white sheets. And then they had chocolate mousse.

It wasn't the kind of meal one recovers from quickly. There was talk of watching a movie, but they hadn't yet decided on the next course.

"What's tomorrow like for you?" Adrianna asked, when she returned to bed. "I mean, besides winning hearts and minds at four o'clock?"

"I should go to something at 12:45," Charlotte said non-committally. "Did you see the Yale reunion is tomorrow at five, neatly conflicting with my session?"

"I did see that," Adrianna said. She was curious about what-ever was at 12:45. Probably some session Charlotte assumed Adrianna wouldn't care about, which was just as well given her own packed schedule.

"I'm telling myself I might go to the ten o'clock morning session depending on what we do or don't get up to tonight," she said. "Or tomorrow for that matter. And I should go to an early modern thing at 12:30 so maybe I'll just plan to see you at your show. And plan not to be in the room between about one and four so you can prep."

"That's sweet of you, baby," Charlotte said. "But if you need to come back, I can keep my shit together. I'm not usu-ally nervous before a talk."

"No," said Adrianna. "I bet you aren't. But even you might

need to get your game face on. And I want to be surprised by your outfit."

"I may have to start repeating some things after this trip," Charlotte said. "A girl can only own so many garter belts."

"Or can she. Maybe we can do a little shopping while we're here," Adrianna said. "It's so low-key compared to New York. There are some great places off the beaten path."

"You sound like you like to shop," Charlotte said. "Whereas I abhor shopping. You might never want to see me again if we go shopping for clothes together. It'd be worse than Ikea."

"Say no more," Adrianna said. This was a novel piece of intel. She wondered how Charlotte managed to look so put together if she didn't spend a decent bit of her time finding and trying on clothes.

"Am I to gather someone does your shopping for you, then?" Adrianna asked. Now that she thought about it the Dior, Marni, and YSL and the precise tailoring would suggest as much—especially on her salary. She'd bought a house with her inheritance and Charlotte had apparently bought dresses.

"You can gather what you want, honey mine. Just don't expect me to willingly trudge through the streets of Chicago with you in search of a new blouse. You're the stylish one. And I happen to like surprises."

Breakfast was delivered the next morning at 8:00 a.m., which turned out to be the worst timing ever. They'd fallen asleep early and as a result woken up early, too. And once they woke up, one thing inevitably led to another.

Adrianna was up first with her jet lag to blame. She was all the way over on her own side of the bed. But when she turned to face Charlotte, there she was, sheets down around her waist and nightshirt conveniently open with one lovely round breast pointed right at her.

Adrianna slid over and put her lips on that sweet dark nipple, giving it the lightest suck.

Charlotte's eyes closed harder before they opened and a smile began to animate her lips.

Adrianna put her hands around Charlotte's breast, holding it to her mouth.

"Mmmmmm, honey, that's nice," Charlotte said sleepily.

"Tastes nice," Adrianna said. "And I'm soooo hungry, baby."

She had started kissing Charlotte's belly, now with both hands on her breasts.

"Well, we can't have that, can we?" Charlotte said. She was more awake now. "Not on the day of my big talk."

Adrianna was beginning to realize that if she wanted to give Charlotte as good as she was getting from her, she would need to be one step ahead at times like this. Charlotte wasn't shy about leading the way when they had sex, nor was she unwilling to let Adrianna be in charge. But ceding control definitely didn't come easy to her—and she obviously got off on giving pleasure. *Thank you, Jesus.* Still, after the way they'd been together in New York, Adrianna needed Charlotte to feel how much she wanted to please her, too.

She didn't provide an answer to Charlotte other than to part her legs and spread her lips a little before she started to suck her pussy, kissing and lapping as Charlotte moaned sweetly bossy things like, "Oh Adrianna. Yes, honey, that's right, lick it right there."

And so it was that when the knock came at the door, Adrianna's head was between Charlotte's legs and Charlotte was gripping the headboard like it was the edge of a skyscraper. And she was not being the least bit quiet. And in fact, neither of them heard the knock at all. But they did hear the telephone a few minutes later when the woman at the front desk informed them that, having tried to deliver their breakfast, the hotel employee had left the cart outside their door and would they be so kind as to bring the trays into the room as other patrons were in need of the cart's services that morning.

"So they only have one cart for the whole hotel?" Charlotte complained. She sounded more skeptical than critical.

"No," said Adrianna, "they just want one of us to come into the hall so they can see who was making the noises you were making or who was making you make them."

"I thought I was pretty quiet," Charlotte said. "Given the circumstances."

"I'd say if we failed to hear someone knocking on the door and saying 'room service,' that's not exactly the case."

"I'd go get the food but I'm not sure I can stay upright," Charlotte said. "Fuck, honey. I think I saw God just now."

"I know I did," said Adrianna.

She looked both ways when she opened the door. And sure enough, at the end of the hall, she saw a young uniformed person of indeterminate gender peeking out from the supply room.

They ate their eggs and toast and turkey sausage at the table in front of the window. They'd almost finished when Adrianna reached over and pulled back the sheers.

"Lake view my ass," she said.

At half past noon, Charlotte left the Blackstone for the Hilton. It seemed silly to wear a coat and gloves and scarf merely to cross the street, but it was snowing again, and the temperature had taken a dive into the single digits overnight.

As soon as she got inside, Charlotte took everything off and put on her ID. She had looked up the interview suite on the website and knew, more or less, where she was headed, which was important in a complex that felt more like a space station than a hotel.

No matter the year or the city, there were certain predictable occurrences at the annual conference of the College Art Association, chief among which was that whoever you least wanted to see, you would see. And probably at a moment when you least wanted to see them.

Often this translated into a scenario such as, you've just bombed a semifinal when you find yourself on a twenty-floor elevator ride with a former peer who you blew off more than once back in grad school and who now has a job at the place you just interviewed. Or you've eviscerated a fellow scholar's book in a recently published review only to find yourself unwittingly flirting with their partner—or the scholar him/her/themselves—at the fishbowl of a fake Irish pub in the lobby. And so on.

What happened to Charlotte, however, simply defied the imagination.

She had just come off the elevator and was walking down the hallway toward the suite in which her Piedmont interview was scheduled when who should she see but fucking Hadley Fairweather emerging from what she could swear was the room where she was headed.

Hadley Fairweather with the toast-worthy job. At USC. What possible business did she have trying for Piedmont?

Leverage? Gluttony? Spite? It made no sense. Like a scared animal, Charlotte looked around for a way out. But it was too late. Because as soon as Hadley looked up it was as if they were locked in some sort of imminent collision course, like comets or strategically deployed missiles. Neither could reasonably turn around. The closer they got the less possible it became not to acknowledge the obvious.

Charlotte had to hand it to Hadley when she did the only classy thing one could do as the two of them strode past each other a dozen feet from the door.

"Break a leg," Hadley said, sounding strangely sincere. Charlotte simply stared at her and stopped to take the deepest breath possible at the threshold.

Charlotte had wondered whether the search chair, formerly introduced to her as Peter, would mention their previous encounter. When he didn't, she gathered that they were both meant to operate as if this was the first they knew of each other's existence. That Esther, Charlotte thought. If this was what she did for a friend, what might she do for someone she was in love with?

Aside from the initial awkwardness of a pretend first meeting, the rest of the interview went smoothly, and perhaps, Charlotte thought, even well. They seemed impressed with her curriculum vitae and had paid close attention to the shows she'd been involved in. Better still, they seemed keen to learn more about the shows she'd proposed but hadn't gotten to curate—especially the shows around race and identity. Their collections were not as comprehensive as the Woodley's but they had the advantage of working closely with the Huntington and other eminent collections from which Charlotte—or the person in the position, Peter said, correcting himself—would be free to request loans.

She felt she didn't do as well as she could have on her competence as a teacher. It had been a long time since she'd been in a classroom and she no longer had the finger-on-the-pulse feeling a good teacher gets from talking to students about their lives and work on a regular basis. When she said as much, the other members of the committee, two art historians and another dean, seemed reassured by her honesty. Nobody likes a braggart where something as challenging as imparting knowledge is concerned. She told them she hoped to publish her dissertation in the next year, which was a bit of a stretch. But again, they seemed to generally like what they were hearing.

"We're interviewing several other candidates," they told her in the final minutes, as she expected. It was often the way they signaled that you shouldn't get your hopes up, however well you thought things had gone. "But we plan to bring the three finalists to campus in about three weeks. We'll be in touch. And please let us know if you are considering another offer in the meantime."

As if, Charlotte wanted to say.

Everyone knew this was one of the two best openings this year—the other being a spot at Princeton, competition for which would be as drenched with bloodlust as a *Game of Thrones* episode. Besides, the poor person who won that job would have a better chance killing dragons—or birthing them—than getting tenure in that department.

She shook their hands.

"We appreciate your time and very much enjoyed talking with you, Dr. Hilaire," said Dean Peter. But who knew what that really meant?

Chapter Nineteen

As Charlotte rode down to the lobby, she realized how right James had been. What she most wanted to do at that moment was text Adrianna about the interview; about the questions she'd been asked—"What makes an exhibition political?" was probably the most provocative—and the answers she'd given. She wanted to text her, but in fact, she could even have sat with her face-to-face and talked about it. She could have told her about Hadley! Instead, she'd missed the chance to be honest about the interview. And now, walking back that dishonesty seemed like a bad idea. It was still early in the process. If Piedmont invited her for a campus visit she would tell Adrianna right away. But now it was still a waiting game. And with Hadley apparently in the mix, she felt far less confident about the outcome.

Back in the room, there was no sign of Adrianna, as promised. She was at her 12:30 early modernist luncheon or whatever it was. Charlotte had the space to herself for a couple of hours. She knew she should do another read-through. Or order lunch. But she felt as if she was standing on one of those lakeshores Adrianna had described to her, with a towering breaker heading her way.

It had to do with the job, she guessed. What if she didn't get it? Would Adrianna return from Spain and go back to work in LA realizing Charlotte was only a drag on her productivity? Would she weigh the pros and cons of a long-term, long-distance relationship and find it wasn't worth the energy and the time and the emotional toll?

James might have asked her if she was projecting just then. Were those really her own fears? She sat down on the edge of the bed. Charlotte had never been afraid of change and she'd never been afraid of work. That people often expected her to be overly delicate or dependent on them had only increased her resolve not to actually be those things.

She was not a fickle person. She knew what she wanted. And something deep in her psyche was telling her that Adrianna wasn't just the woman she wanted to make love to. She was, Charlotte thought, feeling strangely emboldened by the notion, the person she loved.

The Roosevelt Room, site of the session called "Race/Tropes/Tropics: Southern Visual Cultures of the 19th Century" was not large. It wasn't actually a whole room at all since the conference planners had evidently arranged to have an already modest banquet hall further divided by a sliding wall into an even smaller space, a kind of demi-room. There were two banks of chairs with an aisle between them and a podium in front of the screen. But Charlotte could barely get a sense of this when she arrived because, once she politely parted the seas flooding out of the door, she saw that it was standing room only. And not even that, as some people were sitting on the floor.

She found Dr. McNally, the organizer, a mid-career Brown grad currently employed by a liberal arts college in Maine, looking about as frazzled as any self-identified straight white male academic she'd seen. He shook her hand, pointed to her chair and confessed that he hadn't been expecting this.

At all. Charlotte would speak first, always a good thing, as it allowed for relaxed listening or comfortable dissociation for the remainder of the session in accordance with the quality of the content. He had already uploaded her presentation onto his Mac, and they both turned to the screen when her intro slide appeared there: Dr. Charlotte Hilaire, Asst. Curator of American Art, Woodley Center for American Art, New Haven, CT, etc.

The two other presenters gradually materialized and McNally assumed his position at the microphone, urging everyone, as if they were kindergarteners, to find a place and stay there.

From the long panelists' table in the front of the room, Charlotte could see almost everyone, of course. But she didn't see Adrianna. This was upsetting. And while she knew she couldn't afford to be unsettled by it, her mind began to maddeningly veer off in all sorts of irrational directions: Had Adrianna been in an accident? Had she somehow found out about Hadley? Had she run into someone from Piedmont who'd somehow connected the two of them?

Speaking in public was always something of a surreal experience for Charlotte, this time, with a bigger crowd than expected, even more than usual. Usually, her ability to project herself elsewhere even while speaking had the effect of calming her nerves. Not today. Looking out at a largely expressionless crowd of people anxious to get to dinner, she felt frighteningly off balance, as if she were speaking a language nobody in the room understood.

She was reading now without understanding herself, so who knew? It could all have been gibberish at that point. But no, this was why one practiced over and over and over, so that once you were up there you didn't have to worry if a given sentence even made sense. At the height of a mid-recitation internal freak out, you could tell yourself you knew it made sense because you'd rewritten the paper and practiced the talk until you could almost have recited it without the print-out. Or in your sleep. And happily, there was the printout, in your hand—reassuring you that you weren't losing your mind regardless of the looks you were getting from the people in the chairs.

It was only as she had nearly finished and was closing in on page ten that she realized that Grayson himself was in the room. Her boss hadn't mentioned he was going to the conference at their last staff meeting—it wasn't something he normally did, even when the conference was two hours away at the Hilton in New York. Charlotte had glimpsed him during a choreographed pause, while she advanced to the next slide from the penultimate page, gathering momentum for the conclusion about racialized caricatures in animal form. She looked up, continuing to read from memory and, she felt, successfully conveying the mastery of her material. But as she looked across the room her confident gaze was shaken by the jowly face and ubiquitous striped bowtie of the director of the Woodley, one Giles Grayson III, looking back at her cold as ice.

For the remaining two talks, concerning painted natural histories of Caribbean flowers, and illustrated versions of *Uncle Tom's Cabin*, Charlotte was deeply distracted. Completely imploding would be a more accurate description. She felt a burning compulsion to read back through the pages on the table beneath her clammy hands for any remark or characterization that might, from Grayson's point of view, reflect badly on the museum. She also wanted to look at her phone, just in case Adrianna, who she still couldn't locate, had texted her with an explanation for her absence. The other talks seemed to go on forever and she was miserable for every minute of them.

And then, finally, it was time for Q&A.

The audience was quite taken with the talk on flower imagery, which, according to the art historian from Georgia who gave it, a bespectacled woman about Charlotte's age, was rife with subliminally coded sexual—but surely *not* racial—language. They also had questions, mostly biographical, about Beecher Stowe's aesthetic education. Nobody had asked Charlotte anything about the connections she had drawn between African folk tales, the hunting of fugitive enslaved people, and portrayals of Brer Rabbit. Nobody, that is, until a hand went up in the second row.

"I always appreciate a history lesson. But mightn't we, though, merely enjoy the virtuosic illustrations in these American children's books—and they were originally just that, diversions intended for American children—as simply great American graphic art, without devolving into modern-day culture wars? In other words, can't our singularly American Brer Rabbit simply remain Brer Rabbit?"

There was a loud silence followed by the kind of shifting and mumbling signifying that whatever came next would give a decent indication of the state of the field.

"I assume this question is for me, Dr. Grayson," Charlotte said evenly, to which Grayson nodded.

"Part of what I want to convey, and I say this as a Southerner by birth and affinity, is that Brer Rabbit never was American Brer Rabbit. He was African before Uncle Remus and he was African before *Song of the South*. And he was part of the culture of enslaved storytellers before he was stolen and transformed for entertainment and profit. And to my mind, there's nothing simple about that."

"Hear, hear," said someone, to which a handful of people, mostly the handful of people of color in the room, clapped in acknowledgment.

"But you see this is exactly what I'm talking about," said an undeterred Grayson, booming his voice at the audience from his seat. "And I want to take this opportunity to state that my young colleague's views do not in any way represent the institution that employs her, which seeks, or will as long as I run it, not to mire itself in whatever the latest flavor of the month political trends might be."

"Which is itself a political stance," said a voice from the back.

Charlotte was shaking. So much so that the woman sitting next to her had placed her hand on her arm, ostensibly in a show of support.

"Are you OK?" she asked.

"I'm fine, thank you," Charlotte said, without turning her way.

"To suggest that you can divorce art from historical context is political," continued the voice. "And the historical context of this art is the proto-Jim Crow South, plantation slavery, and white supremacy."

It was Adrianna, all the way in the back. Charlotte was sure of it.

"Could the speakers identify themselves, at least by standing?" McNally interjected.

"I'll stand when he stands," Adrianna said.

"No, no," said McNally, regrouping. "I think that's fine, as it happens. Well, who says these sessions are dull? Anyway, it would be great to be able to continue this important discussion but unfortunately, we're out of time. Or fortunately, perhaps. In any case, thanks to everyone for attending. We want to be sure to have this space clear for the next session, so feel free to take your conversations into the lobby."

Or out to the alley.

Charlotte had no idea what to do. If she stayed there, she

feared Dr. Grayson might come over to find her—possibly with a pink slip in hand. And the way she felt, she couldn't be sure she wouldn't say something to him that she would truly regret. Or would she? It seemed highly unlikely she'd have a job to return to on the other side of the conference, anyway.

She wanted to find Adrianna. But she wasn't sure what that might mean for either of them. If Grayson didn't know who had challenged him, he could and would find out from his many Americanist spies. But what could he do to Adrianna? What had she just done to him was more like it, judging from the groups of white people gathering around the few black and brown faces in their midst. One of the latter was a major scholar of contemporary black art—who was disengaging herself from her admirers to walk toward her right now. Charlotte rose and came out from behind the table to greet her.

"Ardelia Quincy," she said, reaching for Charlotte's hand. "I'm at—"

"Leeds," Charlotte said, "I know. It's such an honor to meet you."

"The honor is mine," said Dr. Quincy. "That was very brave what you just did. And I want to say, I fully support you and, should you run into any nonsense with that awful man, please do not hesitate to enlist me. I'm afraid I have to catch a plane. Stay the course, Dr. Hilaire!"

And with that she swiftly disappeared back into the crowd, which had finally started to overflow into the wide hallway outside the stifling chamber. The room was emptying out fast with no Grayson in sight, thank goodness. Charlotte took a moment and returned to the table for her coat and bag, hoping to make a hasty retreat.

As soon as she got there Adrianna appeared at her side, holding Charlotte's coat out for her. After she put it on, Charlotte turned to Adrianna. But instead of hugging her, Adrianna whispered in her ear.

"You know all I want to do is kiss you right now. But not here. Let's get back to the room before someone tries to corner you. Or me."

Chapter Twenty

If there had ever been a bankable benefit to not staying in the conference hotel it was in those next few minutes. For as Adrianna led Charlotte past the hangers-on, most of whom were encouragingly supportive, giving her thumbs up as they walked by, they quickly realized others, who glared at the two of them as if they had crashed an exclusive party—which in some ways they had—were not. It was best to get as far away from the mob of worked-up art historians as possible.

"I shudder to think where we'll be in another few years," said an older man in a louder than necessary voice. "It's all identity-this and identity-that now. Forget the formal qualities of the art, even the rabbits have to have their say."

"Fucking idiot," said Adrianna, not as quietly as she should have.

"You're right," Charlotte said with a rueful smile. "Best get back to our room."

Riding up in the Blackstone elevator, Charlotte held Adrianna's arm, not permitting herself to lean on her the way she wanted to. There were other people with them. Among whom, judging from the lanyard, was yet another of their number on the lam at the better hotel.

As soon as they got into the room Adrianna gathered Charlotte into her arms and kissed her, not in her usual unquenchable way, but tenderly and gently. They stood for a while just inside the door.

"You probably thought I'd burst into tears as soon as we got in here, didn't you?" Charlotte said.

"*I* almost did, so, I guess I might have thought that. You know I'm here for you, babe. Cry all you want."

"While I was sitting in that room, after Grayson tried to take me down, I thought I might. I could feel it coming on. But then you said what you said. You were so far back, I wasn't sure who was talking at first. I didn't know if you were there at all. And then when you said the second part, about Jim Crow, I knew it was you. And then I almost cried because it was so, I don't know, noble. And it meant so much to me that someone was saying it and that someone was you."

Adrianna's eyes were shining. And when Charlotte saw a tear escape, she kissed it away.

"After you said what you said, I didn't feel like crying anymore. I just felt angry. And that's how I feel right now. Sweet Lord, Adrianna. What are we doing? How can we have spent all this time trying to advance in a field dominated by people who think we are less? That what we do doesn't matter or isn't real. I'm just so goddamned tired of it."

Adrianna took Charlotte's hands and kissed them. "I know, baby. I know."

They had a dinner reservation. The idea had been to celebrate Charlotte's success and see a little of the city—at a good restaurant in Logan Square. After all that had happened, neither of them felt like going out. Charlotte, in particular, was awash in a sea of conflicting emotions. Not only was she genuinely afraid of losing her New Haven job, she was worried about just how desperately she wanted the Piedmont position.

Had anyone from the search committee made it to her talk? She could only hope they were still interviewing their "several other candidates" because if they had seen the rela-

tive uproar—by CAA standards at least—Charlotte had initi-
ated, they'd never want to hire her. Most museums couldn't
stand being in the limelight around "political" issues. How
naïve she had been to think that a paper about the ways white
writers and artists tried to represent enslaved people could do
anything but blacklist her. As it were.

"Toni Morrison would have approved," said Adrianna.
"That's what kept going through my mind."

"Well, I'm no Toni Morrison," Charlotte replied.

They were sitting at a table in the front of the restaurant,
with two-tops on either side of them.

"It was a fucking brilliant talk," Adrianna said. "And everyone who isn't terrible thought so. I was in the cheap seats,
I heard the reactions."

"You're sweet to say it," Charlotte said. "But biased."

"Not on this," Adrianna said.

The server, a muscular guy with a sleeve of bat tattoos, kept
coming back before they were ready.

"Two minutes," Adrianna said, when he hovered in their
vicinity again. "I'm sorry this isn't more fun and celebratory,
baby. You did great. If you were up for a job this year, that
talk would have gotten it for you. Trust me."

After they ordered, Charlotte felt a surge of guilt. She knew
it would be impossible to enjoy herself even in the best of circumstances, let alone with this hanging over her.

"Can I tell you something?"

"As long as you're not breaking up with me, sure," said
Adrianna.

It was an odd response. But telling, Charlotte thought. And
it reminded her that Adrianna was more vulnerable than Charlotte sometimes expected, or even realized.

"Why would you say that?" Charlotte said. "You defended
my honor today. You were amazing and I…" She almost said

it. Adrianna had looked up at her with hopeful anticipation and she had almost goddamned said it. But not quite.

"I've been a coward, though. And I need to tell you how."

"Damn, Charlotte," Adrianna said, suddenly looking exasperated. They'd been headed in such a nice direction and Charlotte hated to ruin it. But wasn't it better now than later?

"Are you sure this is the night for whatever this is? Do you really need to tell me right now?"

Charlotte wasn't sure at all.

"Go ahead," Adrianna said. There was an almost defeated expression on her face. "I'm already losing my appetite."

"I had a job interview."

Adrianna narrowed her eyes and frowned. She still had her reading glasses on for the menu. But now she flipped them onto her head.

"When?"

"Today."

"With?"

"Piedmont. The museum."

"Well isn't that some vintage O. Henry–level shit?" Adrianna said with a smile that Charlotte couldn't read.

"As in the writer?" Charlotte answered.

"He's more your period than mine. Spent some time in New Orleans, I believe," Adrianna said.

"Please don't tease me, honey. Not tonight. I only know the Magi story, anyway."

Adrianna looked her in the eye. "Right. The one where you apply for a job in my city and I apply for a job in yours."

Charlotte's head was reeling all the way home on the car ride. And not from the Manhattans, which had only partially taken the edge off. For some reason, Adrianna was even angrier than Charlotte had thought she would be—and that was before Charlotte had any idea that Adrianna was being courted by Yale for a position that would start the coming fall. About which Adrianna, too, had said nothing.

"I don't know why you're so mad," Charlotte said. "How is what I did different? Some would say what you did was worse. You actually have an offer. I'm not even at the campus visit stage."

"It's not a firm offer," Adrianna said. "And I don't care what *some would say*. What if I'd said yes to surprise you?"

"And what if I'd said yes to surprise you?"

"It's Yale who would be asking," Adrianna said. "Snyder says there'd be nothing to deliberate over."

"And maybe I don't care what Snyder says," Charlotte said, aware that dismissing the opinions of Adrianna's alternately beloved and detested doctoral adviser was akin to firing a shot across the bow.

The driver's erratic and overly quick lane changes had a silencing effect on them for the next few miles. He turned on the music.

"When were you going to tell me?" Charlotte asked pissily, as they pulled up to the hotel.

"Happy Valentine's Day," said Adrianna.

It is particularly unpleasant to be in a fight with someone while confined to a small space. An airplane may be the worst location for true domestic disputes, but a hotel room runs a close second. When they returned to theirs it was late, but not as late as when they'd typically go to bed. It was also their last night together with no plans in the works for the next visit.

Without discussion they began their usual bedtime rituals. Adrianna got the bathroom first and came out, teeth-brushed and pajama'd. Then Charlotte went in, took a very quick shower, and emerged scented with lemon verbena.

Her reappearance was not acknowledged by Adrianna, who sat rigidly at the desk answering her email. *What the actual fuck?* Charlotte thought, as she stood outside the bathroom door watching her angrily rat-a-tat-tat away. She felt her throat closing and her eyes welling and she contemplated silently crawling under the covers in hopes that all the day's exhaustion and frustration would help her fall asleep quickly. So quickly, that she wouldn't have time to contemplate this being the end of them, the feared last night where Adrianna broke up with her.

But that wasn't really her style, Charlotte decided.

She had procured a splendid black silk negligee, stitched by the equivalent of virgin nuns in Paris, for her special night with Adrianna. And damn it, she was going to get her money's worth.

First, she turned off the overhead lights, eliciting an angry sigh from Adrianna. Then she walked herself over to the desk and summarily flipped Adrianna's Mac closed with no warning whatsoever, eliciting a "What the hell, Charlotte?"

"Really?" she replied.

Adrianna whipped her head around only to be struck more or less speechless. It was perfectly comical really, to watch her pupils dilate, rather like a cartoon character's, when she saw what Charlotte was wearing.

"Happy Valentine's Day," Charlotte said.

"You look like a bonbon," said Adrianna, staring at Charlotte from across the room after the first round. She was bringing them bottles of water from the mini fridge.

"And you know what to do with a bonbon, no?" she said in French, climbing back onto Adrianna.

"I'm not sure I do," Adrianna said. "They always look too pretty to eat."

She pulled Charlotte down to her and they kissed.

"I'm sorry," Adrianna said after. "I should have told you. And I shouldn't have gotten so mad. I just. This is so crazy-making. I guess I wanted to get it over with and start thinking about this new life back there," she paused. "With you."

Charlotte didn't respond right away, she was too busy kissing Adrianna's neck. "And I just wanted to figure out a way to start over. And do something I want to be doing. Near you."

"And you think you could do that in LA?"

"Of course, I do," Charlotte said. "But not if you're in New Haven."

"You know what would suck the most?" Adrianna said.

"If you didn't get the Yale offer."

"And you didn't get the job at Piedmont."

"So basically we'd be where we are right now," Charlotte said.

"True," said Adrianna. "But I don't think I want that."

Adrianna slid her hands beneath the negligee, leaving its intricate lace to cup Charlotte's breasts. "You don't?"

"Do you?"

"I'm the one that applied for the job in California," Charlotte said, continuing to kiss Adrianna's neck and jaw between her words. "So clearly I don't. But what do we do about it?"

"We see if you get the Piedmont job and go from there," said Adrianna.

"And if Yale makes you the offer first?"

"I guess we'll just have to cross that icy bridge when we come to it," Adrianna said. It was her turn to kiss Charlotte now.

Chapter Twenty-One

By Passover, Esther and Stephen had finalized their divorce. She was clear on her many demands and Stephen, in a perpetual state of post-coital cheater euphoria, had acquiesced to almost all of them, including the house—and even his precious new convertible, which she had added last-minute merely to show him the meaning of pain and suffering.

The divorce had slowed her progress to the judgeship, however, with the governor assuring Esther she'd be up for the next appointment as soon as things in her "personal life" smoothed out. As a specialist in employment law, Title IX in particular, she assured the governor that she'd hold him to his promise. In the meantime, Esther had found herself looking for a case to keep her focused on the law and distracted from her recent transition into single motherhood. And she seemed to have found just the plaintiff.

The woman had emailed her several weeks back, with some very general information about a series of work-related interactions with which she was uncomfortable. She'd gotten Esther's name from a friend of her mother's who'd been at Harvard with Esther, but who Esther could barely remember.

At any rate, Esther was intrigued by the chronology of the events and the possibility of getting someone powerful punished for doing something terrible—her favorite Judith and Holofernes scenario. She didn't need the billables. It was the process and the law that she needed and missed. She could tell the woman was intelligent and, being a soon-to-be transplanted New Yorker, as Esther had more or less once been, won points with her potential attorney, as well.

She officially retained Esther as counsel. They had written back and forth and had a couple of five-hundred-dollar telephone conversations. But they hadn't met in person because the woman was still in Manhattan doing some kind of fellowship at MoMA or the Met, she couldn't remember which.

But this weekend, the woman had sent her a short but sweet email. She'd be in LA for the equivalent of spring break, scoping out the neighborhood where she'd rented an apartment and generally getting the feel of the place. Feeling munificent, and a bit bored, Esther had offered to meet with her new client off the clock, as a substitute for the initial in-person consultation they'd never had.

It was a Saturday and Fisher was at a friend's house with some classmates directing a one-act play he had written for history class. This kid, Esther thought affectionately, not knowing how she could have gotten through the past couple of months without his Owen Meany–like calm and precocious wisdom. She was in her study, reading a blog about sexual harassment at her alma mater, when a car pulled up across the street. An Uber or a Lyft, as predicted; nobody from New York wants to try LA driving anytime soon.

A woman got out, slammed the door, and immediately took out her phone. She walked a few steps then stopped in the middle of the street, typing. Almost immediately a car peeled around the corner and practically mowed her down. Not looking particularly concerned, she ran across to the curb. But she also went right back to her phone—with the vigilance of an investment banker closing a deal. Or a bulldog with a rope toy. Just these few actions could denote anything from admirable focus to unplumbable narcissism, Esther reflected, hoping for the former.

The woman on the phone was tall, slender, and blonde—pretty much what Esther expected, given her voice and manner of speaking. She wore black from head to toe, another East Coast endearment, and she was finally heading Esther's way.

The doorbell echoed through the house like a grandiose peal at the end of a royal wedding, something Stephen had always liked but she found ridiculous. Esther made a quick note on her to-do list: "change chime," before answering the door.

A few minutes later the two of them were midway through a lively debate about the pros and cons of the electoral college and Esther wasn't even sure how they had gotten there. She'd been right about the woman's intelligence—she was fast on her feet and seemed to have an almost encyclopedic knowledge of voting systems. With this as the improbable icebreaker, she'd now turned to the subject at hand.

"So, I do think there's a case," Esther said. "The guy on the search committee walks you to the hotel lobby and in effect, suggests that he come back later for a quid pro quo of job offer in exchange for sex. We can't use the recording, but if he knows it exists that's helpful. Less helpful is the fact that you were, in fact, offered the job. Which makes it hard to argue retaliation. It's sexual harassment, of course. And definitely meets the standard of Title IX."

"So do you think I should sue?" the woman asked. "Or should I just try to get out? I can't imagine sitting in meetings with this ass. And he's tenured, so what are the chances they'll fire him? Even if this is proof. I'm not privy to the things you know. But from what I can tell these cases rarely result in firing the guy who commits the crime."

Esther paused. "That's a fair assessment, disgustingly enough."

"But then there's the question of whether another department will hire me, especially if this went public," she said, looking suddenly despondent.

Esther had been watching the woman closely in order to determine when a moment like this might occur, for she knew it almost certainly would. A complaint, a lawsuit, even a newspaper story about one's victimhood might seem a reasonable enough and even necessary course of action until the hypothetical rubber meets the concretely legal road. At that point, the prospect of subpoenas and witnesses and reporters looking into one's life gets very real, very fast. And the truth, that you, the victim, did nothing to deserve what happened but will continue to suffer from it nonetheless, burrows deep inside your head in a way it previously hadn't.

Esther could see all of this playing out across the woman's face almost as if her thoughts were being projected like subtitles on a screen. First, the animated light that had accompanied her sallies with Esther about Acts of Parliament versus changes to the Constitution went out of her eyes. In place of the light there was a gleam, but it was the shine that comes from approaching tears.

And just like that the waterworks were unleashed.

A discrimination client's embarrassment was almost the worst part for Esther—the fact that this young, confident, accomplished woman was now unable to look Esther in the eye because she'd been humiliated by an established, seemingly untouchable senior colleague was pretty hard to take. Esther had almost forgotten what it felt like to be near the victims.

She stood up from her chair and went over to sit by the woman, but not too close. This situation was also tough—what you didn't want to do was unintentionally sexually harass or appear to sexually harass a client in a sexual harassment case. Even when what you also wanted to do was give the person a hug and tell them it was going to be, somehow, alright.

Esther offered her a box of Kleenex and sat back down in her chair on the other side of the room.

Although she had not yet told Adrianna about her new client, Esther thought today's conversation might provide the occasion. They had been talking to each other fairly frequently since the divorce proceedings and Adrianna's possible move to Yale had become worthy topics for discussion.

Esther had never seen her friend so head over heels and it filled her with optimism. Knowing Charlotte at least a little also made it easier to understand Adrianna's worries about making a life with someone at a different stage of their, let's just say, journey.

"Any news on Piedmont?" Esther asked.

"She'd probably rather tell you herself," Adrianna said, sounding buoyant. "But since you asked. Yes! She just got a campus visit. Surprise, surprise."

"Fantastic!" Esther said. "So, wow. She'll have to come back out here again."

"Yeah, next week, in fact," Adrianna said. "I can't believe I won't be there for the second time. It's a good thing she has you to drink with in the off hours, if she has any. I'm just sorry she's not really seeing the city. No offense, but Pasadena is not exactly representative."

"None taken. Chalk up my current zip code to another spineless concession to Stephen's Westchester pretentions. Alas, it may not always be so. But surely they'll have someone drive her around a little—at least show her the Norton Simon and maybe LACMA," Esther said.

"Listen to you," Adrianna laughed. "Who knew you were so in the know?"

"Which brings us to the next order of business."

"Proceed," said Adrianna.

"Against common sense and all that I know to be right, I think I might be seeing someone. Or starting to see someone."

"Ah, the intermezzo," said Adrianna. "Not to be confused with the rebound, of course."

"How could you possibly arrive at such a conclusion? Given how I framed it," Esther laughed self-deprecatingly. "But Addie. I'm being very, very serious when I say that I need you to be gentle with me on this. I'm not even sure I can tell you."

Adrianna couldn't recall being cautioned by Esther before in such a manner, which gave her a sense of how exposed she must be feeling. She wondered if it could possibly have to do with the single dad of one of Fisher's friends, whose name had come up more than once over the years. Whatever it takes in the short-term, Adrianna thought, as long as the guy was decent at a minimum. Or hot. Esther deserved something good.

"Tell me," Adrianna said. "Whatever it is, I won't judge. Judge."

"Too soon," Esther said. "OK. No more stalling. I'll give it to you straight. Well, not exactly. Shit, I knew it must be hard to do this with people but I'd never really thought about why. It's like you're saying: the person you know, that's not exactly me. I'm actually this other person."

"Go on," Adrianna said. "Who is this other person seeing?"

"A client?" said Esther sheepishly.

"OK. And who exactly is this client?"

"I can't name names, naturally. Particularly given the particulars. But let's just say she's an academic who will be moving here next year."

"OK," said Adrianna. She was trying not to let the enormous smile on her face alter the sound of her voice. "So she's a she. That seems worth taking a moment for."

"Oh, shut up," Esther said. "Are you shocked?"

"Do you want me to be?"

"Good question. I'm not sure. I think I'm shocked."

"Have you kissed?"

"Oh my God, really? Is that how we're doing this?"

"Oh, absolutely. Give me the long version. And don't be gentle."

"Fuck off."

"Start at the beginning."

Almost an hour later, Esther had caught Adrianna up to her second date with the woman she would refer to only as Dr. X. The date had involved a visit to the nearby Norton Simon Museum—hence the sudden familiarity with that collection—culminating in a reportedly epic make-out session on one of Esther's many couches.

"Well, you can't still represent her, can you?" Adrianna asked.

"I shouldn't," Esther said. "But then again, I want her to win. And I am the best."

"Has she been with women before?"

"Why?"

"I don't know. I'm sure you think I'm being a downer, but I just want the best for my girl. My other girl."

"I know you do," said Esther, with proper solemnity. "She has, actually. But she's also younger. Took a page from your playbook, far as that goes. Look, it's not like we're engaged. I have no idea where this is going. It just feels right. I think we connected the first time we talked on the phone. It sounds idiotic. But as soon as I heard her voice I knew it was just a matter of time."

Chapter Twenty-Two

Charlotte was ecstatic about her campus visit, of course. But not as ecstatic as she would have been if she'd known for sure what Adrianna was planning to do about Yale. They had agreed not to talk about how a decision might be made until things with Piedmont were completely resolved. So far, the Yale people had been remarkably understanding of Adrianna's request for more time to consider the potential offer while she completed her research in Madrid.

But Charlotte knew Adrianna. And she knew the lure of a job in one of the world's top departments—at an Ivy whose resources far outpaced those of even a flagship UC—would be hard to turn down. They say you can't go home again, yet Charlotte feared Adrianna just might want to try.

It was weird to be again making a version of the same drive from LAX to Pasadena that she'd made at Christmas. The seasons had changed but the weather was the same. Sunny and mild with no good reason to be uptight or stressed out. This was California.

Of course, like New York, there was the other, more desperate, side of a city of dreamers where so many people came to get discovered or make their big break. Charlotte was feeling a bit of that energy. Curating and teaching somewhere where the students and the institution valued the things she valued was almost past imagining. Now that she'd had some time away from the Woodley, she could see how much she had allowed her own interests, her own commitments, to be compromised. The closer she got to Piedmont, the more she dared to think this might be her time. It was a year for admitting what she wanted, Charlotte let herself inwardly declare. And a year for making it so.

A campus visit is a protracted species of the job interview unique to higher education. In general, a school will winnow down its shortlist to three or four finalists, often from hundreds of initial applicants. The three are invited to the place where they could, if all goes well (or not so well, depending on one's perspective), spend the next two to three decades of their lives. If a candidate search is handled properly, the campus visit is a kind of reciprocal vetting. An elongated professional hookup, if you will. If at some point in seventy-two hours the two parties don't achieve the mysterious but universally sought-after goal called "fit" the visit is a dud. There will be no third date let alone a commitment ceremony.

From the candidate's side, it's like entering a veritable minefield. Opportunities to fuck up a good thing await with every move made and every breath taken. At the heart of the campus visit is the "job talk," an extended version of the kind of research presentation that Charlotte had given at the conference. Beyond this demonstration not only of one's knowledge but one's ability to convey it, is a relentless onslaught of lunches and coffees and student meetings and facilities tours and drives around prospective neighborhoods and meetings with administrators and finally, the intimidating social equivalent of the job talk that is the posh restaurant dinner with department faculty. It seems like fun after a long day's work, until you realize the day isn't nearly over yet.

To say it's a grueling three days that is knowingly intended, especially at some institutions, as a kind of hazing, is an understatement. For Charlotte, however, it was a walk in the park.

What's so hard about being wined and dined by people who want to hear you go on about art?

It was no comparison to sitting in an unheated room or making small talk with the guys in shipping and receiving for hours on end. In sum, Charlotte enjoyed every minute of it.

"If the library's open, I'd love to see the stacks," she said to Dr. Emilie Panciatichi, the department chair and a genial and shockingly down-to-earth-seeming medievalist who'd been there for going on thirty years and was currently leading Charlotte around.

"You don't tire easily, Dr. Hilaire, do you?" she said. "It's that building right over there. I'll leave you to it. The driver will take you back to your hotel in about half an hour and then we'll see you at dinner! Oh, and while I have the chance, I just want to say how much I enjoyed, and learned from, your excellent talk."

"Thank you," Charlotte said. "I'm looking forward to dinner tonight. It's been wonderful being here." And off she went, making every attempt to appear the proactive and energetic scholar she felt she could be in this setting.

The stacks were basically what you'd expect. Shelves of books—but lots of them—surrounded by tables, and cubbies, and carrels, and cubicles infested with all manner of students at 4:30 in the afternoon, no less. This was a good sign.

But what she'd really wanted to find in the library was a few private minutes to herself to read her messages.

It was 1:30 in the morning in Madrid. Negotiating the time difference between there and California was a new kind of terrible and Charlotte thanked God that they weren't forced to contend with it for more than a few days at a time. She was relieved to see that Adrianna had written to her before she went to sleep with a brown fingers-crossed emoji and well wishes and later, with congratulations for a talk that she was certain had gone well.

They would be indescribably lucky to have you. Like me

Charlotte got a little emotional reading Adrianna's words. Time would tell. But with the talk and the interviews over, all that remained of the campus visit was the dinner. And while she wasn't unconcerned about that, it was largely beyond her control whether they liked her or not in whatever venue they'd chosen. All she could do, all she *would* do, was be herself.

The next day at Piedmont was completely open and unscheduled. The best return flight she could find had been an overnight departing around 9:30. The Piedmont people seemed delighted to know that Charlotte planned to use the day to see LACMA and maybe the contemporary collection at the Broad.

Adrianna had assumed she'd want to see Esther, who Adrianna had informed about the job situation. Charlotte was of two minds on that for the same reasons she hadn't wanted to contact Esther when she first saw the job advertised; the less she knew the better. And with this recent news about the enigmatic new love interest, she was doubly unsure how to feel. One thing was certain, she hadn't been wrong about Esther not exactly being the straightest woman in the world.

There seemed no way to get around seeing her in the end. Esther had very kindly volunteered to drive in from Pasadena to meet Charlotte at a bar in Silver Lake, so that Charlotte could experience the city for a couple of hours.

She was a little self-conscious at the beginning, as Charlotte suspected she might be. But then again, she was also Esther.

"Of course I'm mortified about our last conversation," she

said, after a half a glass of wine. "I really think I was out of my head. Though I definitely didn't realize it at the time. I hope you'll forgive me someday. Divorce does things to a person. I'll be a much better lawyer after this."

"There's nothing to forgive," Charlotte said. "And it all makes sense now that you've pledged our sorority. You have pledged our sorority, haven't you?"

Esther went beet red.

"I have yet to declare my allegiances," she said. "But I do feel like certain parts of my life are becoming clearer in ways that finally make sense to me."

"Funny how that works," Charlotte said. "I came out at the tail end of college. But up until then I'd never so much as dated a guy. No proms, no homecoming, nothing. And that whole time the possibility that I was a lesbian didn't enter my mind in a way I was willing to admit. And I'd kissed girls plenty by then. Plenty. It just wasn't an option."

Esther nodded. "I suddenly feel as if I've been checking out women my whole life. Only I was calling it something else. Competitiveness. Or jealousy. Or keeping an eye on people my husband seemed to be overly attentive to. In retrospect it's nuts. Like an *L Word* episode or something."

That she had watched said program might tell a person a thing or two, Charlotte thought.

"And you like this mystery woman? And she knows what a catch you are?"

"I don't know about that," Esther said. "But I like that she's very much her own person. And I like that she's thoughtful. I mean, it's folly to compare. I know that. But the other night something happened and she asked me if I was thinking about Fisher—which I absolutely was—and before that she asked if I was cold, which I also was. I realize it's probably a testament to how bad I'd let my marriage get, but I can't remember the last time Stephen cared if I was cold. Or hungry or bored or burning up with fever, let alone desire. I don't think he ever operated with me at that very basic level of just wondering how I was doing. There's something about the way she treats me that feels totally new. It's almost like I've never been taken care of. Not by someone I'm sleeping with."

"Good. You deserve to be taken care of," Charlotte said. "Plus, from what I hear, she's hotter than Satan's housecat."

Esther rolled her eyes.

"Am I right?"

"Well, you're not wrong," Esther said.

A few hours later when Charlotte finally had a free minute to talk to Adrianna, it was again too late. Or too early. When she boarded the plane, ready to pass out for the duration of the flight—on Piedmont's dime in coach—she knew Adrianna would still be fast asleep. She couldn't wait to get back to New Haven and talk to her girlfriend in the privacy of her own home.

It was instructive to be on the same overnight flight from California to Connecticut that either or both of them would theoretically be taking should their long-distance relationship continue that way once Adrianna returned to Los Angeles. At the beginning of the flight, her forehead jammed into the window and her neck propped up almost comfortably by her trusty neck ring, Charlotte could imagine doing it fairly regularly. After seven hours next to a snoring businessman from La Jolla, she took a rather different view.

It was the essence of draining. Travel always was. Even if you recover physically, something happens to your mind when you go from one place to another, and that takes time to process. As it was, she would be home by midnight and expected at work by 9:00 a.m. Not a lot of built-in recovery time there.

By some marvel, however, better-than-predicted headwinds had blown her east ahead of schedule and Charlotte found herself in her own bed just after 11:30, still too early for Adrianna. But not by much. She decided to stick it out until they could talk, texting Adrianna to see if she would call basically as soon as she was conscious that morning.

It was still pitch dark at 6:30 a.m. but Adrianna didn't care. She'd set her alarm in hopes of catching Charlotte as soon as she got in. They hadn't spoken in days and she was dying to hear how things had gone in Piedmont. And she wanted to hear Charlotte's voice tell the stories not only because they would be better that way but because she would know, from the way she emphasized a word or laughed after a description, how she felt about the visit and whether it was a place she would want to be.

Charlotte answered immediately.

"Hey there," she said, her voice sweetly drawling as it did when she was tired.

"Hi, baby, how are you?"

"Good," she said. "Better now. I missed your voice something fierce."

"Me, too," Adrianna said, relieved to think she'd felt that way, too.

"I'm sure you're so tired, but I wanted to say good-night and see if you had any highlights."

"Oh, I have highlights," Charlotte said. "They have a budget almost twice the size of the Woodley's. And they acted like they all work on race or decolonizing or disability or gender. I know it can't be the actual promised land, but it felt like another universe. They were really nice."

"I'm so glad it went well," Adrianna said, trying to keep casual and upbeat. "Did they give you an idea on the timeline?"

"I'm pretty sure I was the last candidate," Charlotte said. "Sometime next week is what they said. Fuck. Now I'm really scared."

"Do you feel like they saw who you are and what you can do?"

Adrianna could hear Charlotte considering. "I think so? I hope so. Not much else I could have done. So in that sense, whichever way it goes, I'm at peace with it."

"You are not," Adrianna said, laughing.

"Damn straight," Charlotte said. "I want that fucking job."

Chapter Twenty-Three

Adrianna was onto something. She'd been transcribing the diary at a furious pace and she'd had an epiphany about Sor Epiphania. It had to do with the last Aha! moment, when she'd found a passage mentioning a painting sent to "her" love at the convent in Valladolid. Adrianna had assumed, less from a grammatical than a decorum standpoint, that Sor Epiphania was referring to the recipient as someone she, Sor Epiphania, loved. But a more recently discovered passage had thrown this theory into question. It was an entry dated almost a month after the one about the squirrel painting. And it read: "In gratitude for the small painting on copper [squirrel], an escudo, her own, for S Mg.t from her love." Reading this entry alongside the previous one, Adrianna was struck by the only logical conclusion, namely, that the painting—and probably all the other gifts—had been sent by way of the nun from their true source, her Majesty—Su Majestad—the Queen.

This was the kind of discovery one was both glad and not so glad to have made. She could easily predict the kinds of resistance she'd encounter for the suggestion that the Austrian Queen of Spain had a transatlantic female lover during the first few years of her reign. Even the more moderate types would be the first to remind her that "her love" could mean many things in previous centuries. Surely the queen's so-called love was merely a subaltern, a nun no less, in whom she had taken a matriarchal or imperial interest. At the moment, the existence of an *escudo*, a kind of painted shield the nuns wore, typically decorated with a saint or a biblical scene, was the thing principally firing Adrianna's imagination. For if this precious object existed in a collection somewhere, it would be among the first of its genre to make the trip from Mexico to Spain.

There was so much more to do. Yale or no Yale, Adrianna would need more time in Madrid. And how would her own love react to that?

Charlotte was afraid. There was no other word for it. Since the fateful conference Q&A in Chicago, she'd been waiting for the shoe to drop. Make that the guillotine. Requesting emergency time off hadn't helped—though James had made a strong case for Charlotte deserving special treatment in consideration of being stranded in Los Angeles over Christmas. And then the previous Friday, a memo had come down from Grayson ostensibly concerning "important changes" in the museum's oversight at the board level. In fact, however, buried in the third paragraph of that missive emailed at 4:59 was the line: "likely restructuring measures, including non-renewal of contracts, will be announced at the next staff meeting."

That staff meeting was today and it would take place, as always, at 11:00 a.m. sharp.

Charlotte and James had reviewed the possibilities at length in a long call over the weekend. Titles held by a single staff member seemed safer than those with multiple contenders. James was the only controller; Charlotte was the only assistant curator of American art, so his theory was that they'd be safer than the flock of development assistants or junior registrars. When Charlotte had described to him the events surrounding her conference paper, he seemed disconcertingly concerned. But if he had heard anything damning about her future at the museum, James wasn't telling.

The meetings always took place in the conference room, a space too small to hold the museum's entire sizable staff. As such it provided a useful metaphor for the needed downsizing to come. Whoever got there first was able to score an actual seat at the table—as long as the VP-level latecomers were saved a place—but everyone else was forced to stand around the edges of the room, leaning uncomfortably against the sharp, projecting paneling. Patriarch that he was, Grayson would normally occupy the head of the table, with the associate director—Abigail—at his right and the head of operations, a nice enough guy named Michaels, at his left.

The gathering was uncharacteristically quiet, some might say somber, when Grayson arrived, laughing his jocular laugh with Abigail, over something that no doubt only they would find humorous.

He sat down at the table and placed both of his palms flat on its polished mahogany surface.

"I'll cut right to the chase," he said. "Times are tough for all regional museums and we are not exempt. Exhibitions are the way we educate the public and offering the right kinds of exhibitions is how we maintain our stature as one of the leading institutions of our kind. But to do what we need to do, we have to be lean and smart and on the same philosophical and aesthetic page."

The very bad feeling Charlotte was having started to worsen when she looked directly at Abigail, who cravenly turned away, refusing to meet her inquisitive gaze. Deciphering another few lines of the writing that was now on the wall was James, who, standing behind Charlotte, put his hand on her shoulder in a comforting gesture that was anything but. Grayson bellowed on.

"I like to think I've captained this ship effectively for twenty years based on a clear mission and one which I have every intention of shoring up in the years to come. All of which is to say, regrettably, the following contracts will not be renewed after the fiscal year ending June 30th. Ackerman, Ball, Gregorio, Hilaire, and Leverton. We thank all of you for your hard work and your time with the Woodley and we wish you the very best in the future. Please see HR with any questions you might have."

The Woodley Five, as they designated themselves, were in need of a drink. Each of them had a favorite local option, but they agreed for the purpose at hand on a quirky little bar called the Anchor Spa a few blocks from their soon-to-be former employer. Most of their colleagues, except those who had decided to fire them, joined the group there to buy the first few rounds. Now, countless Manhattans later, it was down to just Hilaire and Leverton.

"You saw this coming, but to be blunt, I had no fucking idea," said James.

"They had reason, at least Grayson did, with me. But how will they ever replace you? Why would they try?"

"Oh, they won't have to," he answered.

"You mean you're irreplaceable or you mean they'll have to drag you out cackling and chained to your safe?"

"I mean, I have more than enough to nail that pretentious, bigoted, social-climbing asshole to the wall. When I get through with him, he'll wish he'd never heard the word *cocksucker*. Or *pansy*. And definitely *mulatress*."

"*Mulatress?*" Charlotte said.

"I'm afraid so," James replied, shaking the remaining cubes of ice in his all but empty glass.

In some ways, Charlotte was relieved to know that James

had a battle plan. That he not only had a strategy but ammunition. But she also knew that these things were never as clear-cut as presenting evidence of wrongdoing and having that wrongdoing understood as such and punished. Presenting the kinds of evidence James suggested he somehow possessed might even require lawyers.

If only Charlotte knew of an ass-kicking employment lawyer who specialized in discrimination.

"You have to call Esther," Adrianna said when they spoke later that night. "If James has proof that Grayson referred to the two of you with slurs like that, he needs to find out how to handle it. If you won't call her, I will."

"No," Charlotte said firmly. "If we're going to involve her in this, I'm the one who will call her. And I get to decide that. What if I want to wait and see on Piedmont and, if I get it, just let this mess go? What if I don't want the strain and the pain of some kind of legal case? It's my decision."

Adrianna was silent for a long moment.

"You're right, baby. Of course you're right," she said in a voice tight with anger. "It just makes me so fucking angry that that horrible man could get away with doing something like this to the woman I love."

This time Charlotte was the silent one. *The woman I love.* Had Adrianna said the real L-word? To hear that phrase, even indirectly, made her weak. Sure enough, she felt the sudden burn in her throat that was always there just before she broke into tears.

"Did you—?" she started.

"Did I just tell you I'm in love with you?" Adrianna said. "Is that what you were going to ask me? Because I did. And I am. Of course I am, Charlotte. You must know that."

"Oh, honey, me too," Charlotte said. And then she really did start to cry.

★ ★ ★

Rare as it seems, justice does prevail sometimes. And in the case of James Leverton v. Giles Grayson III there wasn't much of a fight. The reason was quite simple. In his twenty-three years at the Woodley Museum, the past two decades of which were under Grayson's reactionary rule, James Leverton had kept a record of absolutely everything.

The man who had hired a younger James, fresh out of Wharton with his MBA, was also his first true and committed lover. They had enjoyed a very happy two years together until a jealous associate curator, passed over for the director's job, hired a photographer to track his supervisor's extracurricular movements. Once he accumulated a sufficient number of incriminating images—James and his lover dancing shirtless on Fire Island or exchanging a quick kiss in the alley behind the museum—the director was shamed into resigning. It was a conservative institution, and one that would never have knowingly hired an "open" homosexual as its leader at that time.

But as terrible as that chapter of James's life had been, things only got worse. His lover had managed to save James's job—he was never sure under what agreement. But when he couldn't find another position for months, and finally years, the museum's former director sunk into depression and drugs and ultimately took his own life.

To say James had never recovered from the tragedy was not accurate. He had worked very hard over the years to do just that. But he had never forgotten Roger and he had vowed, when Roger was laid to rest, to someday do to Grayson what he had done to them.

From a practical standpoint this meant that James had affidavits and email messages and photographs of his own showing Grayson to be the lying, racist, queer-hating excuse for a human being that he was. And knowing that it was finally the time and the place to bring that evidence to bear, James had done what any good watcher of thrillers would do: he'd sent one copy of what he liked to call his "bulging dossier" to a reliable journalist and the other to the chair of the museum's board of trustees. Then, he'd invoked the whistleblower statute that even their backward organization had been forced to include in its handbook.

Within the hour of receipt, the board chair's "representative" had called James and within the week a settlement had been negotiated, a proviso of which was that James wouldn't lose his job. And neither would Charlotte. And neither would the other members of the Woodley Five, all of whom were also, as it happened, either people of color and/or gay.

"It's almost disappointing not to get our day in court," James said.

They were sitting at the bar at One Fifty-Five very near the spot where Charlotte had first seen Adrianna making out with the ardent grad student.

"Almost," said Charlotte. "How does it feel to be a hero to the people, Norma Rae?"

"Butch, please. I like to think I'm more of an Erin Brockovich," James said.

"You mean more of a Julia Roberts."

"Like I said," he agreed.

Chapter Twenty-Four

Adrianna was in the National Library's basement cafeteria scoping out a place to eat. She wasn't, apparently, the only visiting scholar who liked to go there the last thirty minutes or so before the place closed, knowing it would be far less cacophonous than even an hour earlier when most of the employees took their lunch hours.

Tables, even the little ones, were at a premium. On her second pass, a man in an expensive-looking camel blazer looked up from his newspaper. "Feel free to join me if you want, I'll be gone as soon as I finish this story."

He was reading the *New York Times*.

"Anything happening over there?" she asked him, hoping he'd take it as a joke.

"Just the usual bullshit," he said. The vagueness of his response left her no real choice but to inquire further, against her better judgment.

"A black student was attacked by campus security at my institution in New York for, you know, walking through campus."

This was a surprise coming from a white guy, probably an academic, who looked like a lost Kennedy. "Was he hurt?"

"It says the altercation didn't get beyond them pinning him to a wall. But it was like him versus five rent-a-cops. Place is fucking fascist. Pardon my profanity."

"In the city?" Adrianna asked.

"Regrettably. Of course, I'm lucky to be there. They just suck in a lot of ways. Your place any better?"

"The UC? Yeah, I guess in that way for sure. Definitely not perfect, though."

"I'll take your average temperatures over perfection any day," he said. He folded up the paper and grabbed his tray. "It's all yours. Happy hunting."

Adrianna nodded a goodbye and moved her plate into the space left by the New York guy's three-course lunch tray. She took out her phone to check what would be her morning emails from the States.

And there it was. An official-looking communication from Yale University, with the subject: Offer of Employment. This was unexpected. When she'd last talked to the department chair she'd suggested that they would have another "exploratory" conversation before the real offer came her way. It was too soon, Adrianna found herself thinking.

She clicked on the message, which consisted of a dense chunk of borderline adulatory prose explaining how, as discussed, Adrianna's research and publications had distinguished her as a scholar and how much the department would benefit from her return. She felt a little guilty. She's always been proud to be a Yale PhD. There was something about being able to leave it at "Yale" when people asked where you were a grad student or where you got your doctorate. No need for explanation or qualification. This was what you got from an Ivy. If she was to go back she'd be a tenure-track faculty member at Yale. Not that there was anything to apologize about where UCLA was concerned. But as a public institution the school would never pay her as well or facilitate her connections in the same way.

Then again, at Yale there was always the question of whether a new professor, especially a woman, would be granted tenure. They didn't have the best track record. But surely they had no business asking her if they didn't think she was likely to succeed. And if, God forbid, she didn't get tenure, she'd be in excellent company, and ideally find a good position somewhere quite happy to take New Haven's academic hand-me-downs.

Yale, she kept saying to herself. On the faculty at Yale.

The chair went so far as to put a time clock on the offer in question. Adrianna would have until the end of the following week, a mere eight days, to verbally commit. The sudden urgency brought all sorts of situations to mind, not least of which was the scandal at the nearby Woodley Art Museum.

Although Grayson's racist and sexist and homophobic record had not been made public, the art history department was almost certainly in the loop on his words and deeds. It would be in their best interest to brown-up a little in view of the cautionary tale down the avenue. She'd always had very mixed feelings about becoming a "diversity hire." But no one had said this was the reason for the department's interest. At least not yet.

Almost reluctantly, Adrianna clicked on the contract. She knew its most exciting content would likely be the salary offered, so she let her eyes move there first. Good. Neither pandering nor insulting. Fair but on the generous side for a woman of her age and experience but who was also relatively young in the field. She skimmed the language about relocation, not wanting to think about that, until her eyes hit a line near the middle of the page. The course load would amount to almost a third fewer classes than her current one. So much less teaching. She loved teaching. But as she was learning on sabbatical, she also loved not-teaching. Think what she might be able to accomplish with both time and resources. Her old department had done everything in their power, or at least made it seem that way, to make her an offer she simply couldn't refuse.

Charlotte was on the edge of her emotional seat. No news from Piedmont yet. And no amount of furious cycling between her email and the wiki was helping. They had said it would be a week or so. And that was last Thursday. And today was Friday. And if they were going to honor their promise and also get the offer out before the end of the week, today would be the day.

The wiki was "crickets" as its habitués termed it on a day with no activity.

If there was an actual recipient of the job offer, that immensely fortunate soul was not yet willing to put the other two contenders out of their misery by posting "offer received," the life-changing words that only a small minority of recent or not-so-recent PhDs would ever be able to type on those tear-stained digital pages.

Charlotte wondered what Hadley would do. There was no way to be sure if she was one of the three finalists, but Charlotte suspected it. What art history department wouldn't want a gregarious bisexual blonde complete with an attitude, a political dynasty, and the wardrobe to match? More importantly, she was smart and justifiably ambitious, as even Charlotte had to concede.

To her credit, Charlotte was herself a zealous wiki-updater. She recalled from experience what a difference it made to know, going into a weekend, that the job on which you'd set every fiber of your heart had been offered to someone else. Updating the wiki was a merciful gesture; a ripping off of the Band-Aid. A gift.

Adrianna was eager to talk.

Charlotte had come straight home, poured a glass of wine,

and settled on the sofa with her computer poised on the big stack of books on her coffee table.

Adrianna picked up immediately. She had her hair pulled back and her pajamas on. "So, I got the Yale offer today," she said, as if she had to get it out immediately.

"Oh. Wow. Early. You don't sound excited. Was the money bad?"

"No, the money is great, actually. It's about what I expected, a bit more with all the bells and whistles. If you like bells and whistles."

"When do you have to give them an answer?"

"End of next week."

Charlotte didn't know what to say. She hadn't really let herself get to this point in her head. This point where Adrianna was deciding whether to move back to the city where they met, at least in part so that they could be together. Being together for more than a few days sounded almost too good to be true. It also felt like a door closing on her future.

With a fast-track to tenure job at an Ivy, Adrianna would be at the zenith of her career. Stuck in an entry-level curatorial job, Charlotte would have to stay where she was until she was either promoted to associate at an institution she'd never felt especially invested in—or supported by. Or until she found something else, somewhere else. Which was possible, but unlikely to result in an easy transition to coupledom—they'd almost certainly revert to long-distance status that way, too. It was so much simpler when she hadn't allowed herself to dream.

"What are you thinking?" Charlotte asked.

"I'm thinking I wish Piedmont would give you the good news," Adrianna said. She was sweet to take this tack. Even if Charlotte didn't get the job, it was nice to feel Adrianna's belief in her while she waited to find out.

"Or any news," Charlotte said. "I was sure it would be today. The wiki is quiet, anyway."

"I bet you'll know by midweek," Adrianna said.

"But what if I don't? What do you think you'll tell them?"

"I think I need more information," Adrianna said. "I need to know if you get the offer. If you want the job and to move to LA. All of that."

"Of course I want the job and to move to LA," Charlotte said. "Except if the Yale job is your dream, and that's what you really want. Then I guess I don't know."

"Right," Adrianna said. "I don't know, either."

"I really miss you," Charlotte said, not exactly meaning to. "I wish we could stop thinking about all this for a while."

"So do I," Adrianna said.

Charlotte hoped she'd add something to make her feel better. A clue about what she was really feeling. What she was truly planning.

"I miss you touching me," Adrianna said.

Charlotte knew what that meant. But she was suddenly feeling weird about things becoming sexual tonight. She was the exposed one right now. Adrianna held all the cards. It wasn't the way she liked things to be.

"Not in the mood?" Adrianna asked a few seconds later. She looked disappointed but like she understood.

"No, you know I'm always in the mood," Charlotte said. "I don't know. I'm just stressed. And, I guess, a little vulnerable, if you really want the truth."

"I always want the truth, baby," Adrianna said, coming closer to the screen. "Tell me how else you feel."

"I feel like I have no control right now," she said. "And you know I don't like that."

"I do know," Adrianna said. "What if you tell me what I

can do for you tonight? Maybe that will help. You know I need you to tell me."

Charlotte felt a sharp twinge of arousal hearing Adrianna put it like that. Seeing her say it. Thinking of the way it might be if they were together.

Adrianna was in her bedroom at the apartment. Almost surely in bed. Charlotte could tell.

"Take off your panties and spread your legs, honey," Charlotte started.

Adrianna did as asked.

"Are you hot for me?"

"I'm so wet, Charlotte," Adrianna said. "You always make me so wet."

"Touch your clit the way I touch you," she said. "Rub it for me."

Adrianna began to touch herself, rubbing her clit in hard, fast circles until she was on the edge of orgasm. Charlotte watched, feeling her own excitement building to a peak. Adrianna was looking into the camera with abandon. Brave for her, Charlotte knew.

"Oh, fuck. I'm coming so hard for you, Charlotte," she said. "I'm coming so hard for my sweet, sweet Charlotte."

"That's right, honey," Charlotte said. She was touching herself, too. "You come for me now. You know how much I want you."

Adrianna was moaning, a tangle of sheets between her teeth undoubtedly for the neighbors' sake.

"Oh, God," she keened. "I miss you so much, baby. So, so much."

They say no news is good news. But when Monday came and went with no contact from Piedmont, Charlotte began to entertain a notion that no candidate really wants to consider.

Door number three: an offer is out and it's not to you.

In this scenario, the institution has attempted to hire one of your competitors and while you're not necessarily totally out of the running, you'll never have been the top choice, either.

The wiki had nothing to offer. But with every passing minute, Charlotte became more and more convinced that an offer had been made. And that offer had gone to Hadley Fairweather.

And what if it had? Well, if she took it, metagaming things out, at the very least Hadley's jumping ship at USC would open up a job there, probably next year. Charlotte could always apply for that. Next year.

She felt herself going down a deep and very dark rabbit hole of sadness.

No new email. And once again, the wiki had nothing to offer.

But it was only noon Pacific Standard Time. Plenty of hours left.

On a whim, Charlotte walked down the street to the over-priced café and got a large piece of black velvet cake to go. She took it back to her desk and, rather than decamping to the break room as required, dove into it right there.

Since she'd been fired and rehired, Charlotte was feeling a sense of devil-may-care about her job at the museum. With Grayson's sins revealed, they didn't dare touch her. Not that they had had any objectively valid reason to let her go the first time. But just as she grasped the new level of job security she had attained, she realized how little she liked her job. How little it had to do with what really mattered to her in life.

She rechecked the wiki. Wait. What was this? A few lines down. Beneath the update she had kindly provided the previous week: "finalists invited to campus"—and the +1 +1 that the other two finalists had (apparently) added was something new. "Rejection received" someone had written with today's date. Oh no. This was bad. Not only was an offer out, the offer had almost certainly been accepted. Unless. Unless the rejected party was not a finalist in the first place and Piedmont had charitably cut them free with an "abandon all hope because you definitely didn't get it" letter. At least she hadn't gotten that letter yet. Unless it had been sent the old-fashioned way. If so it could be lying in wait for her, even now, in the un-lockable brass mailbox in the vestibule of her apartment house.

The cake was dry. Her coffee was cold. She wanted to be kissing Adrianna. She wanted to be fucking Adrianna. She wanted to be walking on a beach with her hand in hand. Outside her narrow strip of window, it looked like it might snow.

Chapter Twenty-Five

On Tuesday, Adrianna received an email from the chair of her current home department. Seeing the woman's long and indisputably Scandinavian name in her inbox proved oddly unsettling. She was immediately racked with guilt, as if this Borg queen ensconced in the cube that was UCLA was intuitively aware of the wayward intentions and possible disloyalty of a member of the collective who had gone off-planet. As if she knew exactly what Adrianna was up to with Yale.

But surely not. She was being paranoid. It was probably just the latest procedural update about her tenure case—one of those creepy seventeen-point missives crammed with dos and don'ts and what-ifs and you'd-better-hope-nots. It was too soon to be the decision on her application for a sabbatical extension. Anyway, that would be coming from the Graduate Division.

And yet. The first line of the message was eerily up to speed. "I trust you're enjoying your time in Madrid," the chair wrote. "We here in the department acutely feel your absence. As do your students. And I hesitate to interrupt you with anything but good news, which I hope you will deem this." And which, in fact, it certainly was.

The chair had written to let Adrianna know that, in acknowledgment of her recent archival discovery and the probable approval of her request for an extension by the Graduate

Division, they had decided to advance her name for an endowed chair. If all went as expected with her tenure case, she would be named to the Hall University Professorship, as an associate. Some of the perks she should expect when/if appointed were a new (and presumably better) office, additional research funds, and eligibility for another sabbatical in a mere two years. Surely they must know about Yale, is all Adrianna could manage in terms of a response. But also: Holy Fuck, it felt good to be wanted. And not merely, or at least not so transparently, on the basis of her skin color.

Things were getting interesting. But they were also getting hard.

Charlotte was waiting in line for her coffee at Jojo's when the call came at just past 6:30 California time. Seeing the unfamiliar yet familiar area code, she was immediately confused. Since when had the Piedmont people decided to communicate before their own business hours? Talk about a rude awakening.

But then she realized that it wasn't the number they'd previously given her. Though it was a California number—and the caller had just now left a message.

Esther. She was apparently calling from a landline. And she sounded very upset. It was Fisher, she said, beginning a long and very rambling recording:

"He was over at a friend's house last night, too late. I told him to come home before dark or I'd come to get him. But then I didn't hear from him—I was prepping for a big interview for the judgeship—and he had fallen out of a tree!" Esther's voice was shaking. "And then the other mom called me. And I went to the hospital having no idea what to expect. But he's OK now. He's out of surgery. I'm calling because I left Adrianna an even more lunatic message than this before he went in. And she hasn't responded. And I'm hoping you can let her know he's OK. Compound fracture. But he's out of the woods. In every way, I guess. Charlotte. I'm sorry. Call me if you want."

She hung up. Or possibly ran out of time. Charlotte couldn't tell. But she fully understood Esther's panic and she was just glad to hear that Fisher was evidently OK. She texted Adrianna.

Did you get Esther's message?

And got an immediate response.

No. Text or email or ?

Phone, I think. You should listen to it

God. Is she alright?

Yes. Fisher was in an accident. But he's OK. He's going to be fine.

Jesus!

Yeah. She sounded insane. But understandably

How are you?

OK. No news yet

☹ I'm sorry, baby. Don't lose hope. I'm going to call Esther.

OK. Give her my love. Xoxo

Charlotte texted Esther that she'd call her back later at a time of Esther's choosing. She wanted to let Adrianna talk to her first. Poor Fisher, she thought. He was a good kid and she liked him a lot.

Esther responded to Charlotte's willingness to talk to her later with a particularly obtuse text:

Call me after 2pm your time. Not before. Will be ready for some good news.

Whatever that meant. Rough start to the day, Charlotte decided, definitely deserving of a pastry.

By the time Adrianna had packed up her things and found a quiet spot in one of the cavernous hallways outside the cafeteria, almost an hour had passed. Esther didn't answer the first time. But she called back a few minutes later. She did indeed sound delirious. She'd barely slept and was naturally still recovering from the shock and a night of worrying. But they'd assured her that Fisher's arm would heal with just a slight bend and his traction time would be short. More good news: it wasn't his writing hand.

"He's been much braver than me, as you might predict," Esther said. "He blames himself. Which this time he should, the little jerk. I told him not to climb in the dark."

"Poor guy," Adrianna said. She felt ill at ease in situations involving healthcare for people under eighteen. "Is he sedated? Does it hurt a lot?"

"God," Esther said. "Yes, he's sleeping comfortably, as they say. Instead of, you know, 'Your son is heavily sedated because he was in excruciating pain.'"

"Sorry," said Adrianna.

"It's OK. Only-children without children get a pass."

"You know I have a brother," Adrianna said.

"He's such a prick, it doesn't count." They both laughed. "Hadley has three brothers so she's been great; says this kind of thing happened like every year to one or the other of them growing up."

Adrianna did a mental double take. Had Esther just said the word *Hadley*? And if so, was there any possible way...?

"*Who* has three brothers?"

"Damn," Esther said. "You caught that, did you?"

"I sure as shit did," said Adrianna. "This wouldn't by any snowball's chance in hell be Hadley Fairweather of whom you speak?"

"Damn again," Esther said. "She knew you'd figure it out if I gave you any details. Such a small world you people inhabit. So I didn't. But yes, she's who I've been seeing. We only discovered we had you in common on the third date. Or the third whatever you'd call it."

Adrianna knew she needed to be careful. "I thought she was in New York."

"She's sort of taking a breather from the Met fellowship."

"You're not still representing her, are you?"

"Not officially, no. But the case is being investigated and I'm watching over things from afar. She retained counsel other than me, if that makes you feel better."

"It does," Adrianna said. "And you two are..."

"Happy," said Esther a bit defensively. "Until last night, yes. I was about the happiest I've been since I can remember. And she's a big part of that."

"Well, then I'm happy, too. I'm glad she's there with you guys. I wish I was. Not that I'm much of a comfort. What does Stephen say?"

"My plan is to keep the two of them apart," Esther said. "He's on his way down from San Francisco. They were there for Easter, or so he tells me."

"Christ," said Adrianna.

Hadley and Esther. What was Charlotte going to think about that?

It was 1:17 and Charlotte was finished with lunch. She was now in need of something to keep her busy until she could check back with Esther after two o'clock. She knew what she should be doing, namely finishing the wall labels she'd been assigned for the new show. But today even the notion of going to look at the paintings was a downer. Not only was the show's focus on the derivative quality of American art a sad commentary on, well, American art, the paintings themselves were mostly wooden and marginally embarrassing. They made the Colonists look like revolution was about the last thing they would have been capable of since they could barely paint a recognizable table.

She was just about to get on the elevator when another California number popped up on her phone. This was one she recognized. This was the Piedmont people. She quickly ducked into the bathroom to take the call.

"Dr. Hilaire," said the peppy voice at the other end, "Emilie Panciatichi here, from the Piedmont Colleges. On behalf of the department of the history of art, we'd like to offer you the position of assistant professor of art history and deputy director of the Burrell Museum."

Hallelujah and amen. The words echoed in Charlotte's ear like the final Bachian chord played on a mighty organ. Yes, she wanted to tell her. My answer is yes.

What she said was: "Dr. Panciatichi. It's so wonderful to

hear from you. What fantastic news! I can't tell you how delighted I am at the prospect of coming to Piedmont."

At Adrianna's command she had memorized this phrase. Never say yes immediately, she had told her. Sound ecstatic, even relieved. But say only *I'm delighted at the prospect of taking the job at X.* This signals that you really want it but you're going to negotiate and you might even have leverage—even another offer—on your side.

Women rarely negotiate but they (should) appreciate it when other women do.

Dr. Panciatichi, who had been to the rodeo a few times before, laughed her melodious laugh.

"Of course," she said. "Of course. And we're delighted by the prospect of having you. I wanted to call with the news. But I'll follow up ASAP with a formal offer. You were our first choice, Charlotte. We'd be very disappointed if you didn't accept."

Charlotte was just barely possessed of her faculties enough to apprehend the significance of these gracious words.

"It's really a dream come true," she allowed herself to say. Because it was. "I look forward to receiving the offer. And thank you, again, Dr. Panciatichi. Thank you so much."

It was 1:55 when they finished the call.

Charlotte, who was still in the bathroom, gave herself a good look in the mirror. Deputy curator of a respected academic museum. Imagine that. She couldn't help but smile back at herself as she washed her hands, just for appearance's sake, before leaving. She wasn't more than a few steps away when she realized she'd left her phone on the counter, something she would never have let happen if she were in her right mind—especially since meeting Adrianna. She did an about-face and was just about to walk back in when Abigail, now the museum's interim director, burst out of the bathroom's swinging door. Her face was red and flustered-looking.

Oh shit were the words that came immediately to mind.

Charlotte hadn't physically checked the stalls when she'd run in to answer the Piedmont call. But she had felt sure enough she was alone to stand by the sink as she talked. Had Abigail been there the whole time? Downright sinister as it was to fathom, there was really no other explanation.

In the few moments it had taken to reach this disturbing conclusion, Abigail reached the end of the hallway. She'd not witnessed Charlotte's return to the scene of the crime. Or so it appeared. But now Abigail knew about the Piedmont job. Now Abigail knew everything.

Part Three

Chapter Twenty-Six

Charlotte was on her way home on the shuttle to surprise Adrianna with the good news—which she'd weirdly already shared with Esther, since they'd checked in about Fisher that afternoon—when she received a text.

Out with a few people from the BN. Home in an hour?

What the hell? On the one night when she most wanted to talk, Adrianna was finally permitting herself to socialize. Charlotte knew she had friends from the Biblioteca Nacional—other scholars and researchers who one eventually got to know after passing in hallways, standing at coat checks, and sitting at adjacent tables for months on end. And she was always glad when Adrianna stopped working long enough to enjoy herself a little.

But, in her mind, tonight was supposed to be the culmination of their going on six months of wondering if they could find a way to do what they did professionally in the same place. And if, as their joint efforts to pull up stakes implied, they would have a real shot at being together as a couple.

Then again, an hour was only an hour. Then again, again, once they finally talked, Adrianna would very likely be a little, if not a lot, intoxicated given how scholars liked to tie one on once they finally let loose. Charlotte wanted her big announcement to fall on sober ears.

The shuttle came to her stop and she jumped to the sidewalk over a treacherous bank of sooty snow. The cute little wine store beckoned to her from across the street. Might as well meet Adrianna where she would likely be, Charlotte thought, scampering into the middle of Whitney as she waited for the traffic to pass.

The wine shop was deservedly beloved by many residents of New Haven, mainly grad students and faculty. The former prized it for the knowledgeable staff's willingness to point a person to a good but not prohibitively expensive option for a dinner with visiting relatives or a first date; the latter appreciated that the proprietors were always happy to order a Macallan 18 or a dessert wine from the Central Coast, if by chance they didn't have another special occasion bottle awaiting in the back. Plus the people were just plain friendly. Charlotte had gotten to know the youngish bearded guy who worked there most afternoons well enough that they'd stopped to talk for a few minutes at the Stop & Shop a few days earlier.

"So, you need something that will take you gently into the good night, and do that sort of quickly?" he asked.

"That's about right," Charlotte said. "Something sippable rather than slammable, maybe?"

"What about a really nice Jamaican rum?" he asked, walking over to the shelf and grabbing a very British-looking bottle. "This is a reserve and it's incredibly smooth. One ice cube and it will open up like a bouquet of flowers."

"Well how can I say no to that?" Charlotte wondered whether subconsciously—or consciously—the guy was playing to her Créolité, if he knew she might have a soft spot for things Caribbean.

"Let me know if it does the trick," he said as she walked out.

The trick, she thought, as she hurried into the big yellow Victorian house where she lived, would be to keep things from escalating. She didn't want to put Adrianna on the spot or to view her news as an ultimatum. Adrianna had three days to get back to Yale with her final answer. Charlotte trusted this to make deciding what to say to her old department that much easier.

She had gotten through a good fifth of the bottle of rum by the time her computer chimed Adrianna's incoming call— audio only. Charlotte was lying on the sofa binge-watching *Suits*, her favorite source of ethics-based distraction and role modeling. But combining copious quantities of alcohol derived from sugar cane with formidable women lawyers plying their trade in couture had put her in a contentious state of mind, even before she answered.

It was just past three in the morning in Madrid.

"Hi, baby," Adrianna said, her voice lower and more sultry than usual.

"Hey, honey," Charlotte answered. This had become their usual greeting, a way to put each other at ease and sometimes, to cut to the real conversation by eliminating the "how was your day?" with which their texts often began.

"Did you have fun?" Charlotte asked.

"Oh, you know, a Lit guy from Columbia and a woman who teaches in the Div School at U Chicago, so it wasn't exactly rip-roaring. But they're good people. And queer, as we discovered, so that was funny."

"I'm glad you finally went somewhere besides El Jardin," Charlotte said.

"Who says we did?"

"Seriously?"

"Only for one drink," Adrianna chuckled. "Then we went to the Plaza. What's new with you, sweet bird?"

"I got the job," Charlotte blurted out. She hadn't meant to. In fact, about five fingers of rum ago, she'd decided not to tell Adrianna tonight. But the words just seemed to want to be spoken.

"Damn. You got it?" Adrianna said. "You got the job?"

"I guess I did," Charlotte said, a little put off by Adrianna's reaction. "They called today."

"Wow," Adrianna said, still not sounding nearly as happy for Charlotte, or as congratulatory, let alone excited or relieved, as she had hoped.

"You sound surprised."

"You know I'm not. It's exactly what should happen. I guess I just wasn't quite ready to think about what it means for me."

"It's not like I said yes," Charlotte said. "I told them I was excited, like you told me. And they're sending the formal offer in the next day or so."

"But you're thinking you'll take it, I assume?" Adrianna said. The sexiness had all but drained from her voice, replaced by her "let's figure this out" forthrightness.

"At this moment, I can't rightly say," Charlotte shot back. She didn't like this. Not at all.

"No need to get your back up," Adrianna said. "I'm just asking where your thinking is."

"And I'm just saying, I'm not sure. You don't even sound like you wanted me to get it. Did something happen?"

There was silence at the other end. "Charlotte," Adrianna said, not a little patronizingly, "of course I wanted you to get it. You deserve it. And it's right for you. And it's so good for them. I'm just… I need to work some things out. UCLA has apparently gotten wind of the Yale offer, which is why I think Yale wants me to act fast. It's a tenure-track job at an

Ivy League school, Charlotte. It's a once-in-a-lifetime thing at my age."

And there it was. Now that Charlotte had put a good faith effort into moving across the country to California, upending the only adult life she'd known in the East, Adrianna wasn't sure where she truly wanted to be. Maybe even who she wanted to be with. Not with what she considered a better job in play. Charlotte wasn't saying she wouldn't have applied for the Piedmont job before they met. Of course she would have. But she simply wouldn't have been able to put her heart and soul and every last drop of gumption she had into getting it—not like she had with Adrianna as her motivation.

"I realize that," Charlotte said, tears building. "Well, I guess you've got until Friday, right? I'm sure you'll let me know."

"Don't be childish," Adrianna said. "This is my career."

"Is *that* what this is?" Charlotte replied. "It's late. I'm gonna let you go. Good night."

And she ended the call.

Charlotte cried herself to sleep. And when she woke up, a wicked hangover to contend with and a job to get to, she thought how little she recognized the woman behind those words last night. *Don't be childish.* The phrase cut her to the quick. Was this what she'd been to Adrianna from the beginning, a childish little sex kitten to be dismissed when the grown-ups got together and real life set in? A diversion while she took time away from her all-important work?

It was several minutes before Charlotte remembered that something else significant had happened the previous day: she'd been offered an incredibly desirable position at a respected consortium of schools in a beautiful, warm location at a politically aware, relatively right-minded institution. She had prayed for something like this for years and yesterday, her prayers were answered.

Some of them, at least.

It was bad enough not to be able to revel in her astounding news on her own. And twice as bad not to have felt Adrianna's support and acknowledgment of her achievement as something better than "what should happen."

She threw on her gray worsted wool dress and black tights, twisted her shower-wet hair into a bun, and closed the door on all that disappointment. The sun was struggling to make itself known. Snow had fallen the night before and everything looked new and sparkling under the yellow sky. It was three in the afternoon in Madrid, by which time Adrianna had usually sent her a greeting of some kind. But there was no greeting today.

The brown-inked flourishes on the pages of Sor Epiphania's diary seemed to be playing tricks on Adrianna's eyes. Sometimes when she was transcribing with machine-like efficiency, the meanings of the words or sentences she transformed from Spanish to English only partially registered.

This was not one of those times.

For as soon as she was on a roll with two or three lines in a row, she caught herself reflecting on the author's whereabouts at the time she was writing—was she sitting among the other sisters in the library, was she alone at her personal desk? She wondered about the implications of the words she chose. Or the subtext beneath words in a book ostensibly maintained for Epiphania's eyes only—but which, being a woman of her rank, she must have known might have a wider public someday. What did it mean to write a personal diary for a stranger like Adrianna to read these three and a half centuries later?

Adrianna came to the end of the page but rather than gently

removing the weights and flipping to the next one, she stopped to reread what she'd typed so far.

Today we rec'd a packet of letters from the love of S. Mg.t. Rather, from the colony. These of hers were never sent in her lifetime. To read them now has brought her to tears. They contained much that was unknown to her being at so great a distance and for so long.

Then as now, to be at a great distance from the one you love over an extended period might make the heart grow fonder. But it can also lead to misunderstanding and estrangement. Sor Epiphania had written so empathetically about this that Adrianna was beginning to wonder whether she might form the third side of a triangle, whether spiritual or sexual, or both, she couldn't be sure. Clearly Sor Epiphania was trusted by the queen as well as the Mexican prioress. But perhaps there was more to it than trust. Had Epiphania's own longing for the queen, even from within her own household, helped her understand the queen's longing for the nun pining so far from her, on another continent, in a tiny Mexican town?

It wasn't lost on Adrianna that she had allowed herself to wander into the world of the diary more than usual this day. She took out her phone.

Nothing from Charlotte.

What happened between them last night had left her feeling small, cynical, and alone. Charlotte had been drunk. She had to have been. But Adrianna had been far from sober at the time she made the call. And definitely not in the right place to hear Charlotte's amazing news.

It really had been a fun night. Adrianna didn't know why she'd downplayed that. They'd eaten well and gotten to know each other and traded tales of academic woe. And it felt good to be out with people who were closer to her own age—or older, in the case of the theologian. And she shouldn't feel guilty about that. But for some reason she had.

And she'd punished Charlotte for it pretty unforgivably. Sweet, circumspect Charlotte who laid down her defenses with Adrianna. But also let herself be stronger than she was. And who was tender and fiercely smart but never childish. Adrianna knew she never should have spoken to her like that. Charlotte had every right to be furious; whatever the future held, her reaction to Charlotte's good news—and for her it was exactly that—had been heartless and selfish. And now she couldn't take it back.

Chapter Twenty-Seven

Wednesday passed with nothing from Adrianna. It felt like they were playing chicken at the beginning, but when a whole day, their first, went by without any form of contact, Charlotte was starting to wonder if Adrianna was gathering the courage to break up with her.

The thought of it was more than she could bear. But as she sat peering over the rooftops of New Haven, nursing a therapeutic double whip mocha with coconut syrup at her cluttered desk in the museum, she realized she couldn't even be sure whether Adrianna would have the decency to say no to her before she said yes to Yale.

It was already almost 4:00 p.m. in Spain. Surely Adrianna had given them her answer by now. She was a big fan of buffers. Part of the secret of her success, from what Charlotte could tell, was that Adrianna was always ready ahead of the deadline. If something was due at 5:00 p.m., she'd have it in by noon. It was how she maintained her own sense of control, Charlotte deduced. Even, or especially, when things were well out of her hands.

A glance at her phone produced no text or phone message.

As soon as she'd gotten in that morning, in true and imminent danger of breaking down, Charlotte laid the situation out to James, who chastised her rather severely for not dancing in the streets about the Piedmont position. He was happy for her, she could tell. Happy enough to demand that she leave Connecticut once and possibly for all, and take that job. Whatever happened with Adrianna, he declared, eyes flashing, Piedmont was an opportunity not to be missed.

"Believe me when I say to you again," he had intoned theatrically. "For most of us, opportunities do not grow on trees. In this life, it's catch as catch can."

When Charlotte's eyes had started gleaming, he'd repeatedly stabbed his finger on the surface of his giant rolltop desk. "And if she doesn't see that. She does. Not. Deserve you."

Charlotte had rushed over to hug him, after which he said, "By the bye, Abigail wants to see you at some point today. No idea what about. Maybe she wants you to be the eventual new director. I've already declined, so don't worry about hurting my feelings on that score. But remember, a bird in the hand is what we want in life. Just this once forget about what's in the bush."

When Charlotte left James's office she felt better about the value of friendship if not the power of love. She also reckoned that if she was going to leave her job at the Woodley, she'd want to go out on a high note, with the outstanding work completed to her satisfaction. The likelihood that this would be the last time she helped put a show together there inspired renewed focus. Before anyone had to remind her to do it, she was back in basement storage cataloguing away. Climbing the stairs a few hours later for a late lunch, she realized she'd better check in with Abigail.

Abigail. The one detail Charlotte hadn't revealed to James was that Abigail had eavesdropped—from a bathroom stall—on her call with Dr. Panciatichi. This, Charlotte assumed, was what she'd want to talk to her about. Though she couldn't imagine how she'd introduce the topic and to what end.

A vestige of both another era and another country, Abigail was a curious creature. She was not only an Australian but an Australian educated at Cambridge, which gave her accent and her national and cultural allegiances a distinctive flavor. She was older than James but younger than Grayson, though nobody knew by how much. And while she was reliably mean, she could also be capriciously kind, even generous. As was well known, she was married to the great-grandson of a real estate magnate and was under no financial pressure to work. But with a doctorate from the Courtauld, she not only loved what she did but had the credentials for it. Accordingly, she had, to date, seen no reason either to give up her role to someone younger and/or possibly more appropriate or deserving, nor to change the way she had approached her job for the past twenty-five years.

"Charlotte, come in, come in," Abigail said, motioning Charlotte into one of the poufy twin bergères opposite her desk.

"How are we?"

"Just fine, thank you, Abigail. Are you well? I haven't seen you since…"

You fired me. Ooops.

Abigail gave her a puzzled look. "I'm quite well, thank you. Right, then, I asked you to pop in about your new contract. I know we revised it for another year at assistant, pending a review for associate after that, but I think it won't do not to clarify what comes next."

"I see," said Charlotte.

"Right. Well, in a word, I won't be here forever. Which isn't to say I'm at death's door or anything so grave as that. Literally or figuratively. Merely, when I do retire in about two years' time it would be logical for you to move into this role. Of course we can't write that up contractually. But if you were promoted to associate this year, you'd have just about the same level of experience I had when I became deputy. So there's a precedent of sorts."

Unbelievable. Charlotte had heard about bidding wars for this or that heir apparent of some famous scholar, usually, though not always, male. Princeton v Williams v Hopkins or some such. But she'd never imagined, after coming up short for two years, that two museums might simultaneously be after *her*.

Fuck interesting. This was getting good.

Yet for the second time in two days, Charlotte was instantly filled with what could only be described as bittersweet emotions. Here she was, safely and securely at the top of a mountain she'd not even set out to climb six months ago, but with no one to share the view. Going home after work, she felt at once invincible and completely powerless.

She took a raincheck for a celebratory drink with James at One Fifty-Five, deciding to walk home to East Rock instead. It was sunny for once, and now that it was almost May the snow had given way to rain. Cutting into the middle of the campus, she passed the university museum and the Beinecke so that she could take the long stretch down Hillhouse Avenue. Perhaps because it reminded her of parts of New Orleans, this was her favorite street. It was pretty in any season, with its Gothic mansions set far back from the sidewalk on wide lawns. But it would be especially lovely in just a few more weeks when the trees flowered and densely planted beds of bulbs added riotous yellows and reds and greens to the sober facades. Already it was leafy. Long after its official debut, the season was finally changing. Charlotte could feel it.

Adrianna was almost asleep. She'd decided not to drink until this whole thing with Yale—and UCLA—was worked out.

She'd left the library early and walked all the way home, something she enjoyed in good weather, but which she'd stopped doing once it got cold and snowy.

Madrid was a fantastic city for walking. Whether one preferred the kind of broad European boulevards associated with Paris or Rome or the medieval warrens of residential streets more like Florence or Bruges, a person could wander for hours through parks and plazas and never want for inspiration or hit a dead end. It was just the thing for thinking through a complex problem.

Perhaps as a sort of penance, Adrianna had taken the very long way, down to the Prado gardens along Alfonso XII and back up via the Paseo to Malasaña, where she was currently sitting outside a café in the brisk evening air drinking a coffee. She had one of the heavy blankets provided by the restaurant over her knees but it was getting too cold even for that. Just when she was about to get up and start the walk home a call came in. From Esther.

"What time is it there?"

"You know what time it is here, just about seven."

"So tomorrow is the deadline."

"Which you also know."

"What I don't know is what your goddamn problem is. You need to call Charlotte. Tonight. Her tonight. Before tomorrow."

"How do you know I haven't?"

"Have you?"

"No."

"What possible excuse can you have for leaving her hanging like this? It's not like you to be cruel. Self-indulgent when the mood strikes. Detached when you have your reasons. But not cruel."

"Jesus, Esther. Don't pull any punches. I know. OK. I know.

I've been as shitty as I could be about this. She hasn't called me either, by the way. But look, Charlotte and I are at very different points in our lives. Maybe you haven't felt that yet with your trophy wife, but after a while you realize…"

"Adrianna Consuelo Coates. Will you please shut up?" Esther said curtly. "After a while what *you* should realize is that true love is everything. What I do with my trophy wife is my business, you don't know her well enough to comment. But I know Charlotte and I really know you and I'm calling to tell you that I think you're this close to fucking up your life."

"Oh please," Adrianna said. "Sometimes I think you don't know *me* very well. To be where I am has taken a level of personal and professional discipline and tunnel vision that I don't think, frankly, you can begin to conceive of—even as a Jewish woman judge-to-be. Do you know how many queer women of color get PhDs in art history? The fact that only three and a half percent of PhDs in all the humanities are black might give you an idea. The offer of a position at an Ivy is something I never thought I'd get, not because I'm not good enough but because shit is fucked. So fucked, I know it's something I'll never see again."

"Yes," said Esther. "That may all be true. And it's *bisexual* Jewish woman judge-to-be to you. Do you love Charlotte?"

"You know I love Charlotte."

"But you love your ego more."

"Wow, you're really testing the limits of our friendship here," said Adrianna. "For what it's worth, I don't know what I'm going to do yet. I just need a clear head and some time on my own to decide."

"Honestly," Esther said. "I think you need to grow up."

Easier said than done.

In fact, Adrianna felt more unsure of herself than she had in a very long time. It was tempting to write off Esther's intervention as the product of her newfound sapphistry—newly minted skirt-chasers see lady love everywhere and they need it to be real and lasting. But it was more than that. Esther did know her better than probably anyone else. And it wasn't as if she wasn't hands down the most driven and career-focused woman Adrianna could think of.

Esther had faced the music in ways Adrianna couldn't begin to understand. She was the one who'd been forced to confront her own mortality. If Esther was telling her to stop and take another look at her life, it was likely a look worth taking.

Was this really all about ego?

Did it really come down to true love versus which academic department she was in?

When she thought about it that way, Adrianna could see how things might look from Esther's perspective.

And Charlotte's perspective? She hadn't put the question like that. Charlotte hadn't put it any way at all. She was out of pocket, offline, and for all Adrianna knew, making her own life choices regardless of what Adrianna decided. So far Adrianna's hypotheticals had only included a topsy-turvy world where she was on the East Coast and Charlotte was on the West.

Only now did it occur to her that Charlotte could end up in LA whether or not they figured out how to be together—Charlotte could be living in her city, going to her coffee places and museum openings and women's nights and Adrianna wouldn't be a part of any of that. And if she stayed and they didn't work this out, one day she would see Charlotte across a room, at a restaurant or a lecture, and her heart would explode. And she would be consumed with what might have been. And she would try not to remember what it felt like to be in love with Charlotte Hilaire in the way that she was right now.

Chapter Twenty-Eight

Charlotte hadn't heard from Adrianna in almost two days. If it wasn't for Esther intervening like some kind of angelic mediator, she almost certainly would have lost her resolve. She started texting Adrianna probably a dozen times, only to stop short of hitting the little blue arrow. She'd written half as many draft emails. And she'd definitely come close to pressing call. But Esther encouraged Charlotte not to make the first move. She told her that if Adrianna was going to arrive at the right decision, she'd probably need to get there on her own. If she were in her place, Esther said, she'd never have found the strength not to give in to someone like Adrianna. Hearing this, Charlotte felt good about staying true to herself.

She also found it a little hard to believe. If she hadn't had so much going on in her own life, she knew things would be different. But the point was, she did. And Adrianna could take it or leave it.

Unfortunately, after forty-eight hours of pure despair it felt as if Adrianna had decided to "leave it." And maybe decided to leave Charlotte, too. The period from waking to sleeping never seems longer than when you're waiting for the person you love to give you a sign that they love you back. Or worse, when you wait and wait and they don't even have the compassion and kindness to tell you they don't love you after all when it comes right down to it.

Either way, when Charlotte woke up on Friday feeling broken but resigned, she realized that deeply unpleasant feeling brought with it a small degree of relief that what was done was at least, almost, done. It was already early afternoon in Spain. Adrianna would be giving her response soon and she'd now shown what kind of a person she was capable of being, regardless of what she'd decided.

A day ago, Charlotte would have thought what she wanted most from Adrianna was hearts and flowers and apologies, ideally backed up by an incontrovertibly valid excuse for being so insensitive. But the wound had deepened. Now it wasn't only the possibility, or probability, that Adrianna would answer the seductive fucking siren call of the Yale job, but the fact that she had behaved so callously to Charlotte while she was choosing to do so. This was what she couldn't stomach.

And yet, what could Charlotte do but get on with it? If someone had interrupted her latest festival of tears the previous night, she wouldn't have believed functioning in the world the next day was possible. But here she was, showering and dressing and walking back down Hillhouse Avenue as if the life she knew before Adrianna had abruptly returned. The only difference was that this life, too, was drawing to a close.

Regardless of what the Piedmont offer was, on principle she'd try for the 10% salary increase Adrianna had made her promise she'd politely request. She'd see if there was wiggle room on the start-up funds. But then—frankly, who cared whether they gave her exactly what she asked for—she'd sign on the dotted line. She'd take the job. And a few months later, she'd move to Los Angeles, California, where at least she already had one friend. Two if you counted Hadley.

The Piedmont offer was in her email by noon and it was definitely livable. In fact, Charlotte was hard-pressed to ask for additional salary since what they were offering was nearly a third more than what she currently made. And anyway, she always had what her father left her if she needed it. Still, she'd learned from Adrianna that women aren't generally good at asking for what they're worth so she decided to politely negotiate just to show she had it in her.

Having learned that lesson seemed painfully ironic to her now.

The man she thought of as Dean Peter had asked to talk to her by phone to answer any questions, read, hear her requests, sometime in the midafternoon. When they spoke, Charlotte had maintained her enthusiasm for the job without being overly exuberant; she'd calmly asked about the salary and the benefits, never implying that any aspect of the contract was an issue. At the end of their conversation the Dean said: "If you're as shrewd a negotiator for the museum as you've been just now, we're in even better shape than I thought. I'll be back to you with the answers as soon as I can. I'm confident we can do at least some of this."

With every interaction with her new employer Charlotte felt more like the person she wanted to be.

As much to calm her nerves as to make up for the time she was engaged in negotiating, Charlotte spent the rest of the afternoon in the basement doing condition reports. It was good to be alone if only because at this point her emotions were so raw on the surface she knew she was in danger of breaking into another convulsive crying fit at any moment. Her stomach hurt from clutching and her heart felt physically bruised.

She'd finished writing up a still life with "significant losses" when she realized it had to be closing time. She pulled out her phone. Not only was it nearing six o'clock, but she'd missed *several* calls from Adrianna—owing, no doubt, to the lack of a signal in the museum's bunker of a basement.

Bittersweet.

Not long ago the mere sight of Adrianna's name had been enough to fill Charlotte with anxious glee. Now she was experiencing something else. This was heartbreak, pure and simple. She'd never thought reliable, thoughtful, tenderly considerate Adrianna would let her down. And certainly not this way. And over something so outside their feelings for each other as this.

It was time to go home in any case—being the last one in a museum, especially in the basement, was never the safest feeling. She gathered up her things and headed upstairs to her desk.

Once there, with no one else around, Charlotte thought about whether she should return Adrianna's call. Right now. At the office. Where she might have less of a chance of losing her shit completely. She dreaded the idea of finishing the workday with what could be their last conversation. But it was late and she was beat. And it didn't seem worth trying to make Adrianna as miserable, if such a thing were possible, as living in a state of unknowing had made her feel. Best to get it over with. Best to know for certain that Adrianna's choice was made. Charlotte sat down at her desk and waited for an answer.

Adrianna picked up immediately. "Charlotte," she said, her voice sounding strange and unsteady.

"I didn't listen to the messages," Charlotte said flatly. "I'm just calling you back."

"There is so much I want to say to you right now," Adrianna said quickly, almost as if she was reciting something she'd written out. "I'm sorry for what I said and for just…disappearing like a fucking coward when we needed to be together on this and work things out. Charlotte, you've become the most important person in my life. And I don't ever want to be without you. And I didn't take the Yale job and—"

"Why not?" Charlotte interrupted.

"What? Because if you'll have me, I have to be with you. I can't not be with you, baby," Adrianna said as if it were the obvious and only possible answer.

"What about your career?"

"What about *your* career? What about what *you* want? This is your chance. It's what you've been waiting for. And it's perfect. I've been so fucking selfish. I don't know why I couldn't see that, but I do now."

"You haven't," Charlotte said. She was almost angry at Adrianna for feeling this way. Angry that she had to feel this way. That it had to be one of them or the other whose dreams would come true. And that Adrianna had to feel selfish for striving to achieve what she was hardwired for.

"You've sacrificed everything for this life and worked so hard. *So* hard. And you deserve Yale. Even if Yale doesn't deserve you. I want you to get what you want, Adrianna. And I can't have you resenting me because I took away your dream."

"But you are my dream, Charlotte," Adrianna said slowly. "In every way I can think of."

Charlotte had to let those words live there for a minute.

"I am?"

"Yes, baby. You so, so are."

A little later, once Charlotte was home for the evening and safely ensconced on the sofa they talked face-to-face for a few more minutes. It was way past midnight in Madrid and Adrianna should have been asleep, but she said she couldn't imagine sleeping because she was still so relieved and happy that Charlotte had called back and let her tell her about Yale. Or not-Yale, as the case would be.

After a very long, but very full day at work Charlotte was just glad to be in her apartment where she could see Adrianna's beaming face as they talked about the future. Together. Suddenly she had a new career. She had an amazing girlfriend. And she had a life that was finally moving forward.

"So, there is one caveat," Adrianna said, sounding more serious than Charlotte would have preferred.

"Tell me."

"I said no to the sabbatical extension next fall," she explained. "But I said yes to coming back here for the summer, figuring you'd have time off before you start the school year, too. And figuring maybe I could get you to spend some of it in the Castilian heat with me. The archives are something like air-conditioned. And there's sangria and terrazas and the parts of the museums with the art in them that you never got to see. Hot AF summer in Chueca, Dr. Hilaire?"

"Yes," Charlotte replied, ecstatic at the thought. "Yes, yes, yes, yes, yes!"

Chapter Twenty-Nine

The day before Charlotte's flight to LA, a small package arrived at her apartment via FedEx. By that time, her furniture and most of her clothing had been packed up along with some forty boxes of books. God willing it was all currently trucking across the country to her equally small but much brighter new apartment in Los Feliz, where she would meet the movers in approximately four days.

The old space was basically empty except for the sleeping bag she had borrowed from James, who never explained why he owned such a thing, a couple of empty boxes, and the luggage she would take on the plane. She had ordered pizza of course—New Haven being famous for its thin crust pies—and was planning to eat it alone with her computer and a farewell bottle from the wine shop.

She recognized the return Los Angeles address on the package. Adrianna hadn't mentioned anything, however, so she wondered if it might be that rarest of rare gestures from her girlfriend: a surprise.

Adrianna had been back in LA for about two weeks, her fellowship formally and fruitfully concluded for the school year. The deal she'd told Charlotte about from her department chair provided further research funding for two summer months in Madrid and a reduced course load instead of the extended fall term. According to Adrianna, summer in that city in the heart

of Spain was typically about as hot and dry as Death Valley—
walking a couple of blocks easily left a person drenched with
sweat, she'd said. And hand fans were de rigueur.

It sounded a little like New Orleans without the humidity
and the hurricanes, which was fine by Charlotte. But within
the realm of academic horse trading, the arrangement was
a sacrifice of sorts. Instead of having a full semester away to
continue her archival research Adrianna would be going back
to school along with Charlotte in the fall. Charlotte had tried
to get her to take the time off she'd been awarded—knowing
she was coming back to live in the same city made a big difference—but she just said she couldn't wait to cook breakfast
for Charlotte every morning. For this she got a skeptical eye
roll, even though Charlotte couldn't think of anything better
than spending their summer vacation together.

The plan was to get Charlotte settled into the new LA place
in June. In July, Adrianna would go back to Madrid—same
apartment. Then, at the end of the month, Charlotte would
join her there for a little work and a lot of play. Charlotte was
beginning to investigate Creole identity in Spain prior to the
nineteenth century, and she intended to do some archival
unearthing of her own. She was ready to reinvent herself as
a scholar. And, admittedly, with a little trepidation, she was
eager to find out what it would be like to be part of a couple
who ambitiously pursued their separate careers together.

But first, there was the cross-country move. And saying
goodbye to the old existence.

Charlotte's pizza filled the apartment with lemony vapors
laced with oregano, parmesan, and clams. Her last white pie.
For the foreseeable future, anyway. She opened the awaited
bottle of Sangiovese and sidled up to the box that was her
makeshift dining table.

In some ways it was difficult to conceive of a life beyond

this fascinating and frustrating small Connecticut city, with its stark divides between races and incomes and access. With its boutique hotels, pricey Italian bakeries, and Cuban restaurants; with its ever-growing population of people experiencing life without enough food and a place to live. New Haven had been her home since she was a first-year in college. She'd grown up here.

At eighteen, Charlotte had arrived believing she was finally on her way to living the New England life she'd secretly imagined. Through sheer force of will she'd escaped the parochial confines of her corner of the South, and with it an imposed identity that felt like something from *Showboat*, to a place where she was convinced her intelligence and discipline would propel her ever forward.

It had taken a while. But in the end, she supposed, they had.

Two things surprised her. First, she missed New Orleans almost daily. And second, Yale was far from the land of milk and honey Charlotte had naively imagined it to be; many of the same rules applied above the Mason-Dixon Line, as she soon learned. But New Haven had also provided some crucial life lessons. This was where she came out; this was where she first kissed a girl in public. This was where she was first called a dyke on the street and a zebra in the classroom.

The Piedmont Colleges were sure to have their failings and problems, but what they offered was a fresh start and a place where she might be able to help make things different and better for women like her—and for lots of other kinds of students, as well.

It was a good run, New Haven. But it was time to move on.

After one Netflix episode had flowed imperceptibly into another and she'd inhaled one slice more than she vowed to eat, Charlotte remembered the little package she'd conspicuously deposited in her open suitcase—as a treat for later.

What could Adrianna have needed to get her so urgently that it couldn't wait until she picked her up at LAX tomorrow?

The box inside the cardboard shipper was a little too big to be a ring box. *Hélas!*

Still, it was the size of something small but special. Charlotte almost didn't want to open it yet. But she knew when she talked to her in an hour, Adrianna would want to hear her response to whatever was inside.

Charlotte took a breath. She ran her nail through the tape around the little rectangle and opened it. Inside there was a thin layer of cotton batting, underneath which was: a key. It was old-looking. But not in an antique brass skeleton-key kind of way. It was the key to a car. And Charlotte didn't need to look very closely at the black rubber fob to recognize the heraldic shield that was its logo. This was a Porsche key. She'd guess it belonged to a car from the late '90s or early 2000s, when keys still turned actual locks and ignitions. A small slip of paper in the box read: *"For the next time you want to take me somewhere I've never been."*

Charlotte could feel the waters rising. All the signs were there, from the growing knot in her throat to the warmth in her chest to the pressure behind her eyes. But these were welcome tears, happy tears, fallen-in-love-and-don't-want-to-get-up tears. And goddamn did Adrianna know exactly how to roll out the red carpet. She couldn't wait to drive that car!

Charlotte's trip the next day was an easy one. Mostly because she knew that flying from one coast to the other wasn't about to become a regular feature of her life. The prospect of no LDR was an exciting one!

Remarkably, she had managed to sleep almost an hour on the plane shortly after they took off. But as she moved physically closer to her new life and to Adrianna—whom she hadn't seen in person since the conference—Charlotte vibrated herself awake with a good kind of nervous energy. For the past few months she'd delayed her own gratification. But now it was finally time for the reward. Apropos of which, she made a mental note to herself to think twice before wearing a garter belt on a coast-to-coast flight.

As soon as they touched down, she texted Adrianna, who was on her way to meet her at Arrivals. It was extremely tempting to go straight to the baggage claim. But after seven hours a little freshening up was certainly in order. She'd brought a change of clothes—one of the indestructible Saint Laurent wrap dresses that Adrianna liked so well—to go over the microfiber unmentionables of which she was also pretty fond.

Charlotte emerged from the airport ladies' room feeling ready to take on the world.

All she needed was her luggage.

Down at the baggage claim, she soon had cause to wonder if she would get it. The crowd of passengers had considerably thinned out by the time she got there and nothing new was being coughed up onto the conveyor belt. The same plastic-wrapped millennial-pink duffel made the circuit at least twice, but there was no sign of Charlotte's oversized, packed-to-the-limits suitcase. She could feel her blood pressure creeping.

"So help me," she intoned.

When the belt buzzed disappointingly to a stop she had no choice but to approach the customer service counter. The guy working there, about her height with graying temples and a broad smile, was more sympathetic to her neckline than her plight. But whatever his motivations he was able to determine that Charlotte's bag had been mistakenly rerouted and wouldn't get to LA until later that night. He'd have the luggage delivered wherever she requested—in fact, he was quite willing to drive it there himself.

All's well that ends well, Charlotte thought, trying hard to channel the new, more relaxed, California version of herself. But make no mistake, there would be hell to pay if they lost her favorite two pairs of fuck-me pumps.

Adrianna had meanwhile circled the airport a few times so as not to get ticketed, her righteous anger on behalf of Charlotte's lost bag growing with every pass. Charlotte texted her an update on the rerouting problem and told her she was finally coming out.

What seemed like mere seconds later, she heard the roar of an engine as a red—that's coral red, very rare—Carrera revved into the pickup area, deftly inserting itself between two SUVs. The woman inside, in sunglasses and a pale blue suit, was, of course, Adrianna. Charlotte just about died.

Adrianna quickly cut the ignition, punched on the hazards, and came around to her, stopping short in her driving moccasins when she got the full view.

"Hi, baby," she said, almost shyly.

"Hey, honey," Charlotte responded, quickly coming Adrianna's way to pull her in for a long, very French, kiss.

As Adrianna pointed out, it was a blessing in disguise that Charlotte's luggage hadn't arrived. No Porsche is made for hauling anything or anyone much bigger than a bag of golf clubs and maybe a runway model or two. And Charlotte's hard-sided behemoth would certainly not have fit under the hood. But Adrianna did find a place there for her carry-on. Then, almost immediately, they were on the freeway, rocketing toward…

"So, you know how I am about surprises," Adrianna said. "But you being you, I thought you might like this one. And you're certainly dressed for it. Wow."

"I'm intrigued," Charlotte said with a sidelong smile. "Go on."

"Well, a few weeks ago I told Esther you were getting in

today. And she's got this modest side, as you can probably imagine. And once she knew how close it was to your arrival time she practically let me not find out that her swearing in is today. In about an hour, actually. And I wondered if, since the timing is just about right, you'd mind going before we head back to the house."

"Swearing in as a judge, swearing in?" Charlotte asked.

"Yes," Adrianna said. "At the courthouse and everything."

"Well, I don't see how we can miss an event like that. It's a good thing I wore my garters after all."

"It's always a good thing when you wear your garters," Adrianna said, giving Charlotte's knee a squeeze.

Esther's ceremony, as it happened, was in the Stanley Mosk Courthouse in downtown LA. It had been moved at the last minute from the smaller to the larger presiding judge's court-room because word got around that it would be a very well-attended event. And indeed it was, with over two hundred guests, fans of Esther from her past professional life as a law firm partner—district attorneys, judges, and other lawyers—to her present pedagogical one—including students of all vintages and fellow colleagues, as well as a complement of law school deans. Everyone, in fact, except her less than judicious ex-husband, which was exactly how she wanted it.

As Esther noted in her remarks, none of her grandparents, immigrants mostly from Hungary, had gone to college, so she hoped they would be proud of the path she had followed, being sworn in at a courthouse named after the California Supreme Court's longest-serving justice who was also Jewish—though not as liberal as he should have been, she had added. Fisher stood by his mother's side brandishing his fluorescent plaster cast as she followed the example of the late notorious Ruth Bader Ginsburg by taking the oath with her hand on a Hebrew Bible.

The reception, which was really more of a giant full-blown cocktail party, was unbelievably held at the Disney concert hall. Charlotte felt she'd come a long way from New Haven and she'd only been in California for an afternoon.

Because they'd barely gotten to see them at the reception, Esther and Hadley invited Charlotte and Adrianna to a celebratory high tea the next day at the Huntington. English tea with cakes and light hors d'oeuvres was an old-fashioned, only vaguely authentic, tradition at the gardens. But it was one of Esther's favorite California guilty pleasures and an occasional getaway she had always enjoyed as much for the clotted cream and buttery miniature scones as for the views of the famous roses surrounding the little tearoom.

Charlotte had driven them there. It was exhilarating for her and endearing to Adrianna, who had only partially grasped the depths of their mutual love of fast cars. Charlotte's first was a 1967 Austin-Healey Sprite which survived the first trip from New Orleans to New Haven, but sadly gave up the ghost on the way back down. She hadn't kept a car since, not really needing one in Connecticut and certainly never wanting one when she went into New York.

The drive had been fun all by itself. But for Charlotte, there was the added satisfaction of pulling up in Adrianna's Carrera in front of Esther and Hadley, who were waiting for them on the curb outside the elaborate admissions pavilion. Charlotte had caught a glimpse of *them* too, looking for all the world like an old married couple as Esther gingerly balanced on Hadley's arm to shake a rock out of her shoe.

"Good," said Adrianna, patting the dashboard when Charlotte turned off the car. "I think she likes you."

"Oh, I know she likes me," Charlotte said. "And I love her."

It took Adrianna a minute to clock Esther and Hadley. "Look at this," she said, drily, with one eyebrow raised.

Charlotte turned her way before she opened the door. "We're not going to have a problem here, are we?" she asked, not entirely in jest.

"I'm not sure," Adrianna answered.

It was a more candid response than Charlotte expected.

But maybe not unwarranted. The tables had turned some since they attended the Fairweather fête in Williamsburg. In the first place, Charlotte had gotten the Piedmont job. And Hadley had not. As a result, Charlotte was feeling like bygones might be able to be bygones. Especially after seeing how cute Hadley looked with Esther just now, she was newly of the mind that either Hadley must have changed or Esther must have discovered qualities in her that Charlotte had missed. Or quite possibly both.

Yet Adrianna was now plainly suspicious of Hadley, worried whatever she was doing with her best friend would end with Esther brokenhearted and/or gun-shy, just when she should be entering the hot BMILF dating pool as a serious contender.

"My goal is to pretend I'm meeting her for the first time," Charlotte said.

"We both know you're the nice one."

"I can afford to be," Charlotte said, leaning over to kiss Adrianna's cheek before they got out of the car. "And so can you."

"Your honor," Adrianna said as they approached the two women who, she wouldn't lie, made a very good-looking pair.

"Oh, please. No need to call me that," said Esther. "Judge Adler is perfectly acceptable."

Everyone laughed.

"Last night was amazing," Adrianna said. "I'm so proud

of you. Never surprised, but always proud. Your speech was very touching."

"Thank you for being there," Esther said, eager to move on. "And thank you for coming straight off the plane, Charlotte. That was beyond the call, really. But it was lovely of you."

"It was very exciting. And so glamourous," Charlotte said. "Congratulations, again. How does it feel?"

"I'll tell you all about it over the whipped butter," Esther said.

"Yes, let's get this princess party started," Hadley said, making everyone, even Adrianna, smile.

A few minutes later they were walking in twos through the camellia groves on their way to the tearoom.

Esther had taken Adrianna's arm in what she read as a signal that the two of them needed a few minutes to themselves. Charlotte and Hadley soon fell behind them on the shady path, placing themselves strategically out of earshot.

"Hadley looks as happy as you do. Much more relaxed than when we saw her in New York. Are things going OK with her case?"

"Yes," Esther said. "It's over. They settled. He's out. Preponderance of evidence. All I can say. But she's safe there now as far as he's concerned. We're very happy with the outcome. They handled it well. It's a rarity."

"We?" Adrianna said. "You're at the *we* stage. They grow up so fast."

"Be nice," Esther said. "Anyway, that's on you. You can't blame me for being inspired. You two were clearly made for each other. It took me a while to realize I was seeing you together for the first time last night. But you letting her drive *the car* tells me everything I need to know. Surely that's a first."

"Yes it is," Adrianna said.

Tea was unbelievable—only Americans would turn a modest tide-you-over snack into a lavish, all-you-can-eat petit fours buffet. The best part were the little to-go bags they made for the leftover scones, with tiny jars of preserves included.

But before that it had quickly turned into a joyful, even relaxed, and sometimes hilarious meal. If not between four old friends, then among women who cared about the women they loved enough to make room for new relationships. Adrianna soon let Hadley off the hook, seeing how good she was with Esther, who seemed almost relaxed in her presence despite what was clearly some pretty serious chemistry between them.

People are sometimes entirely different outside their element. Inveterate New Yorker that she was, Hadley seemed to have found a more natural habitat in Los Angeles. Charlotte caught her more than once looking contentedly off into the gardens, following the path of a hummingbird or watching a rabbit disappear into the bushes.

When Adrianna asked about Fisher's arm, a momentarily very serious Hadley had actually answered first.

"He only wants to go to the cast-doctor with Hadley," Esther elaborated. "Apparently, she makes it fun. This from a kid who was one hundred percent convinced the little saw thing was going to leave him bleeding like a perimenopausal law professor. Or maybe that was my take."

"He just likes that I gave him a thumbs-up on the hot pink plaster," Hadley said.

"Yes," Esther agreed, giving her an affectionate look. "We both do."

On the walk back toward the parking lot, they switched it up, with Charlotte and Esther behind Hadley and Adrianna.

Charlotte watched as Hadley, with a black sweater tossed casually over her shoulders, her bare ankles looking especially tan and bony in worn Gucci loafers, listened raptly to whatever Adrianna was saying.

From her body language, Adrianna seemed to be enjoying the conversation and Charlotte felt a sudden infusion of fondness for her. She was so beautiful with her coarse dark hair loose on her broad shoulders, her brown, animated hands gesturing to Hadley, no doubt about a painting or a funny exchange between a pair of seventeenth-century Mexican nuns.

Just then Adrianna turned around.

"Charlotte," she said. "Before we leave, I want to show you the cactus garden."

Once they'd said their goodbyes to Esther and Hadley, Adrianna walked Charlotte back toward the café and down a winding path that led into a fantastical landscape of succulents and all manner of spiky, bristly, otherworldly cacti. Some resembled giant pincushions or needled urchins, others were sleek and slender, tall as trees. A few of the plants were even adorned with bright red blooms or white-petalled starbursts. It was magical, actually, the way such underappreciated, supposedly off-putting flora could be so lush and enchanting, representing every imaginable shade and texture of green, from matte silvery gray to glossy lime. Charlotte saw immediately why Adrianna loved it.

"I've thought about this moment ever since that first trip," Charlotte told her. "Somehow I knew I'd be back. And I knew we'd come here together. I told the cactuses they'd have to wait but I hoped it wouldn't be too long."

After, Adrianna took them home. She drove fast—everyone there seemed to—and very confidently. Riding with her as she shifted and jockeyed through the freeway traffic was about as sexy an introduction to her new Los Angeles life as Charlotte could have envisioned. It was just about dusk when they pulled into Adrianna's garage.

The house was a deceptively pintsized Neo-Spanish charmer

from probably the late '20s or '30s. Red tile roof, pale tur-
quoise trim, Saltillo tiles, burbling little courtyard fountain.
Inside, it was pristinely modern but not monochrome—pale
pinks, silvers, and dove grays with an occasional colorful pop
of vintage wallpaper—striking a balance between chic and
serene.

They sat down at the kitchen table and drank some water.

"I know it's not quite dark yet," Adrianna said, looking
around the kitchen after a long pause. "But what I really, really want is to take you back to bed right now."

"You say that as if I need convincing," Charlotte said. "It's
been a busy twenty-four hours. And don't forget, I'm still on
East Coast time."

"So you're tired?" Adrianna teased back. "Because if you
need to catch up on your sleep, by all means…"

"I do want to catch up," Charlotte said. "Just not on sleep."

Charlotte had already taken off her shoes. And Adrianna had
already popped the Veuve Clicquot. They took their glasses
into her bedroom, where for a time they simply swayed in
each other's arms in something like a slow dance to the muted
Cuban music Adrianna had put on.

Charlotte began to unbutton Adrianna's crisp shirt, kissing
down her neck and across the tan line on her chest. Adrianna
shivered, though it wasn't cold. It all felt strangely different
to her, even more electrifying than before, to be touched by
this woman who knew how much she loved her.

Charlotte was wearing a triple strand of pearls, no doubt a
family heirloom, made more luminous by the darker, warmer
tones of her skin. When she reached back to take off the neck-
lace, Adrianna stopped her.

"No, don't," she said. "They're so gorgeous on you. Leave
it on."

Charlotte batted her long, pretty eyelashes but said nothing. While Adrianna got out of her jeans, Charlotte started undoing her dress. She wanted to kiss Charlotte and watch her simultaneously. She had missed every bit of her while they were apart. It felt as if she should remind her that she remembered the hollows above her collarbone and the unmistakable curve of her waist and the shape and feel of her nipples by kissing her in all these places.

So she did.

They remained by the side of the bed for a while, stopping to talk and laugh every few minutes before starting to kiss again. But then Charlotte left Adrianna standing there and went over to the upholstered chair on the other side of the room. She put her foot up on the seat cushion and carefully slid down her stockings, a sight of which Adrianna would never, ever grow tired. She unclasped and took off her bra, dropped it on the chair, then climbed into her side of Adrianna's bed.

As soon as Adrianna got in next to her, Charlotte moved on top, sliding her thigh between her legs, sucking and rubbing. Kissing her everywhere until, at last, Charlotte was fucking her, making the hot waves at her core deliciously ebb and flow. Adrianna had let go immediately, entrusting herself to Charlotte's care; to her control. She was comfortable here but it was no less of a thrill. The pearls softly buffeted her face as Charlotte's breasts moved over her. All she could think was that she wanted to have this secure, confident, unbelievably sexy woman in every corner of her life. As if reading her mind, Charlotte caught her eye with a satisfied smile.

"Good girl. That's right," she murmured. Biceps tensed, she was focused on her task, watching as Adrianna jerked her hips insatiably.

Charlotte had raised Adrianna's wrists over her head where she now held them firmly with her free hand.

Adrianna's sex suddenly clenched, reacting to the sound of Charlotte's voice. She moaned Charlotte's name again and again, reluctantly surrendering to the pleasure of a very intense climax.

"Just like that," Charlotte purred in her bedroom voice. "My Adrianna."

"God, I love you," Adrianna half whispered, half cried in the throes of her last satisfied thrust.

Charlotte brought her lips to Adrianna's ear.

"Oh, honey mine," she said. "I love you, too."

Epilogue

It doesn't get much hotter than an August afternoon in Madrid. At Adrianna's suggestion, Charlotte spent the day at the house museum of the late nineteenth-century Spanish painter Joachín Sorolla. Sorolla was from coastal Valencia and his paintings felt as if they were born in the sea, brought forth from a frothy clamshell, full of blistering sun and ultramarine light. Once he was deemed a national treasure, Sorolla had spent most of his life in dry, dusty Madrid with his pampered and, one suspected, headstrong wife, Clotilde. In 1911, rich and acclaimed, he built a large and attractive house for them in the bourgeois neighborhood of Chamberí.

Charlotte hadn't landed on anything by the so-called Spanish Sargent that aligned with her Creole interests, but the painter's house was a wonderful place to spend the late afternoon, post-siesta, while Adrianna put in her requisite daily hours at the Biblioteca. They had been up until the wee hours. And they had slept in.

These endless days and nights were a bit like an extended honeymoon.

Once she'd arrived from LA about three weeks ago, they'd quickly settled into a pleasant routine. Adrianna rose early and worked most days while Charlotte slept in until she felt like making breakfast, which she, and not Adrianna, had taken on as her particular responsibility.

They'd sit either at the little kitchen table or, if it was cool and early enough, at the even smaller table on the balcony, from which they could hear—and sometimes even see—the army of neighborhood bells as they soberly pealed the morning hours.

After Adrianna showered and dressed and eventually got herself out the door, Charlotte sometimes went down to El Jardin to read the paper and hammer out some ideas or emails on her laptop along with all the other actual and would-be authors. People were always writing in Madrid—a stolen glance over the forest of screens open on the tables at a given local haunt usually revealed the formatting of a screenplay or a short story or some other necessarily double-spaced literary endeavor.

Charlotte found it encouraging to work among creatives, even if the secret smokers in the back made for a less than healthy workplace.

Walking back from the museum in the relative freshness of the evening, she was glad she'd left early enough to stop at home to drop off her things before she met up with Adrianna.

Adrianna was almost through the seven-page letter she'd first ordered up, having transcribed Sor Epiphania's most recent account of the transaction between her superior, who Adrianna continued to suspect was the queen, and that lady's beloved prioress in the Mexican convent. The prioress was apparently delighted by the little squirrel painting on copper, which Adrianna had determined was likely made by a relatively famous Flemish court artist called Clara Peeters. The queen, emboldened, had commissioned another one—this time a still life with what seemed to be a special request for a rendition of pastries formed in the shape of the prioress's initials. Wouldn't that be amazing, Adrianna thought. And wouldn't it be even more amazing if she could track down that painting—likely languishing in some dank conventual sacristy or refectory in that inland part of Mexico—and show that it was a kind of love letter between two women separated by land and sea and rank and the Spanish church and crown's ceaseless desire to convert and conquer.

All this talk of gifts for the woman you love turned Adrianna's thoughts to Charlotte, of course. The future before them in LA. Working together and, Adrianna was willing to inwardly propose, living together when the time came and it felt right. The month they had spent before she returned to Madrid was good in every way. Charlotte in her little apartment twenty minutes away, getting to know the neighborhood, exploring the city on her own when she wanted to or with Adrianna when they preferred to do that.

So far Adrianna's favorite thing to do with Charlotte—well, her second-favorite—was to wake up early on a weekday and drive over to pick Charlotte up to take her to Silver Lake Reservoir. They'd park up in the hills and walk down to the dog-park side and start the loop from there. Sometimes they would walk together and sometimes Charlotte—in all her spandex glory—would run on her own, lapping Adrianna at least once as she made her own more leisurely (but still brisk) walk around the sparkling man-made lake. For a few weeks after Charlotte arrived there were great blue heron nests in the tall trees on one edge to the water and they'd made a point of stopping to try to catch sight of the babies when they went. It had finally felt like the kind of dream-LA Adrianna wished it could be—nodding at the reservoir regulars, occasionally swearing they had seen some celebrity or another, going for coffee after, taking time to enjoy the California that never failed to remind her she wasn't in the Midwest or New England anymore. Thank God.

Adrianna was already finding it difficult to believe she'd seriously considered moving back to the East Coast for any job.

Today she could have kept transcribing for probably another hour before she reached her threshold of concentration but she was fast approaching a respectable departure. She'd put in the time. What the hell, she could leave early if she wanted to. And she really wanted to. Charlotte and the entertaining, visiting, James from New Haven were probably already at their table on the square.

Charlotte and James had only been there half an hour, but good gravy was it hot. Like fry-an-egg-on-the-street hot. So hot you could actually see the air hovering at the horizon in scintillating waves.

James had delightedly purchased a cheap paper *abanico* printed with a lacy pattern of flowers. Even under the shade of their big umbrella, the two of them were fanning themselves nonstop like a pair of church ladies. They didn't dare rest their elbows on the scalding surface of the metal table, which was surely to blame for melting the ice in the ruby glasses of fruity tinto de verano they'd ordered. A fitting balance to their salty platter of pale, flash-fried calamari, still as hot as if it was right out of the oil. Adrianna would be there at some point, on her way home from another day—now evening—at the library with her nuns.

"We do miss you," James said.

"And I miss you," Charlotte replied. "But you, and you alone."

"LA is a great city, though," he said. "I think it's more your speed."

"I just can't get over how beautiful it is. The palm trees and the flowers and the big blue sky. I almost keep forgetting there's a beach. We've only been a couple of times, but I could get used to that."

"Well, be that as it may, I dare them to best our Hammonasset clam shacks," said James, forking the last trio of squid rings onto his plate. "You'll be back for the fried oysters someday, mark my words."

"You forget where I come from," Charlotte said. "But I'll be back to see you. With or without the breading."

They talked for a while more, until the food was finished and the drinks were long gone. James had a date with someone he'd met on Tinder or Grindr or the gay male museum network equivalent thereof. He was clearly excited, checking the time every few minutes and casting sly glances at himself in the restaurant's glass.

"Go already," Charlotte said. "Before you melt."

"Am I sweating?" he asked in a panic.

"Only on the inside. You look very handsome. Have fun!"

He got up immediately, as if he'd been waiting for permission, kissed Charlotte quickly on each cheek, and headed somewhat hesitantly into the open square, stopping to check his phone again before he was ten feet away.

Charlotte didn't want to make James self-conscious so she looked around to the other tables, filled with mostly couples—of women, of men, of people who probably wouldn't identify with either of these designations.

The talk was relaxed and the poses were languid and everyone seemed down for the kind of endless night out for which the city was famous. They were just getting started.

It felt late to Charlotte but it was only a little past eight.

Here she was again, she thought, suddenly imbued with the variety of déjà vu she had felt at the cactus gardens after she'd first arrived in LA. There, too, it was as if she'd known she'd be back. But now that she was, the place she'd returned to was nothing like the place it had been before. Or maybe she was the one who had changed.

Madrid didn't feel familiar. But she was getting to know it, and maybe even understand it better day by day. She was at home enough here to be sitting at a table by herself in the middle of a foreign city of millions of people and still not feel awkward or lonely.

Of course that had everything to do with Adrianna.

This life they were living was unlike anything she'd experienced. She'd never lived with a girlfriend. Never come close. Never gotten past the stage of closing the bathroom door or lying about who wanted to get up first. The ease of it might have had something to do with knowing they'd both be in their own apartments when they returned—to the same state! The current situation was temporary, which made it fun but also freeing. They both seemed to be enjoying themselves— together and apart.

Just then Charlotte looked up from her phone, where she'd been perusing the latest art film offerings at the Circulo de Bellas Artes. There, striding into the plaza in her linen suit and porkpie hat, was Adrianna. She paused in the middle of the pavement and took off her sunglasses, scanning the sea of tables until she saw Charlotte's wave.

The expectant smile of recognition she returned was full of tenderness. Lord, she was stunning, Charlotte thought, watching Adrianna head for her table.

"I hope you haven't been waiting long, my love," Adrianna said when she got there, kissing Charlotte fully on the lips without the slightest hesitation. She was so very much herself. And so very much hers, Charlotte thought, with the blissful knowledge that Adrianna felt that way, too. She was every bit Charlotte's.

"How was your day, sweet bird?" Adrianna asked, not bothering to sit down.

"It was perfect. The museum was a great idea," Charlotte said. "Did you get done what you wanted to get done?"

"Enough for one day," Adrianna said. "But now I'm ready to get out of this heat and be home with my girl."

"Maybe take a nice cool shower?" Charlotte said.

"Maybe," Adrianna answered with the look Charlotte knew and loved.

She stood up and reached for Adrianna's hand as they began walking.

The incorrigible Castilian sun was finally giving way to the moon's more temperate influence. They cut across the plaza, around the corner, and down the street to the apartment, where they made themselves dinner, went to bed, and didn't go to sleep for a very long time.

★ ★ ★ ★ ★

Acknowledgments

Writing this book was consolation at a difficult moment and I am infinitely grateful to the wonderful Kerri Buckley at Carina Adores for bringing more queer of color romance into the world, and to my supremely incisive, exacting, and food-loving editor, Alissa Davis, for helping me make this the story I wanted it to be. Jessica Alvarez at BookEnds is that rare combination of guardian angel and Amazon. I can't imagine a better—or more savvy—agent and I am so appreciative of her support and wisdom. I wrote my debut romance when for the whole world travel, eating at wonderful restaurants, exploring new cities, being with friends and family—and meeting the love of your life face-to-face—had suddenly become distant memories and seemingly impossible dreams. I am thankful to have had a safe home in which to shelter and a partner and pets with whom to weather the hardships of isolation and illness. I was fortunate. But my heart goes out to those who lost family and loved ones and health and work. I hope we begin now to reckon, heal, and understand each other anew.

Author Bio

Verity Lowell writes diverse contemporary stories about smart, driven queer women falling hard for each other in all sorts of cities and settings. Born in the Rockies, she has lived on both coasts of the US and several states in between. Travel, libraries, coffeehouses, oceans, and many kinds of music are among her enduring loves. Also: museums + cats, though she grew up with dogs and likes them a lot, too. She holds a PhD in the history of art and is a former Fulbright Scholar. To see what Verity is up to visit www.veritylowell.com.

*All Mason wants to do is fall in love, get married,
and live happily ever after...but it turns out the traditional life
he expected has some surprises in store.*

Keep reading for an excerpt from
The Life Revamp *by Kris Ripper.*

Tim was perfect. He was everything I looked for in a partner: employed (hello, *doctor*), stable (no crazy exes lined up around the block or stories about how he wanted to punch people), and kind. He didn't drink too much or spend all night fighting with strangers on the internet or say passive-aggressive things and then gaslight me when I called him out about it. He had a retirement fund. He always found interesting things to talk about.

He was *perfect*.

We'd been dating for almost six months and it seemed like now was the appropriate time to Get More Serious. To be honest, at this point in my not-quite-disastrous but also not-quite-fruitful dating life, I wasn't even sure what getting more serious was supposed to look like. I guess we'd go exclusive and, having done that, we'd make more of an effort to see each other? Move in together eventually, get married, combine our finances, buy a house, adopt a kid or two?

It was a little heteronormative and cookie-cutter, but that didn't trouble me much; whoever it was who said that thing about no battle plan surviving contact with the enemy could have said it about relationships. All of my friends had fallen in love and paired off, and their relationships took whatever shape made sense to the people involved—not necessarily the shapes they would have predicted.

Tim and I would find our way. That was how it worked, at least judging from observational data.

Which was why, when he said, "Should we discuss where this is heading?" over wine at a fancy restaurant, smiling at me with all the assurance in the world, I should have been elated.

Wasn't this what I'd been waiting for? Wasn't this exactly what committed adult dating looked like? Two grown-ups, fancy restaurant, having a Serious Conversation About Their Relationship?

So why was there a heavy sensation in my gut, a weight that held me back from all the excitement I'd expected to feel in this moment?

"Yes," I said, or forced myself to say, pushing down that feeling and willing it to disappear. "Let's do that."

"Well, Mason—" Tim lifted his glass "—I really enjoy what we've been doing and I'd like to do more of it."

"Me too," I echoed, clinking my glass against his. He was a busy doctor. I was a less-busy-but-still-working-full-time-with-a-solid-social-life bank sales associate. We saw each other once a week. It was not like he was going to give up his doctoring to see me more—and I wouldn't want him to—so I guess that meant… I'd be giving up things in my life?

But no, I was just being paranoid about this after the many, *many* times I'd dated people who expected me to make all the allowances for them without getting anything in return. Tim wasn't like that.

Tim was the perfect guy. Who was now looking a little uncertain.

I was officially screwing this up. "Sorry, a lot on my mind. Let's definitely do more of this, um, of everything." I smiled at him, which wasn't hard, because Tim was the guy you smile at. We'd met through a dating app, and from the first texts back and forth, he was always easy to smile at, even when he was just words on a screen.

He shook his head slightly. "I'm doing this all wrong. I was so caught up in having this conversation I skipped over all the usual catch-up things. How was your week? Is everything all right?"

"Yeah, everything is all right. Sorry. Just having an off night, I think?" I wasn't going to compound my weirdness by inventing a crisis. That was a thing younger Mason might have done, and while I slightly envied his willingness to make something up when he didn't know what to say, I was no longer that careless with the truth. At least that was what I told myself as the silence grew awkward.

"My timing is terrible," Tim said. "I apologize. Let's table this for right now and revisit it when we're both fully present. But for the sake of future reference, this *is* something you want to revisit, isn't it? It's completely okay if it's not! Only, I would appreciate knowing that now."

"Definitely." The relief of being let off the hook made my voice firm. "Very definitely."

"Okay, good. Now let's pretend I never brought it up." Self-conscious laugh. "I just signed up for a training I thought you might find interesting. If you want to hear about it?"

I did want to hear about it. More than that, I wanted the conversation to return to something completely neutral, which didn't demand I have to think about my feelings.

We went back to my place after and had exceptional sex—Tim wasn't just a pretty face, let's be clear, he had the skills to back it up—and then he went home because he had early appointments the following day.

And I nominally went to bed. By which I mean I stared at the ceiling for a long time. And then sent a Snap to my best friend. I was too lazy to turn on the lights, so it was just a shifting pattern of darkness and less darkness while I spoke, though I turned on a sparkle filter to give Declan something to watch.

"Okay, date recap, I fucked everything up? He wanted to talk about our relationship and I froze like—" I paused, trying to come up with a really good metaphor. And failing. "Like a freaking deer in headlights, Dec. What is *wrong* with me? He's perfect. He wants all the things I want. He's a doctor. He's nice. He's stable. Why am I not over the moon right now with an exclusive boyfriend, picking out table toppers for my wedding Pinterest board?"

And send. That was how I'd pictured this moment, when I'd imagined it, but now that it was here, I couldn't even be happy about it.

I'd expected Dec to be asleep and get back to me in the morning, but a few minutes later my phone buzzed.

He was using a filter that gave him a cowboy hat, which was a funny juxtaposition against the rainbow shower curtains in what was clearly his partner Sidney's tiny apartment bathroom. "Wait, what happened? I'm confused. Also, ohmygod, make Sid stop editing. I'm sooooooo tirrrrrrrrred. But tell me what happened, because I don't know what you fucked up and I want to be supportive." He pointed. "Supportive face. Now tell me how I'm supporting you."

I was just about to reply when a new series of Snaps came through.

"Also, nothing's wrong with you. You say he's perfect when you know there's no such thing. If I'd drawn a picture of who I thought was perfect for me, it'd be a picture of you, which is obviously not true, and I'd have never been open to Sid, and then we'd all be super sad. Romance is not a formula in a spreadsheet, Mase!"

One more Snap, this time no cowboy hat, just Dec with his hair mussed in front of a plastic rainbow.

"This is me not apologizing *again* for leaving you at the altar. Please note my emotional growth." Then he stuck his tongue out at me and added, "I haven't grown *that* much."

I flipped on my lamp and said very solemnly, "I see your emotional growth and I appreciate it." I left a long pause where I did not stick my tongue out in return even though he'd be waiting for it, just to mess with him. And I really didn't need him to apologize again for leaving me at the altar when we were twenty-two. "But seriously, why am I like this? I've been hoping that dating Tim—or anyone—would get to this point, and now that it has, I can't even be happy about it? Am I self-sabotaging? Should I call him right now and propose? Ahhhhh."

Snapchat is like a super sped-up version of the telegraph, where you send a message and then wait for the other person to watch it and then record their own, then they wait while you do the same. Sometimes I kind of like all those pauses. The lack of immediacy can be perfect and allow me to virtually chat with my friends throughout the day while actually hearing their voices.

Right now the lack of immediacy was super annoying because I wanted Declan to tell me how to fix this thing with Tim.

Which he didn't. He did send four entire series of Snaps, this time from Sid's kitchen, with a chicken on his head. Not an actual chicken, a filter of a chicken, which was one of his favorites and also let me know that he was trying to reassure me with a calm, meditative chicken filter, even though he himself was pacing and gesturing and couldn't stay still.

"Okay, first, you are *amazing*. You are an amazing human being, there is *nothing* wrong with you, you're wonderful, and

of *course* Dr. Tim NoLastName wants to lock that down, because you're a fucking catch, Mase, okay? So stop acting like
he deserves better than you! He doesn't. Literally *no one* deserves better than you, you're the fucking best, and I say that
as an authority on the subject."

New Snap. "Second, you should definitely not call him
up and propose, ohmygod, don't even *say* that." He shook his
head violently and the chicken filter glitched trying to keep
up. "Seriously, take it from me, that is the exact wrong thing
to do. I know ambivalence is scary when you think you have
everything you want, but *listen to it*. You're not doing anyone
any favors if you pretend you're more into something than
you are."

New Snap. "And Sid totally backs me up on that, FYI,
but anyway, I don't think it's self-sabotage. You just need
some time to think about it, and you're allowed to need that.
Just because a guy seems 'perfect'—" aggressive air quotes
"—doesn't mean he's perfect *for you*. Like maybe he is? But
you don't have to decide that tonight."

New Snap, with his face closer to the screen. "Ummmm…
also, Sid's done editing, so we're kind of on our way to bed—
or going to do something bed-related, anyway—but I'm totally
here for you. Both of us are here for you. But don't propose to
Tim. Just take a bath and read a book or something, okay? I
love you sooooooo much! There is *nothing* wrong with you."
He got even closer, his eyes slightly out of focus. "Mase, you're
incredible. I'm so lucky you're my bestie." He blew me a kiss.

By the time I'd seen all the Snaps, I had a text that read,
Also if you need me, we can phone?

In other words, he'd put off having sexy times with his
partner if I was freaking out. Which was sweet, but no. I'm
fine, you two kids go have a good time, I sent back.

And I was fine. Mostly. Just confused.

Ambivalence? Was that what this was? This…this feeling of *meh* when I expected feelings of *yay*? But I did like Tim. We had fun. I respected him. He respected me. Sure, it wasn't a formula in a spreadsheet, but when you added up all the good things, shouldn't that still equal *hell yes, let's take this to the next level, baby, I'm totally in*?

Don't miss The Life Revamp *by Kris Ripper, available wherever Carina Adores books are sold.*

www.CarinaPress.com

Copyright © 2021 by Kris Ripper

IF YOU ENJOYED THIS BOOK WE THINK YOU WILL ALSO LOVE

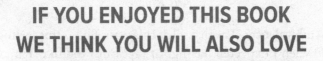

Carina Adores is home to modern, romantic love stories where LGBTQ+ characters find their happily-ever-afters.

Discover more at
CarinaAdores.com

CARADORES2021 TR

Discover another great contemporary romance from Carina Adores

All Mason wants to do is fall in love, get married and live happily-ever-after. The hunt is beginning to wear him down…until he meets (slightly) famous fashion designer Diego. Everything sparks between them—the banter, the sex, the fiery eye contact across a crowded room.

There's just one thing: Diego is already married and living his happily-ever-after, which luckily (or not) for Mason includes outside courtships.

Mason thought he knew what would make him happy, but it turns out the traditional life he'd expected has some surprises in store.

Don't miss
The Life Revamp **by Kris Ripper,**
available wherever Carina Press books are sold.

CarinaAdores.com

CARKR1221TR